THE FORTRESS WALLS WITHIN

A NOVEL

KEN JACKSON

Order this book online at www.trafford.com
or email orders@trafford.com

Most Trafford titles are also available at major online book retailers.

Printed in the United States of America.

ISBN: 978-1-4669-6963-6 (sc)
ISBN: 978-1-4669-6964-3 (hc)
ISBN: 978-1-4669-6965-0 (e)

Library of Congress Control Number: 2012921911

Trafford rev. 11/27/2012

 www.trafford.com

North America & international
toll-free: 1 888 232 4444 (USA & Canada)
phone: 250 383 6864 ⬧ fax: 812 355 4082

Vision without action
Is a daydream

Action without vision
Is a nightmare

—Japanese proverb

A Life Can Be Changed Forever
In A Moment
By Those Never Met
Events Never Expected
And Worlds We Never Knew

FOR

The friends who said I should
My wife who thought I could
And the One who knew I would

Robert Henry was an ordinary man. Nothing special had happened in his life; at least nothing that stood out as extraordinary. His successes were important ones but few and far between. What he had accomplished was nothing any other man in his situation would be expected to do.

That would all change the day a small boy he had never met before walked into his life, as much by accident as destiny. Robert would learn things about himself, others and even the universe that he never believed he was capable of. He would help to leave a legacy behind that he had searched for but never found. Nothing that would happen to him would be the way he imagined; still the journey would lead him in directions he never knew possible.

It was a journey he would not take alone. That's where the story begins.

PROLOGUE

An old man stood at the edge of the field looking into the morning mist. The dampness of the air inflamed the arthritic pain he suffered everyday. He pulled the collar of his jacket as close to his neck as he could and sipped from the coffee cup held in his hand. The sensation of hot coffee contributed little to the coldness he felt but the familiarity of the taste offered comfort for moments of easier days. His body told a story of the pain and suffering of age but his mind could share stories of greatness and happiness. There were stories of sadness that could fill his mind too just as with any living being; but it was the good things in life he had learned to focus on as he became older.

Sometimes the simplest things can trigger memories of a time in one's life that added value to a person's past even if it was years before it could be understood. The taste of coffee reminded the old man of his time when life became different for him. Even the cold could not take away the warmth of those memories.

He continued to look past the season colors of the area before him and the fallen leaves hinting at the winter soon to arrive. What he saw was much greater than that. The image was important to him any time of the year; at any point in time. It was a vision he had learned to embrace even when the picture did not lie in front of him.

The man could not believe he had been a part of such an event or understand why he had been chosen for the task. It seemed like such a simple thing at the time, miniscule by most standards and life changing for others. It had caused him to re-visit his life and this place many times for reflection and understanding.

He shifted his weight to his right leg and leaned harder on the cane he carried with him always. Not yet ready to leave and half of his coffee remaining he ignored the feeling of dampness and moved closer to what he had been a part of. What he had built. What had defined his spirit and added meaning to his life.

Everything seemed so long ago. Where had the time gone? Should he have done more? Would he be remembered as someone who gave more than he took? He shook his head and chuckled to himself. No one was there to share the moment so he did not have to explain that more often than not his thoughts were often those of a rambling old man moving closer to the end of his life wondering what he could have done different.

These were the type of doubts that he believed many people often experienced even if they did not have the courage to admit it; but in this moment; in this place he had no doubts. It was here that he most believed he had made a difference. It was in this spot that he knew he had contributed and that his life did matter.

Gazing at what lay before him he saw his past, his present and maybe even his future. Then again maybe he was just an old man lost in his memories. What could he know that others didn't?

The thought made him smile and provided him with warmth inside that coffee would never re-produce; a warmth that morning dampness would never defeat. Taking a final look at his accomplishment he drank the last of his coffee then turned to begin the walk to his home. He walked with a discernable limp but with happiness in his soul that few people often got to see; but those that did reveled in the experience.

So he was just an old man to the uninformed; a young heart to others and someone to be respected by many. His part of a life story may be forgotten but will always make a difference. A difference no one could have anticipated; least of all the old man himself; at least when it was happening. It is a story many people would wish they could have of their own to share with the world. If only they knew.

CHAPTER 1

Mine was a story that could have happened to almost any average person living an average, simple suburban life, but it didn't happen to just anyone. It happened to me. The story began simply enough. Many great events do.

My life to this point had been normal, with few if any big things to celebrate other than the odd wedding and childbirth. Don't get me wrong, I was grateful for those special days. Those memories made it possible to have a grounded, healthy view of my life, giving me direction and purpose. I guess I lived a normal, uneventful life, just like many people in my part of the world. I went to work like everyone else to pay for the life I chose to live. I had my hobbies and routines that gave me some moments of happiness, and when I looked back at my life to this point I was basically satisfied with most of the things my family and I had accomplished. In many ways, I was quite happy about my life. I just never stood out any more than the next guy. I was ordinary.

My parents had named me Robert after a grandfather I never knew. For some reason I could never tolerate being called Bob or Bobby when I was younger, so I would always correct people. As I grew older, it somehow seemed less important, so I didn't go to the trouble of correcting them anymore. Funny thing was I couldn't remember the last person who called me anything except Robert. Maybe the less important I made it, the less often it happened.

Robert Henry sounded simple and strong to me, even if it did seem strange when I was a small boy to have two first names. There was a time; I was about four, when I thought Henry was a brother I never got to meet. Every time my mother or father called me by both names, I thought they were calling for me and my "brother" Henry.

It didn't take long though to understand that being called by both names usually meant I was in some kind of trouble. That was when I really wished I did have a brother Henry, because then he could have taken the blame from time to time. He could have had the spankings that went with it. Believe me I wouldn't have missed them. Even with two first names and the confusion it caused me in my early years, I still felt much more fortunate in grade school than some of the other kids in my class who received nicknames that stuck with them all the way to junior high. No one really got around to giving me a nickname based on either of my names.

As I got older, I was forced to get used to being called Mr. Henry by service clerks, gas attendants, and other people who were younger than me. I tried to tell myself that it was out of respect rather than because of my age; then I didn't feel like time was slipping away.

To know me and understand my story people had to know about my family. I had great parents. I loved and respected them but they were disciplinarians and I always knew there was a consequence for anything I did. That's when the spankings became a big part of the process. If I did something wrong—and got caught—I knew for sure what the punishment would be. I never had to wonder when it would happen either, it was immediate and firm. The question in many ways "Was the reward worth the consequence?" I was young so often I figured I wouldn't get caught and if I did so what? It wasn't like I was stealing cars. What was the worse that could happen, another spanking? I could handle my parents discipline and there were times that I did get away with misbehaving. That's when I thought I had outsmarted everyone, but of course I hadn't, I had just got lucky. Funny thing was that even at this stage of my life, the use of both of my names makes me feel nervous. I suppose their form of discipline kept me out of getting into any amount of serious trouble. I'm sure they would say they did it for my own good and it hurt them more than it hurt me. Parents always said things like that but given a chance I would tell them I thought they had made "my own good" too much of a priority. I would also have challenged them on their statement. I was sure my butt hurt more than their feelings had!

It was true that I had grown up in the "me generation" and believed that everything was mine for the taking, just like many people who made up the back end of the baby boomer population. I did not have the same opportunity to go to college that most of today's middle—and upper-class children do today. My parents had made work ethic and responsibility important things in my life. It was okay to fail as long as I did my best and lived with the results. I felt I had worked hard throughout my life and was just as proud of my failures as I was of my successes, because I felt both made me stronger. My father taught me that.

My family wasn't poor but we didn't have a lot and I had memories of my own happy times when imagination was all I had. They were some of the happiest days of my childhood. My world was as big as I wanted to make it back then. Nothing was impossible.

I was taught a work ethic by my parents. Chores and responsibility were a part of my childhood. When I took that work ethic and applied it to my adult life I was able to obtain most of the things in life that I wanted. They also taught me to never forget the value of family so my wife and daughter meant the most to me. My Dad used to tell me how important is a big house without a family to share it with? I learned to understand what he meant and tried to remember it every day.

In the end my parents discipline had helped me carve out a good life for myself. For that I was grateful. Unfortunately my greatest enemies had become complacency and boredom. I lived an above-average middle-class life, where I had too much to lose and felt I was too old to take the big risks anymore to get to the next level. In many ways things were too good for me. Sometimes good can block the path to great and keep a person from making that big step forward so if I wasn't going forward was I going backwards? That was where I was in my life.

Now, I'm not complaining. I had built a comfortable lifestyle for myself and my family. We had a nice house, which my wife, Marie, had made into a warm home. She had planted flowers, added the right curtains to our windows, kept the house clean, placed candles everywhere, and made sure we used fresh towels every other day. It was her efforts that made our house a home. She especially made sure we had clean sheets every week. I always teased her about that; asking her if she thought we lived in a hotel or something. (Of course I don't know what hotel I would stay in that only changed sheets once a week!) Her answer was always the same "to keep the "bedbugs" out." I couldn't be sure she wasn't talking about me, and I didn't see any advantage in asking her. With her odd sense of humor I never knew what her answer might be.

She made the best meals, did all the "little things" and kept our house a warm place to come home to, even while holding down a full time job of her own. This was important to her and something I believed she saw as one of her roles in life. She had told me more than once that helping her wouldn't kill me. I told her I couldn't be sure of that; so why test it? In the end I didn't know what I would do without her.

To be honest the truth was that many of the things she asked me to do just weren't important to me. All I really needed was a bed, television, and enough food to get me through the week. Throw in the occasional golf game or sporting event and I thought the world was great. That doesn't mean I was a cave man. I had been doing my own cooking and cleaning long before I met my bride to be. None of it had been very good, but I had survived. Over time I came to understand how much our home meant to her and I learned how to help out where I could. In the end what was important to her became important to me.

I think I never told her often enough how proud I was of her. It seemed that we missed a lot more of those opportunities than we should have over the years of marriage to remind each other how much we really did care for each other. Life sometimes just got in the way.

Marie had also invested many frustrating hours trying to help me become a good enough husband, whom she could take out into the world and leave unattended from time to time. Her reasons were always well intentioned, albeit annoying for both of us.

One example was how quickly it became important for me to put the toilet seat down after I was finished in the bathroom. It was a small thing, but it minimized the chance that she would fall in by mistake in the middle of the night while half asleep. I learned that one the first time I heard loud cursing directed at me one night at about 2:00 a.m. in the third month of our marriage. I hadn't heard my new wife swear like a trucker before (and it wouldn't be the last time), so I definitely paid attention and quickly learned the value of bathroom etiquette.

She used to give me a look from time to time that made me feel that she was happy with the man I had become, but there was still work left to do. Maybe she just didn't know if she would have enough time.

Marie and I had done well enough through our twenty-five plus years of marriage. Our life had been a happy one, for the most part. There had been times of course, as in any strong union, with two strong individuals, where the two of us had not agreed. It was often the small things, such as what I was supposed to wear to a wedding, the color to paint a bedroom, or her plans to redesign our backyard, but we had found ways throughout the years to forgive each other for the unimportant things that made us angry.

We never seemed to disagree about the big things in our lives, such as where to live and how to help our daughter when she needed us. I believed that successful marriages included compromise. If a person didn't give in once in a while, then the battles would never end. Fighting forever was not something I wanted to do. Make love not war was my motto. Well it was a motto I wanted to at least try and live by. I have to admit there were times early on when a good fight seemed the way to go. It made the love all that more rewarding!

Family conversation had come up from time to time. We often disagreed on issues involving both sides of the family and would find ourselves angry at each other over events that ultimately didn't matter in the first place. They just became bigger problems than they needed to be. I guess most families have similar problems when it comes to those things and I always used to say that I married the woman first. I wasn't always sure where the rest of the family fit into the picture after that.

I wouldn't say that we had a perfect marriage either—far from it. We both had human frailties and had argued many times often ending up with no answer we could agree upon. I said it before—anyone who said they never went to bed mad was lying, never needed sleep or was divorced!

When things seemed out of control I would always remind myself of the old saying: "What doesn't kill us makes us stronger." Sometimes the logic of the quote seemed inspirational, but at other times it just seemed like death would have been easier.

Then there was our daughter, Anne. We called her Annie, after her mother's grandmother. I was not totally in favor of the name choice, but I was relieved to have a healthy baby daughter, and it seemed important enough to Marie, so I went along with her wishes.

As she grew from baby into a young woman, she would often manipulate my good nature, using the "daddy's girl" card to her advantage. I would raise my voice occasionally and pretend to be the disciplinarian, but Marie would always wait until our daughter had left the room and say something like "I guess it doesn't take much for daddy's girl to get what she wants." I would get my back up and go to the living room to watch television, or outside for a walk, until I could go back into the same room with my wife and feel like I could defend myself with dignity. I realized that she was just teasing, but it still annoyed the hell out of me.

If I was being honest with myself, I would have to say she was probably right. Instead I would tell myself, "Hey, there are worse things than being loved by your daughter, even if her love sometimes comes with the price tag of a new pair of jeans!" Annie thought she was special and I wouldn't be able to say no. She was right. I knew what she was doing but her happiness was everything to me. Besides I didn't think she ever abused the privilege.

My protective nature made it stressful when Annie began to date. Like everything else, I tried to learn how to let things go, suppress them, or at the very least set them aside long enough so that she was able to have some form of normal social life. At times I didn't do so well. I'm sure she had to explain my attitude to some of her dates, but we both seemed to have gotten through her teenage years without too many scars.

The truth was that I was more roar than bite. I tried to act tough in front of the young men, but I was really just a softie who wanted to see his own beautiful daughter end up with a good man someday—just not now. I thought she might even find one as good as her father. Of course, I never put it that way to Marie. Her laughter at the idea of my own perfection as a husband would not be accepted well by me. I decided to let it be my private dream.

Marie and I were proud of our girl. Not only had she been a great child growing up, but she was now following a college dream of becoming an engineer. I thought it was an unusual career choice. It was a field women were not often a part of. The fact that she was taking on a challenge like that made me proud of her.

At times I wondered if my daughter was really meant to be a son. I didn't think that because I secretly wanted a boy; that was not the case at all. It just seemed that Anne often took on challenges more often chosen by men. The world had changed dramatically, even in my own lifetime. Women were now lawyers, engineers, and soldiers. A woman in today's world could do anything a man could, and a man could do anything a woman could. Our society was on a path of equality; total equality may not have yet arrived in every home on the block, but it was definitely in the neighborhood.

My daughter was part of that next generation of change. She did not worry about what everyone else thought, not because she didn't care; rather, she just wasn't going to let people's narrow mindedness stop her from making her mark in the world. I wish had been as enlightened as she was. Spending time with Annie helped though, even if she didn't always change my mind. I liked to think that listening to what she had to say made me a better husband and father, or at the very least smarter than the day before. The interaction might keep my mind active enough to stop my brain's aging process. Learning slowed forgetting.

Annie was in her second year of university and was enjoying the challenges that her learning was bringing. I used to tease her all the time that I hoped she did well in school and became a world-class engineer so when she got her degree she could help me redesign and rebuild my bank account. "Oh, Daddy," she would say in a lighthearted way that made me think she knew something I did not. She probably did.

As I said, we were both very proud of our daughter, even though we couldn't really understand what she was studying. Marie and I were not uneducated people. I had always felt that I had been a good student and wanted to participate in the learning process. I could not, however, even pretend to know most of the things Annie talked about. I tried to ask her questions to help me understand but quickly gave up when she began talking about all the courses she was attending. I figured it was better to be quiet and let people wonder if I wasn't all that smart than open my mouth and prove it.

Annie never made me feel that I was stupid or talked down to me. She just accepted the fact that engineering would be something we would never really share. It meant more to me to know that she respected her mother and me enough not to demonstrate any arrogance about her knowledge; that kind of respect meant a lot to me and made me feel that we as parents had taught her well. Maybe our training wasn't as good as college courses, but a child needed life courses too.

She lived away from home and seemed to have a normal student life. She enjoyed the campus experience, made new friends and enjoyed the occasional social event. Her main focus always remained her studies though. I liked to think some of that was from her father's influence and determination.

Although I always saw myself as an ordinary man, I felt I had inherited a certain drive to overcome my shortcomings and find a way to succeed—well, my version of success anyway. I think Annie also had that drive to do better. It just appeared that hers were better focused than mine had been. In the end I hoped she would do better than I had because of it. I knew she would because she also had the same inner strength of her mother. How could she fail?

I had strength of my own, but for some reason I often put myself down before others got a chance to do it. I hoped that my daughter would not feel that she had to do the same. I don't know if it was just a defense mechanism to keep people from making fun of me or because I could laugh at myself easily enough; I just wanted to have control of the joke.

I hadn't met all of my goals. How many people ever do? Then I would tell myself that there were many people in the world who had reached new peaks of success in their fifties or sixties. There were many examples of human beings who had discovered themselves later in life. They had taken on new adventures and succeeded. That meant that there should still be lots of time for me, right? I don't know if I really believed that, but it was important for me to give myself hope that something great was going to happen in my life.

I had given up my dreams of being an NBA basketball star (not that I ever had a chance anyway) and my singing only made deaf birds cry, so I had come to understand that there were probably some things I would not accomplish in my life. There had to be other things left to do, right?

And then I met Andy Bell.

Up to now I've only offered a snapshot of my life. Meeting Andy is where my story really begins, because meeting him would set off a chain of events that would force me to see things I didn't want to. It would cause me to admit things to myself I never thought I would. It would remind me of things I had long forgotten. It would make me feel better than I ever could have imagined, then bring me such pain that I could not fathom the depths of the emotion. It would open doors I wanted to keep closed and close doors I thought would always be open. It was a day that I never looked for, a day that found me. It was a day that made me question everything in life to that point and wonder where things should go from there.

And I almost missed it.

CHAPTER 2

I was in my garage the day I first met Andy. My family knew that I had claimed our garage as my domain and turned it into a small workshop. We had been living in our current home for almost thirteen years, and it had become very clear in the first few months that Marie had little interest in whatever projects I was working on, as long as she was able to have a place to park her car. Anything else was up to me.

The fact that we owned a house with a triple garage and had only two vehicles made carving out my niche much easier. It was important to Marie that the work area was cleaned up from time to time. I could understand that and tell when the time had come for clean up. Just a sideways frown as she walked past me or a comment thrown my way as we pulled the vehicle out of the garage would indicate the mess was beginning to bother her. She was usually right.

I had thought of building a wall to make it harder to see the mess, but it always seemed easier just to clean the area. At those times I would just sweep everything up in the next day or two. It made the dinner conversation a little bit more pleasant, and I would often discover some long lost tool or bracket I thought I had lost forever. I wanted to think it was a positive process for both of us.

Marie was a very forgiving person who gave me lots of room to be my own man. She never really fit any stereotype of a nagging wife, so I never saw doing the little things that made her life happier a chore. I guess that was one of the good things about our marriage.

My workshop had a table saw, workbench, tool area, and a place to store miscellaneous bits of wood. It was all I needed. More than anything it gave me a place to hide, somewhere I could just shut out the world, with all its daily pressures. I could be alone, listen to music, think about anything I wanted or do nothing at all. It was a strange freedom I had learned to enjoy. I assumed many people my age had the same fantasy.

Living in the city provided me as much anonymity as I chose. I had come to know the neighbors on each side of us over time, and we had even become friends with both couples. We got to know their children and made sure we also had special Halloween candy bags ready for them each year. The extra candy was appreciated. I just did not feel that I had to be friends with everyone on the street. This didn't mean there wasn't some neighborhood gossip from time to time; no community was immune to gossip. Listening to it was sometimes fun, even if I didn't know the people.

Both families next to us had been living in their homes when we moved in. Annie was close to their children in age, and since she was an only child she often played with the neighborhood children. It had been fun to watch each other's children go from babies and young people to the adults they were becoming. They often spoke of us like an aunt and uncle. Having our own daughter, we knew the value of that kind of trust from children. It was a respect that I hoped we had earned and it wasn't just due to the extra candy! Their respect was our gift.

We were always blessed with good neighbors wherever we lived. We would check on their house, collect their mail or shovel their walks when they were gone. They would do the same for us. But that was about as far as it went.

We had developed our own circle of friends over the years. They did not always include our neighbors, and I was not even able to tell for sure who else lived across the street, three doors down, or a block away. For that matter, I could barely identify any of the people on our street other than a friendly nod or hello as we passed them during a walk or bike ride. I liked to think that was not unfriendliness, just a way of minding my own business.

That's why I was so surprised when Andy approached me on that spring day.

I usually left the large door to my workshop open so the dust would blow outside. I used to have a family dog that would join me in the workshop. He never seemed to mind the sound of the saw or hammer and in most cases just slept through everything. Maybe he just enjoyed being included.

He had been a quiet, friendly dog, and I always told people he had more rights in our house than I ever would. I know I could never have done some of the things he did without being punished. Then again, I also couldn't lift my leg over my head to check my rear end out so maybe he was more special than me. When I acted jealous of the attention he received my wife would remind me that he was just a dog. I would tell her that I believed she thought the dog was cuter than me! She would often laugh at my joke, but I never remember her disputing my statement. In the end he was a friend I enjoyed having.

A pet is often good for the soul. Their love is so unconditional and they react to the owner's actions. If a pet was treated well they trusted the owner and enjoyed the environment they lived in. A happy pet added to a happy home. I always enjoyed my dog and gave him a lot of attention. I was rewarded with a friendship that had put little or no demands on me. As long as I fed him, walked him and gave him a little attention from time to time he was happy. I know it sounds a bit silly but he was like a pal, someone I could always count on to be there through good and bad. Sadly my pal had been hit by a car about a year ago and I had to put him to sleep. I still missed him. Someday I might get another pet, but not yet. Friendship like that was hard to find.

So I was working on a small planter box for the backyard, attempting to get the proper angle to one of the key pieces. My dog friend no longer shared my work space but I still really enjoyed my hobby even though my woodworking skills were somewhat suspect. Woodworking was never anything I would have been able to make a living at that was for sure. Finished carpentry to me meant that I was done! My "rough carpentry" wasn't much better. For that matter, my projects might have been done faster and better if I had paid someone else to do them. But where was the fun in that? I was intently focused on calculating the proper way to attack the piece of wood sitting in front of me when I heard a strong but young voice coming from just outside my door.

"Hey, mister."

I didn't see anything when I first looked up, because I was momentarily blinded by the sunshine, which provided morning heat and comfort to my workshop. I always liked the way the sunshine brightened my garage and loosened my muscles while I worked. Sometimes it felt like a warm protective blanket adding value to my day. Then there were times like this when I should have been wearing sunglasses. It was the sound of his voice rather than the site of the child that turned me in his direction.

"Hey, mister, you got any bottles?"

I looked down at a little boy standing in front of me. He was eight, maybe nine years old, dressed in ordinary looking oversized blue jeans, a shirt, and a ball cap that was too big for him, making his head look much smaller than it was. It appeared that he was wearing some hand-me-downs that he had not yet grown into.

What caught my attention was the small wagon sitting behind him. I was more used to boys his age going past me on skateboards, roller blades, or walking in groups loudly laughing and ignoring the problems of the world. Instead, here was this little boy standing in front of me with a friendly yet determined look on his face, pulling a small wagon, the kind of which existed more in my time than his.

"Bottles? What kind of bottles?" I replied.

"Any kind that I can take to the bottle depot. I need money, and my dad says I have to earn it myself, so I'm trying to collect pop bottles for the refund. Got any?"

This determined young entrepreneur now had my attention, and I wondered what someone his age could so desperately need money for, or for that matter why his father would make him go out on his own to raise it. I thought I could use a break anyway since I couldn't figure out how to build the flower box yet. I put down my tool; pulled out a stool and sat down. I gave the boy another "once over" before I asked him what his name was.

"Andy Bell. What's yours, mister?"

The boy spoke in a direct manner I hadn't expected but I always believed it to be important to help young children develop respect for their elders—that's why I taught my daughter to call adults by their surname. Maybe that was an antique attitude—I didn't know and didn't care.

"My name is Mister Henry."

He stuck his hand out towards me. "Nice to meet you, Mister Henry; I'm Andy."

I was amused by the formality of this little boy's introduction and yet impressed by the way he carried himself. Someone had definitely instilled respect into this little boy, much as I would have. I shook his hand and since he appeared to be all business I thought I better get right to it.

"I think I might have a few empty pop bottles kicking around. How many do you want?"

"All of them would be fine, Mister Henry."

I chuckled, realizing that he had given me a good answer, in his case more than less was best. He appeared to know instinctively that there was no crime in asking. I just didn't know if his ego was too fragile to accept no as well as yes. Luckily I wouldn't have to test him on that. Besides it was my fault that my question had painted me into a corner. How could I say no to the boy now?

I walked over to a corner of the building and moved a few boards that were in the way so I could pull out a garbage bag of recyclable bottles. I had been storing them until my next clean up day, when I would throw them in my truck and find some time to drop them off at the depot to collect the few dollars the deposit refund would provide. I was actually more than happy to give them away, since the time and effort of taking them to the bottle depot wasn't worth the trouble or the reward. I only did it for the environment anyway, or so I thought. So in a way, little Andy Bell was doing me a favor.

When I turned around I asked, "Why do you need all this money you're collecting?"

"I'm building a fortress for me and George. Dad said that since this was something I wanted then I had to get my own money."

Teaching him a lesson like that was good but as I looked at this future builder of grand projects I wondered why his father would not offer more help? Why wouldn't he be walking around the neighborhood with him? I decided not to pursue my curiosity and let the moment pass. It was none of my business anyway.

"Sounds like a big project. You sure you're going to get enough money?" I didn't know why I asked him that question. It wasn't like I was going to offer anything except the bottles.

"Oh sure; Besides George is helping me."

"So, who's this George?"

"He's my friend. He's older than me and said he will try to help me with the big stuff when we start building. He wants to help me, but sometimes he's busy too, so I'll do the best I can." I had a feeling I was being set up for more than just a bottle drive so I carried the conversation forward.

"How much money do you actually need for this fort you plan to build anyway?"

"I don't know yet, but George and me probably need a lot, because we want to build a big fortress not a just a fort. I can use my grandpa's hammer and stuff, but George says we will need wood, nails, and maybe some other things, so I figure we need at least fifty dollars. That should be enough. He knows what he is talking about."

I was not sure what size of fortress this young contractor was planning on building, but his answer told me that even though he talked as if he was grown up, he had a naive understanding of what fifty dollars would buy in today's world. Before I had a chance to respond I heard him speak again.

"I see you got lots of wood here, Mister Henry," he said as he looked past me into my workshop at the small pile of stacked lumber.

I was right he was after more than just pop bottles, so I grabbed the bag in front of me and told Andy that we better get these put on his wagon so he could get them to the depot while the day was still young. I didn't need some neighborhood urchin hanging around using up my Saturday.

The boy seemed disappointed but turned to help me put his newfound bounty on to the delivery wagon. Placing it on the box area was easy, but I could tell right away there was no way that his load would stay on the wagon. I asked him to wait for a minute.

Then I went back into my workshop and found two tarp straps I kept stored in the bottom of my toolbox.

When I returned he was standing near the front of his wagon looking into the bag I had just given him. He turned towards me as I approached him with a wide grin on his face. "Gee, thanks, Mr. Henry. That's a lot of bottles." His tone was one of pleasant surprise.

"Well you're welcome, Mr. Bell" I said with a mock sense of respect. "Now let's see if we can secure your load so that they don't fall off on your way home." I took the straps and hooked the ends on the side of the wagon strapping the large bag down. "How far do you have to go?"

"Not far. I just live down the street. Is it okay if I use these stretchy things for a while to collect more bottles?"

I assumed he was referring to the tarp straps, so I said to him, "Sure go ahead. But I will need them back."

"You bet, Mr. Henry. I'll bring them back as soon as I'm done."

"And make sure you get a grown up to help you, because if they slip they can hurt you."

"Okay, Mr. Henry. I'll be careful." With that he picked up the handle to his red wagon and headed down the street. He turned back towards me; gave a final wave goodbye and carried on in the direction of his house.

Watching him leave he reminded me of the cartoon character Dennis the Menace. I hoped it wouldn't be my destiny to become his Mr. Wilson. If it came to that I also hoped I wouldn't fit the role of the cranky Mister Wilson too well. I must be nicer than that. Then I wondered why I had not noticed this little boy in the neighborhood before. He said he lived just down the street and the way he talked made it obvious he was familiar with the area so I must have spotted him from time to time. Why had he not stuck in my mind? Actually I found myself kind of happy for the interruption. His visit had been a short one but it had peaked my interest. It made me think of my own childhood days. Simpler times I guess.

So despite the oversized clothes, his youthful innocence and his unattainable goals he exuded confidence for a small young man that made you want to get to know him better. Somehow I felt like I was going to.

CHAPTER 3

Little boy's personalities were often as similar as they were different, despite any kind of home environment. Andy was like most boys his age. He took on the world with an overabundance of energy. Every waking moment was an opportunity, every event an adventure. He lived life the way little boys were made to live it—happy, carefree, and with excitement. Life had not had a chance to wear him down. But it was beginning to.

Andy's family lived with his grandfather. He wasn't quite sure why. He had his own opinions but they were more thoughts than knowledge. His mother and father both worked and they used to talk about moving to their own place. Andy knew this was just a dream, because his parents would always follow any such conversation with a sentence like, "It would sure be nice, but we can't to afford it." He wasn't sure what they meant by that, but he knew enough to know that they were not moving. In most cases the topic ended more as an argument than a conversation. It can be difficult for a young child like Andy to hear yelling when he didn't understand the situation. Actually it could be frightening.

He never knew his grandmother. She had died before he was born so he liked to think they lived with his grandfather because he needed someone to take care of him. Andy could tell this wasn't true just from listening to the things his parents said to each other. Still he liked to think of it that way; after all it was just an opinion. It didn't have to be a fact. Imagination was a little boy's best friend so he tried to imagine one big happy family. It wasn't always easy.

Andy thought his parents argued more than they should. He knew it was true but he didn't know why. He was only nine so how would he understand everything? Much of the strife going on in the home was simple day-to-day adult interactions. Some conflicts were much more complicated. He really couldn't tell the difference. To him a fight was a fight and hearing his parents yell at each other made for an unhappy home. His life experiences were limited by his age and maybe if he had been older his parents fighting wouldn't have seemed so important. But he wasn't older. He was nine and still unable to understand why the fighting went on. He made guesses but this was when his imagination worked against him. He could imagine things that were never really there and sadly some that were.

So the yelling that went on in his house made Andy want to hide in his room or go outside to find his friend George and run off to play together. He felt that he would not be missed anyway. Those were the times when he dreamed he had better parents. The feeling didn't make him happy and he couldn't really imagine what different parents would be like. He just wanted the yelling to stop.

There was one last thing that worried Andy the most, the times when his grandfather or mother would tell his father that he was a no-good drunk. Andy knew this was bad just by his father's reaction. He had never seen his father hit anyone, but at times like those he wondered. He worried about what would happen if his father did get drunk enough to do something bad. A nine year old boy should not have even known what being drunk looked like; but he did. Drunken fathers could be hard for their sons. Andy never knew what he would have to do if his father ever did get violent. He knew that he wanted to protect his Mom but he was just a boy so what would he be able to do? Would he have to fight his Dad? Would his grandfather be able to help? This was when his imagination worked against him and these were the type of questions that rambled through his brain during the times when his father was most out of control. These were the times he was most scared.

That's why George and Andy were going to build their fortress. A fortress was something most boys dreamed of and Andy was no different. George said it would be something that they built together and something that was his own. George explained to him what a fortress was. How it kept bad things out and could be a good place to defend from. He wasn't sure what George meant but he could tell it was a good thing. The fortress was exactly what he needed. Once it was done he would have a place to run and hide when he felt the need to, a place where he could feel safe and a place that as George said could be his own. He didn't know how important that place would be. That would be another day.

Most of the things Andy felt about his life were not thoughts as much as "feeling" about how things were. Understanding the feelings was more complicated.

For now Andy was happy. He felt his morning bottle drive went well. Many of his neighbors were willing to give him what he was asking for, and he felt content with his anticipated reward. He had not had a chance to count the bottles he had collected, but he knew it would add up to a great start for him and George. Although his collections had went well, it had been more difficult than he had expected. Andy had gone to more than twenty homes telling people the same story. He was surprised at the resistance of some of the adults in the neighborhood to share even a small amount of their abundance with him. It never occurred to him that he would hear no from some of the neighbors but it didn't stop him. He was on a mission. When someone said no he thanked them just like his grandfather taught him to do and moved on to the next home. He was going to build his fortress and he needed money for that and for him this was the only way to get it. Besides he felt that most of the people he met were friendly enough to him.

When he had walked away from Mr. Henry's house he had a large bagful of what he was looking for. He had enjoyed talking to Mr. Henry, and something told him that he would see this man again. Talking to him was easy. Mr. Henry took the time to listen to Andy and he liked that about him. Most adults didn't take the time to listen to him, especially his parents.

As he walked down the street Andy was busy thinking about how grown ups treated him. Usually adults would tell him to go off and play, ignore him, or tell him simply to shut up. This seemed to happen even when he had something important to say. He felt his own parents often did not listen to him.

He tried every day to talk to his mom and Dad, but usually they were too busy or were arguing about something. Andy figured that his dad had an important job, even though he really did not know what it was. He tried now and then to ask his dad what he did, but he was just told that he wouldn't understand. After being turned away a few times, Andy figured he must be right, so he quit asking.

Andy could tell that his parents had a lot to do. His mom went to work every day and she had to take care of him and his baby sister as well. They told him that they had lots to worry about. They had to put food on the table for the family and did not always have time to play. He tried to understand.

None of that mattered however on this spring day. Mr. Henry had been easy to talk with. He was definitely the nicest grownup he had met during the day's adventure. This man had made it easy for Andy to ask him for what he wanted. When he left the end of the driveway, Andy felt he had accomplished something special. There was a connection he had made with Mr. Henry, something he felt would be good for him the next time he saw him. He just wasn't sure what that was yet.

Andy struggled to pull the wagon, which his father had given him. He was making several trips back to his house because he could only carry so many at a time. Each time he went home he felt stronger because he was working towards his goal; the fortress. Pulling the wagon may have been seen as a struggle to someone watching the boy but to Andy it was a reward for what he was doing.

His father reminded him that it was important to take good care of the wagon, since he and his grandfather had both used it when they were his age. The boy could tell that he meant his grandfather on his Dad's side and even though he had never met him Andy felt special on this day to be allowed to use the small family wagon his own father had used when he was the same age. It proved to him that even though his dad did not seem able to make time for him, he still trusted him. At least that was what he wanted to think.

On one of his trips back to his house he looked to his left as he was walking down the sidewalk and saw his friend George crossing the street to join him.

"Hi, George," he hollered as the boy ran up to him.

"Hi, Andy; How's it going?"

"Great. I think we did real good today. You'll be real happy with all the bottles I collected."

"Really? How many?"

"Well, I don't really know for sure," Andy admitted, "but it's a lot. I think we can start building our fortress real soon," Andy said with excitement in his voice.

As Andy's older friend, George felt part of his job was to keep him from getting carried away. "Let's not move too fast" he said. "We want to do everything the right way. You don't even know how many bottles we have or how much money they add up to. Let's just start by taking everything to the bottle depot so we can see how much money we have to work with. Okay?"

Andy was momentarily crushed by George's response, but he looked up to him. He trusted George, because he was his friend and he would not lie. As well, he was sure that George knew more than he did, because he was much older than Andy, which made George smarter than he was. If George said to wait, then he would wait. He was only talking a day or two anyway, right?

"Okay, George. I'll go home right now and start counting out the bottles," said Andy. "It's going to be a strong fortress you know. We'll have lots of money and it will be a big strong fortress. I just know it."

"I know it will," George agreed. "It will be the best fortress we ever built. It will protect us from everything."

Andy just nodded his head, happy to hear George agree with him. He gave George a big, happy grin and continued pulling his wagon of dreams on down the path towards his house.

CHAPTER 4

Saturdays around our home were simple, a day for catching up on chores from the previous week, housekeeping and yard duties. I admit that I had been a classic procrastinator early on in my life, but I soon saw no advantage to this path. I would often end up in a big argument over some small thing, such as mowing the grass or folding towels. Then the two-day weekend would be spoiled by tension and sarcastic remarks. I usually ended up doing the chore anyway.

There was enough tension and sarcasm at my workplace. I sure didn't need it at home too, so I learned to get things done as quickly as possible. Besides, I had discovered that Marie was a pretty understanding household supervisor as long as I was making a true effort. More importantly, she was often right. I wasn't going to give the satisfaction of telling her that, though.

I would occasionally volunteer to do more than the basics from time to time. I would tell my wife I just wanted to help out. The truth was I was banking some "good time" to cash in at a later date, when I wanted to do something fun like golfing or finishing one of my projects. This Saturday was a nice day, with a great weather forecast, and I just wanted to get through my basic chores and get back to working in my shop. I wasn't looking to do anything extra.

Our yard was something we took pride in. I felt the work Marie and I put into keeping it look good was well worth the effort. The grass was full and green because I always made sure it was fertilized properly not to mention providing the right amount of water.

When I looked around the yard I saw Marie's bright flowers in bloom, the raised flower bed I had built several years before and the play center I had built for Annie when she was young was still standing. It stood alone unused since she was a child. I just didn't have the heart to tear it down because it was one of my better projects I was most proud of. It was things like those that represented signs that it was my family that lived here and that it was our home. Just looking at my yard gave me a sense of satisfaction.

I had finished trimming and mowing the back lawn when I decided to go inside to get a drink of water before moving on to the front yard. Both the front and back areas of our house were a bit larger than normal yards in the neighborhood so taking a break half way through made it easier for me.

I was pouring a glass of water from our cooler when Marie walked into the kitchen.

"How's it going?" she asked.

"Not bad. The weather is great. It looks like it's going to last all day."

"Uh huh, The Weather Network says I that it will be quite warm today."

"That's good; can never use enough good weather."

"What have you been working on outside?" she asked.

"Oh just the usual; trimming and mowing; you know, Saturday stuff." I had drunk my first glass of water but I was still thirsty so I went back to the cooler for another one.

"That's good" she said as she continued to wipe down the counter. She seemed to always be doing something. I called it puttering, she called it being busy.

"What have you been doing?" I asked.

"Laundry mostly" She answered. "Washed the sheets and towels—you know Saturday stuff." She smiled at me coyly as if to say I wasn't the only one to do weekend chores.

I didn't want to take the bait so I pretended to take a large gulp of water and mumbled "Uh Huh."

"I'm going to be coming outside to water my plants before it gets too hot."

"Good idea" I said.

"They take a lot of work you know." She stated.

"I know. You do a good job that's why they look so great" offering a compliment.

She glanced my way without saying anything. I think she was trying to decide if I was making fun of her or actually complimenting her. It was unfortunate that sometimes it was easier to accept a comment from a stranger than from someone you knew. I used to tell Marie that many people seemed to think that I could be quite funny; she had just seen the lounge act too many times. My wife never tried to dispute my argument!

She chose to ignore my comment which was actually okay with me because I wanted to go finish my chores anyway. I downed the rest of my water, put the glass in the dishwasher and turned to leave the kitchen when I heard Marie ask me another question.

"Say, have you seen that little boy recently?"

I stopped to respond "What little boy?"

"The one you met a couple of weeks ago outside, the boy who was looking for pop bottles. The boy you told me about." It occurred to me that I had not seen him since that first meeting.

"Oh that boy. No, I guess I haven't."

"I thought you said he just lived down the street."

"That's what he told me."

"What did you say his name was?"

I had to pause for a minute while I researched my memory banks. Then I remembered the mental trigger I had implanted when I first heard him speak his name. I had equated his first name to Raggedy Andy, because his clothes had never really fit him, and his last name to a lunch bell, because I thought a boy his size should never be late for lunch! I know that would have sounded mean to some people—that's why I never verbalized the memory triggers I used.

"Andy Bell. I think his name was Andy Bell. Why?"

"No reason. I just wondered why you wouldn't have seen him once in a while. You're outside enough in your workshop."

I was beginning to get annoyed. All I had come into the house for was a drink of water before carrying on with my day. I didn't know where Marie was going with our conversation, and I wasn't sure I wanted to. Was she trying to give me a jab about spending too much time on my woodworking projects? She was usually supportive of my hobby, often because I volunteered to make her something to aid in her hobbies. What difference did it make to her if I had not seen a small neighborhood child for a couple of weeks?

"What difference does it matter?" I blurted out. "I only met him once."

My tone of voice seemed to make Marie angry. "It doesn't matter! I was just asking."

"Well, if you want to know so much, why don't you go find him? I'm sure he's around somewhere."

"You know, sometimes you can be a real jerk! I was just making conversation. What's the problem?"

"No problem. I just wanted a glass of water. So why don't you just let me do my chores."

"Fine!"

"Fine!"

Marie turned and stormed out of the kitchen. I stepped out the back door in an angry mood myself thinking "there goes a feel good Saturday."

I reviewed in my mind what had just happened. There appeared to be no good explanation for the altercation. Marie and I usually got along well enough. Saturdays never presented a problem. Since we both had things to do, interaction throughout the day was usually intermittent and friendly. So why did we just have a useless argument about such a simple thing?

I could never understand why Marie and I had these small spats in the first place. It wasn't as though I thought she was a bad person; in fact, I had fallen in love with my wife almost the first night I met her, like in some romance novel one gets lost in during a rainy day of reading. I could have a temper from time to time but I was also a hopeless romantic.

I met her at a local dance many years before. She was wearing a bright red summer dress, standing off in a corner talking and laughing with some friends. I spotted her while I was sitting with my own friends, who were telling all the "big man" stories I had heard a hundred times before. Hell, I had probably even told some of them myself. Of course, their method of storytelling was not nearly as romantic or eloquent as mine.

I found myself annoyed with their conversation, and like a bull attracted to the red cape of the bullfighter, I spoke up, saying that I was going to go ask that pretty girl in the red dress to dance. They turned their heads to look in the direction of the girl and laughed. The event itself and the conversation came flooding back from my memories.

"Good luck," one of them said. "You don't have a chance with a girl like that."

"Yeah," said my other friend. "Don't worry, we'll order you another beer. You'll be back soon enough—it won't get warm." He then punched my other friend in the arm and they joined each other in a sarcastic laugh.

"Well, we'll see," I shot back. "Just remember, telling the stories don't make them true stories!" I walked off towards this beauty in red feeling quite smug that I had put them in their place, but at the same time nervous that she would refuse my request to dance. If that happened, the walk back to my table was going to be much longer than the walk there.

I approached her with a youthful brashness and introduced myself.

I opened with a confident "Hi I'm Robert"

"Marie" was her simple response.

Deciding to act like I knew what I was doing and not give her too much time to think about anything I replied "Well it's nice to meet you Marie. Would you like to dance?"

She appeared to give me a "once over" and I waited for what seemed like an eternity for her answer. It was actually just a few seconds; I'm sure because I could feel my heartbeats.

Fortunately, the lady in red, Marie, accepted my request to join me on the dance floor, albeit with apparent nervousness on her part as well. Thank God I didn't have to make the walk back to my friends.

I liked to tell myself her nervousness was due to my dance moves and that my handsomeness that day made her weak in the knees. I never asked her to explain her reaction so my myth could never be shattered.

After the band stopped for a break we returned to her table where her friends sat. She didn't offer a formal invite or anything we just seemed to drift back there. I was happy and turned to give my buddies a big grin as if to say "told you so."

"Do you need a drink" I had asked.

"No thanks I still have this one" she said reaching for the glass in front of her. I didn't know it then but I would find out soon enough that it was just a soda drink. Marie didn't like alcohol much and didn't drink it often. Truth was I was happy with her answer because I was short of cash and didn't have a lot to spend that night.

I tried to make small talk "So what kind of work do you do?"

"What makes you sure that I work?" she said with a tiny smirk on her face.

I of course didn't know her age yet so maybe she was a student. It was the only thing I could think of so I asked "Are you a student?"

"Kind of" her answer came in a cryptic manner. Then she added "and kind of work too."

"What does that mean?" I asked a bit confused.

"It means that I work during the day and take classes at night. You know kind of work and kind of study."

Since I couldn't tell if she was trying to tease me . . . or confuse me . . . I decided to take her answer at face value. "Okay what do you work at during the day and study at night?" I questioned with what I hoped wasn't an obvious level of smug satisfaction.

"Nothing important; I work at a clothing story and just taking office courses at the local college."

I knew which college she spoke of because we only had the one so that made one less question I could ask. "Sounds important enough to me; not many people can do both at the same time." I was sincere in my compliment and hoped Marie could see that. She must have felt the same way because she continued talking with me. I figured the longer we talked the better my chances were to get to know her better. There was something about this girl that was almost spell-binding to me.

The night had moved along with more dancing, light talk, laughing, and a sense that this was a special night for me; both of us actually which I would find out soon enough. We didn't run off for a one-night stand or anything, which was important, because I already had respect for this young girl. When the night was over we realized that we wanted to see each other so we made a date for the next day. That date led to another date, then another and before long we were a couple.

Ironically I had even told a friend only days after meeting Marie that I was going to marry this girl—she just didn't know it yet! The fact that I only had $100 to my name never even came into my mind as an excuse but it had made it hard to buy the ring she deserved.

I desperately needed her to say yes, so the way I asked was going to be important. Somehow I believed it would all work out—I just did not know how yet. I just wanted to do it right. It took some time but I was finally able to win her over and with some hard work I found a way to buy the ring I thought she deserved. I don't know which was harder, finding a ring or getting her to accept. Moving from dating to engagement was a big step for both of us and there were times like now when I wasn't sure she might not have regretted giving in to my romantic intentions.

The memory of our first meeting was always a good one, and a highlight in my life, so as I began to become less angry I began to accept that Marie could be right: sometimes I was a jerk. For most of my life I had thought of it as a strength that would help me fight my way through problems and situations, but it also pushed people away. Was I pushing my wife away this day?

Then I thought to myself, so what? I had a habit of becoming self absorbed; didn't we all? That's why it was easy to tell myself that I was a busy person. Even though my daughter was off to university and I no longer had the responsibilities of taking her to school plays or sporting events, I was still a busy man. So what if I forgot something as insignificant as a meeting with a neighborhood entrepreneur? I had put in my time with kids. I had earned my free time.

Annie had been a high-energy child who kept both of us busy. She was an ambitious girl who wanted to participate in as many activities as she could. This also meant that her mother and I were busy running her from one thing to another.

With those thoughts in my mind it was easier to feel self righteous after I argued with my wife and feel that I was the one that was right. Even as I went back to my chores I found my level of annoyance growing again. If I left things alone they usually went back to normal in a short time; but even though I knew that I wasn't always good at doing it. Why did everything have to explode into a big deal, anyway? I reminded myself that I didn't want to be drawn into the busy life of another kid like Andy Bell? I was just too tired. Maybe I should explain that to Marie. Would she understand? Would it even matter to her and most of all why had my chance meeting with the child stir up so many questions anyway? Had Marie accidentally opened a door I didn't know was there?

I didn't know the answer, but now I couldn't get the damn question out of my mind.

CHAPTER 5

I heard the sound of running coming up the pathway as I reached down to pick up the trimming tool. I was still miffed at Marie and I wasn't interested in talking to anyone so I didn't look up to see who it was. As far as I was considered whoever it was could go away.

I was busy telling myself that it was my Saturday job to take care of the yard, and that's all. It wasn't part of my job to entertain every street boy that came along. So what if I hadn't given a second thought about a boy I had meant only once. Big deal; she could be as mad as she wanted. I would enjoy the quietness! Apparently I wanted to keep the hurt alive a bit longer and embrace my old friend—self pity. Besides I was getting good at holding onto anger. It was something I wasn't proud of and worked on when I could— today just wasn't one of those days.

I tried to look busy so I wouldn't be bothered but then I heard his voice and could no longer ignore him.

"Hi, Mr. Henry; Whatcha doing?"

I turned around slowly to find the same little boy standing in front of me that I had just struggled a few minutes earlier to remember. It seemed more than a coincidence.

He stood in front of me with the same carefree naivety I had seen the last time. As I looked at him, I felt another twinge of guilt for not remembering him. Again I couldn't understand why it should matter either way to me but it did. I would never admit that to Marie however. I wouldn't allow her the satisfaction.

"I brought back your stretchy straps," said Andy. "They sure helped. Thanks a lot."

I knew it was too late to start my lawnmower and pretend I had not heard him. Besides, my argument with Marie was not his fault, and I didn't want to snap at him or tell him to go away. He hadn't done anything wrong.

"They're called tie downs," I said. "Not stretchy straps."

"Oh. Okay. Well I'm bringing them back anyways."

"Thanks, Andy" I grunted as I reached forward and took the tie downs from him. I thought I should call him by name, since I had just gone through so much in the last few minutes to remember it. "I appreciate you returning them."

"No problem. What's wrong, Mr. Henry?"

It surprised me that a small child could so easily tell that something wasn't right. Why or how he could sense the emotion was mystifying so I thought it would be better simply to change the subject to avoid any further explanation.

"Nothing is wrong. I'm just busy—that's all."

"Oh okay, what ya been doing?" Andy asked. I was amused at how easily the attention of a young boy could be changed. It was actually a relief because it allowed me to move the conversation in a different direction since I wouldn't want to have to explain my mood to the lad anyways. I decided to answer his question with a simple response rather than ignore it then move on to the only activity I knew the boy was involved in. I figured that would change the conversation quick enough.

"I am just doing yard work. I do it every Saturday," I answered. "How are the plans for your fort coming along?"

"Well, it's going slower than George and I thought it would," Andy said in a frustrated voice, "And it's a fortress."

I ignored the obvious correction of my reference to his project and continued with a simple "Why's that?"

"Well, it will probably cost more than we thought, and we still need some real plans to work with. George says we'll get it done— it's just going to take longer than we hoped."

I was once again impressed by the way this young contractor with such little life experience spoke to me; such confidence.

"Well, I'm sure everything will work out," I said, attempting to make him feel better. I was ready to go back to the work that lay before me and was hoping he would move on.

"I hope so," he continued. "We have already got the place picked out. We just have to get going."

He did not seem in a hurry to leave. I just assumed that he was planning to build his fort in the backyard of his family's home. Apparently, the two boys had bigger plans. "Where do you plan to build this fort of yours?"

"We've got a spot picked out down by Johnson's Pond." I knew where the boy spoke of; everyone in the neighborhood knew of Johnson's Pond. Since we lived in the suburbs and we were on the outskirts of a city, there was still some rural area close by yet to be developed.

I took a moment to remember what I knew about the spot. Johnson's pond was still one of those undeveloped areas that many people saw as "greenbelt area." There couldn't have been more than twenty acres left and the land had no real use to it, until the day came that land developers found interest in it. That would still be several years away, though, and I could certainly understand the area's attraction to a small boy like Andy.

I knew the property was owned by an old man who had most likely inherited it as part of a farm at one time or another. Of course I was just guessing about the inheritance part. He was somewhat of a recluse and no one knew much about him. The area was named Johnson's Pond because that was his last name. I doubted that he himself called it that. The name made the area sound much grander than it was. There were still many attractive indigenous trees, birds, and local plants living in the area and it stood out from the rest of the neighborhood. The "pond" itself was more of a slough than any kind of beautiful water park. The spring runoffs would add freshness to the spot each year, but the water would become more stagnant as the summer dragged on. There were times when Marie and I would take a walk around the area and I could even see some kind of moss or something floating on top of the water; still though the property had a certain attraction and definite possibilities.

The twenty acres or thereabouts was not the perfect world of greenbelt land, but it was a safe enough area. I could see where Andy and his friend George would find some interest in building a fort for themselves in the trees of this hideaway. I had been a small boy myself at one time, so I still had some distant memories of places I grew up around that were similar to Johnson's Pond. I remembered some of the fun I had playing games with my friends in a secret place of our own. I hadn't forgotten everything I enjoyed as a child; I wasn't that old. I was sure that Andy would enjoy similar adventures.

"Well, that sounds like a good spot to build some sort of tree house," I said.

"Oh, it's not going to be just a tree house," Andy stated. "Like I said, it will be a fortress where George and I can kill off the dragons that come to fight us. We're going to play games, talk and anything else we want to do. We'll do lots of stuff. It'll be great"

Again amused by his imagination and determination, I had no doubt that he would win whatever battle came his way. I had not met his friend George, but the look on Andy's face told me for sure that he was quite serious. If his friend was equally strong, then who knew what fights they would win or discoveries they would make.

I had become more invested in the conversation and began by saying "Well that sounds like fun. Do you think I will be able to come and visit you once in a while?"

Andy was too young to understand that I was teasing him, so his answer was straight forward and strong. "You bet Mr. Henry. You can come anytime you want—after we build it."

Then something occurred to me. "Hey, have you asked Mr. Johnson's permission to build something on his land?"

"Not yet, but it won't be a problem," Andy stated confidently.

"Why is that?" I questioned.

"I know he'll like us."

"Oh is that so?" I couldn't help smile. "Everything will be okay on his side of things then?"

"Sure. It won't be a problem at all."

I looked down at the boy wondering if life could be so simple. An odd sadness surrounded me for the briefest moment. I wished my life could be that simple. I must have taken too long to reply because his voice brought me back to the moment.

"What's the matter, Mr. Henry?"

I looked down at the boy as I gathered myself and put my actor mask back on.

"Oh nothing . . . just thinking."

"About what?"

"Just things, nothing important," I tried to say nonchalantly while changing the subject. "So when are you going to see Mr. Johnson about building your fort?"

"Don't know," he stated. Then the boy got a worried look on his tiny face and said, "Guess I better do it soon if we want to get building."

I wanted to be encouraging, so I found myself putting my hand on his shoulder while telling him not to worry. There would be lots of time. It was in that moment that my charitable human nature—plus my big mouth—painted me into a corner. As I heard my voice say the words, I wondered what had prompted me to make such an offer.

"Just come see me if you need any help."

"Really?" Andy said, his voice perking up. "Would you really help me build the fortress?"

I had just meant that I would help him talk to old man Johnson, at most. Truthfully, I didn't really want to help him at all, since I knew it would interrupt my own comfortable routines. I was just trying to say something that would make the boy feel more optimistic. I had forgotten how literal children took things. I took a second look at this little guy, wondering how innocent he really was—or was he just smarter than me?

"It would sure be great if you could, Mr. Henry. You see, George can't help me with everything, and you probably know about my dad." He didn't expand on that issue and I was glad he hadn't. "We could go see Mr. Johnson tomorrow."

I knew that backing away from my offer or making any excuse now would crush Andy's feelings. I had already hurt enough feelings for today.

As well this little guy somehow appeared to have latched on to me for some reason. I felt his boyish admiration growing for me. It had been a long time since I had felt that kind of importance, and I liked it. What the hell, how much work could it be anyway? Kids got bored easily, so it might be something that he would only stick at doing for a week or two, and then I would be free again.

"Sure, we could do that, I suppose." I hesitated briefly. I knew that my wife and I would be going to church in the morning, if she was talking to me by then; and I wanted to watch some sports on TV later in the day, so I told him, "Tomorrow's Sunday, so let's go over in the afternoon about two o'clock, okay?"

"Sure!"

Then something came to me. "You know how to tell time, Andy?"

"Just about," he said, "but Mom knows how, so I'll just ask her."

"I have a better idea," I said, now realizing that I was about to take on a project with a young boy I had met only a couple of times. In today's mixed-up world I sure did not want people in the neighborhood, especially his family, to think that I was heading off to a pond alone with this little boy for any reason other than the construction of his fort. "How about if I come down to pick you up at your house? Then I can meet your mom so she knows where we are going and what we're doing. Make sure that it's okay with her. Sound good?"

"Okay!"

"Where do you live?"

"Three blocks that way," he said, pointing. "Just down the street. Our house is white with blue windows. We got a big tree in the front yard. I'll sit outside and wait for you so you don't miss our place."

"Wait," I said before he ran away. "What side of the street are you on and will your mom be home?"

I could see Andy was getting ready to make his escape when he said, "Same side as you. Mom's home every Sunday, so you can meet her then."

"What about your Dad?" I questioned.

"Probably not. He's not home much." I sensed that the boy was less eager to have me meet his father than his mother and that was fine with me. From what little I had heard about the man I wasn't sure I really wanted to meet him anyways.

35

I didn't question him any further. I figured with the kind of information he provided I should be able to find his house. If I didn't find him, I had a feeling that he would make sure that he found me!

"See you tomorrow," he hollered back as he went running down the street. He took off in the opposite direction full of excitement and happiness.

I couldn't keep from smiling as I picked up my trimmer to continue my work, knowing that I still wasn't completely sure if I had not been fooled by a young boy into helping him. Then I thought to myself "what the hell?" I didn't care if I had been taken in. My life had become so mundane that it might feel be good to give something back, do something different from my normal routine. Who knows maybe I would even enjoy it.

Then my analytical dragon began to come alive in my brain. I seemed to always have too much time to think and overanalyze but it was who I was. I began to think of the times I had spent with my own daughter when she was that age. Being a parent held many responsibilities as well as joys. I remembered how cute she had been but also how adamant she could be and how much energy she had drained from me, much more than I would have in my favor today. "No" was just a word that caused her to try a different approach to asking me. She could be demanding of my time and small disappointments to her were as big as a crashing car accident. How many times had I found myself putting my own duties aside to take care of her demands then going back later on to finish my own work. I remembered how tired I was at the end of a day of her child adventures. Of course I was much younger then.

"Geez am I too old to chase after this lad?" I mumbled to myself. "My God, now what did I get myself in to?"

"Who are you talking to?" I heard Marie ask. I had been deep in thought and never even heard her come up behind me.

"No one" I said; "Just thinking out loud."

"Oh okay."

It was obvious by her tone of voice that our little argument was forgotten. I could never stay mad at her for very long either. Why we bickered never seemed to make sense anyway. Many people would just say that was a part of marriage. Unfortunate if that was true.

"What are you up to?"

"Just taking a break from my garden" Marie said. "Wanted to see what you were doing."

I noticed that she had a glass of water in her hand and offered it to me before I asked if she had brought it for me. I was grateful for the drink because it was becoming quite warm outside.

"Usual things; trying to finish my grass trimming and stuff; I keep getting interrupted though." I grinned at her to show her I was just teasing. "Of course I never seem to be working when the supervisor arrives."

"Yes I noticed that" she said with a wry smile of her own.

"I thought you might" I laughed.

"So was that the little boy we were talking about leaving here?"

"Yeah it was. His name is Andy Bell; I remembered it as soon as he came running up."

"Seems like an excited little guy" Marie said.

"I'm sure you're right. He just got me to agree to help build his fort."

"How did he do that?" she questioned.

"Probably tricked me" I chuckled.

"Aren't you smarter than a young boy?" she said with a laugh of her own.

"Apparently not" I stated attempting to look chagrined. Marie knew me too well though and could tell I really wasn't upset about the whole thing.

"You'll probably enjoy it anyway" she offered.

"Why do you think that?"

"Well you like building things and he obviously wants something built."

"You're right about that! However I have a feeling that it is going to be a bigger project than he thinks it is."

"You'll be fine."

"Really? Why do you say that?"

"You're good with children Robert. I remember how patient you were with Annie and you've only mellowed as you got older."

"I thought I was always mellow" I laughed with a false sense of indignation and hurt look on my face. "And who said I got older?"

Marie laughed before replying "Have you looked in a mirror lately? Notice any gray hairs?"

Grateful she had not also pointed out my growing belly as well I decided to simply agree and move on. "Gray can mean wisdom you know."

"Uh Huh" she nodded. "What do you think it means for you?"

"Boy you're really funny aren't you? Ever think about taking your act on the road?"

"Maybe I could open for your act" she teased.

I could see I wasn't going to get the better of her today. First a little boy is smarter than me and now my wife; what was the world coming to? Marie's sense of humor was every bit as good as mine. I don't know if that meant we both had a strange sense of humor or just a good one. For me I chose the latter.

I handed her the empty glass with a quick thank you and picked up my tool once again to begin the rest of my afternoon chore. "Well I better get this finished before the supervisor fires me."

"Oh she would never do that" Marie stated.

"Why's that?" I questioned.

"No one else dumb enough to work for the wages my husband pays."

Realizing there was no good answer since I was both the husband and dumb worker I surrendered, gave her a smile and shook my head in one final attempt to keep my dignity. She gave me a smile of her own and turned to walk back into the house. I momentarily glanced at my beautiful wife walking away and wondered what I would do without her. Then I pulled the cord on the weed trimmer, waited for it to start and prepared to finish what I had started. Maybe more days like this won't be so bad after all I thought.

CHAPTER 6

Marie and I had spent some time during Saturday's supper meal discussing my promise to Andy. I filled her in with more detail on what had happened in the afternoon and chuckled a bit in how I thought maybe small Andy had maneuvered me into enlisting in his fortress project.

"I'm not sure yet who the smart one was, him or me?" I stated.

"That's Sunday afternoon right?" she asked "After church?

"Yes dear" I replied making it clear I understood her point "Don't worry I'll be at church. Just like normal."

Luckily she chose to ignore my condescending tone of voice. Good thing too because the afternoon had been perfect so another useless quarrel would not have been fun.

"That's nice, dear," she said. It was clear that was all she wanted to confirm. The rest of my story were just words, I couldn't even tell if she really heard them.

Marie got up from the the table to bring more gravy in from the kitchen. She had a way of dismissing anything important to me with that simple sentence. I don't think she was trying to belittle me, or was even aware that she was doing it, but I always wanted her to ask me questions and show more interest in what I was doing. Sometimes she did but more often she didn't.

I decided to press on so when she came back to the table I asked her "What do you think?"

"About what?"

I took a moment to look at her wondering if she was toying with me "The boy Andy Bell. What do you think about me helping him?"

"I told you this afternoon what I thought about it" she stated with the simplicity of truth.

"Remind me" I replied.

"I said you'll do just fine."

It was obvious to me that I wasn't going to receive any further encouragement so I choked back my ego and decided to just let it go.

Sometimes I wondered why I even bothered to tell her about my plans. It seemed that whatever project I wanted to do was okay with Marie as long as it didn't interfere with the day-to-day running of her house or our life. But I wanted more. I wanted her to share in my ideas. I wanted her feedback, encouragement, and interest. She didn't seem able to give me those things, so I had come to accept her "that's nice dear" as the stamp of her approval.

"Okay" I said bringing an end to the Andy Bell conversation "Just so you remember I'll be gone all afternoon after church."

"That's fine. Annie won't be here tomorrow so maybe I'll do some shopping."

"She's not making it over tomorrow?"

"No. Too much studying she said, plus some kind of paper due on Monday."

"That's too bad" I said with disappointment "I look forward to seeing her."

"Me too" Marie said before adding "School is important though and her exams will be coming up soon. She needs to put in the study time. Her classes are hard."

"I know, I know. It doesn't mean I won't miss her."

"I know Robert; but we'll probably see her next week. We'll enjoy seeing her just as much then."

Even that was something I could agree on.

Sunday mornings came quick enough, the last cherished day off before I went back to work. We came back from the church service, which we attended every week. I must admit I went to church mostly as a routine that my wife had created for our family when our daughter was a child. Although I did have strong spiritual beliefs I had never been excited about the religious part of society. To me faith and religion were two different things. In my opinion you could have one without the other so given a choice I would rather have spent my Sundays watching sports. This was never truer then after a long week of hard work. Instead I joined my wife in the weekly tradition. There were worse things in life I rationalized than sharing my faith with other people even if I didn't always agree on their methods.

There was another reason as well. Since Annie had moved out of the house to go to school, Sundays had often become the only day of the week that we were actually able to see our daughter. We would take her with us whenever she could get to our house early enough. Her visits made going to church easier for me.

Annie was one thing that I did enjoy about Sunday so I was still disheartened that she wouldn't make it to our house this week. The intellectual side of me could understand that part of my daughter's life, but in my heart I was disappointed when I didn't get to see her at least once a week. I could always tell that my wife felt the same way about Annie's visits, and I think it was something we quietly shared as mother and father.

Don't get me wrong, I often enjoyed Sunday-morning interactions with friends or acquaintances even without Annie being present. This Sunday, however, had not been one of those days. I was missing my daughter, and my mind was concentrating more on what lay ahead of me in the afternoon. I still had to deal with Andy. I barely listened to the pastor's words and wouldn't even remember what his sermon was about.

As I sat quietly in the pew surrounded by other people my thoughts were more on my commitment to Andy. I surmised that I couldn't back out of my promise now to help the boy with his fortress project, even though a big part of me wanted to. Marie's confidence in me the night before if only given in an offhanded manner helped me believe it shouldn't be too unpleasant. In truth, if I was to be honest to myself it felt good to see the joy in his eyes when he had asked me for my assistance and I said yes. A child's innocence was hard to ignore. It was nice to have him think that I would be able to help him with something so important to his life. I'm sure his request was bolstering my ego. I just hoped I wouldn't disappoint him.

I had worked on many projects and knew my weaknesses, so I was afraid that he might have put more value on my building skills than he should have. I didn't want him to know that my small shop, which he had seen the first day we met, was meant more as a place of solitude than an actual area of great creations. I had no idea how to build a fortress but there appeared to be no way out for me now without losing face. My pride wouldn't allow that. These were the thoughts and doubts rambling through my mind as the sermon came to a close. Marie touched my arm to get my attention and indicated that it was time to leave. We gathered ourselves to say our goodbyes to our friends and make the short drive home.

"I'll get changed and head out right away" I said as we walked into the front door of our home. "The fortress architect will be waiting for me" I laughed.

Marie smiled back to me as she hung up her coat and joined in with the joke "You wouldn't want to keep a building giant like him waiting. Who knows he may have more work for you later on!"

"May even be a new career for me" I chuckled.

"You never know." Marie then added "I'll make a quick lunch for you before you head out."

That seemed like a good idea because I didn't know how long I would actually be gone. Besides I was somewhat hungry.

After lunch it was time to meet Andy and his mother. I couldn't put it off any longer. I had changed my clothes from my Sunday best to my weekend attire and since it was a windy spring day, I gathered a light coat, my favorite, pulled my walking shoes on, hollered good-bye, and walked out the door. It was almost two o'clock, and I knew that young Andy would be waiting for me, so I didn't want to be late. I headed down the street, following the instructions he had given me and knowing that it should be easy to find his house.

I found it a short while later. Sure enough, he was sitting on the front step of his house, dressed in his best clothes complete with his signature ball cap ready to make his presentation to Mr. Johnson.

He had not seen me right away, so I had a moment to take a better look at the house. It was a simple house, one I had driven by hundreds of times without really noticing it. It was a bungalow with blue windows, just as Andy had said. The blue paint around the window and door frames was beginning to fall off. Spring cleanup had not been done yet, and everything showed small areas of disrepair. The one thing that stood out in this otherwise plain picture was a beautiful birch tree positioned in the middle of the front yard. The leaves were just beginning to bud, and the winter version of this tree could still be seen, but I could tell that this represented the majestic centerpiece of the property. Why had I never noticed it before?

Andy had spotted me. His big smile, combined with the excitement in his voice, told me that he had been waiting for me with less than total patience.

"Hi, Mr. Henry. Glad to see you made it! Are you ready to go?"

"Hello, Andy. Glad to see you too," I said, matching his enthusiasm while trying to keep my own amused smile at his exuberance to myself. "We'll go as soon as I meet your mom. Where is she?"

"She's inside," Andy said. "I'll get her." The next thing I saw was Andy turning towards the front door, letting it slam as he jumped through the opening.

"Mom, he's here," Andy hollered. "Come meet Mr. Henry so we can go." Andy spoke this more as a statement of fact than a demand, and I hoped his mother understood it that way. I didn't want things to start off on the wrong foot. I stood on the Bells' front steps looking around toward the street, waiting for Andy's mom, when I heard the gentle sound of woman's shoes walking towards the front door. Men often walked with more of a clumping sound. A few seconds later I was addressed by a soft voice.

"Mr. Henry?"

"Hello, Mrs. Bell?"

"Please, call me Laura."

"Robert."

"Andy tells me that you just live down the street and that you were kind enough to offer helping him with his big fortress plans?"

I liked the fact that she got straight to the point with a non-judgmental question. Just like her son.

"Well help him may be an overstatement," I said, chuckling. "I just hope he isn't disappointed with my best efforts!"

She smiled back at me with what appeared to be understanding. "Yes, well, he can be quite a persuasive young man when he wants something," she said as she turned to see Andy approach us.

"You met him, so can I go now, Mom?" Andy said with childlike frustration.

"Go get your coat, Andy. I'll speak to Mr. Henry for a moment." Andy turned and ran back into the house, leaving his mother and me on the doorstep.

"Please come on in," Laura said, holding open the door.

"Thanks," I offered as I stepped inside. "So, it sounds like Andy filled you in on my involvement."

"Yes, well I wish his father could help him do it, but he can't," she said.

Couldn't or wouldn't? I thought. But I wasn't about to pry into a stranger's business, especially on the first meeting.

"My father, Andy's grandfather, would like to help him out, but I don't think his health makes it possible for him right now."

"Oh, what kind of problem does your father have?" I asked Laura out of politeness.

"Well, he had a heart attack a couple of years ago. He has recovered, but it's best not to take any risks. I know he would certainly do it if I asked him. I've made it clear to Andy not to ask him. He isn't quite old enough to understand why, but luckily he still does what I tell him. We'll see how long that lasts," she said, sighing.

"They do grow up fast," I said, feeling awkward. It was the first thing I could think to say. I should have been able to offer something more than an overused cliché, but nothing came to mind. "I just wanted to meet you before Andy and I went off to try and construct whatever tree house or fortress he is thinking of building. To be honest, I'm not really sure what kind of a construction undertaking I've actually signed up for." I said this to her with a grin on my face so she would think I was joking with her. Thankfully, she did. However, there was far more truth in that statement than I wanted her to know at this time.

"Yes, well Andy has a habit of enlisting many people in whatever project he has on the go," she said, laughing. "He should be a recruiter for the Armed Services! He's harmless and well meaning, just like most small boys. Just be sure to not let him trick you into wasting too much of your own time."

"I don't really mind. To be candid, I find your son to be a surprisingly polite and respectful young man. We don't find that as often as we should in children anymore. It's good to see. I imagine you're the one responsible for that."

"Thank you, Mr. Henry."

"Robert," I corrected her.

"Robert," she said, obviously thankful for the politeness but cautious about the compliments. She appeared more uncomfortable with familiarity than I would have expected. I didn't know her history with men I just hoped that she did not think I had any special interest in her other then polite friendliness. Not only wasn't I interested in any other woman, but I was obviously past my prime and frankly hadn't been much of a ladies' man when I was young.

I decided to chalk up her uncomfortable posture as a symptom of today's uncertain world. Maybe she just wasn't used to hearing such strong praise of her son or herself from a stranger. I took more notice of the woman standing in front of me. She was plain, although not unattractive. She looked to be in her mid-thirties, with a nice enough figure, hair to her shoulders, which I always found attractive in women, and little makeup.

There was a tired look to her demeanor, however. I assumed that was from raising a small, rambunctious boy like Andy. Andy had mentioned that he had a sister, but she did not appear to be anywhere nearby.

I guessed that she was a fair woman, who took no nonsense from anyone. I didn't know why I thought these things, but they had crossed my mind within the first few minutes of meeting her. I decided that I liked this person.

"No problem," I added. "My wife and I have a daughter who was an active child herself. She was into many different activities. My wife, Marie, and I always seemed to be running off to something every day when she was Andy's age. There isn't much I haven't seen," I assured her. I wasn't trying to impress this woman, just leave her with a feeling of safety while passing her child's activity on to me.

Andy came bursting out to the porch where we were standing. "Okay, Mr. Henry I'm ready! I've got everything I need. Can we go?"

"Sure Andy. I guess we can go now as long as it is okay with your mother."

"Is it okay, Mom? Can I go?"

Laura took one last look at me. "Yes, Andy, it's okay. You can go."

"Great. Let's go, Mr. Henry," Andy said, as if his mother might change her mind if we waited any longer.

"Aren't you going to say good-bye to your mom?"

"Bye, Mom," he offered, the same quick good-bye most boys give when they've got places to go.

"Whoa," Laura said. "Give me a hug good-bye."

"Aw, Mom!" Andy said, embarrassed.

"You know the rule, little guy. A kiss hello or a hug good-bye," Andy's Mom said.

Running up to his mom, he gave her the quickest hug I had seen in a long time, probably since the time when I was a little boy dealing with the same unfair mother's request. Now that my mother had been gone for so long, I wondered why I didn't take more hugs from her. That was one of my own ghosts to deal with.

Andy then turned on his heel, looked at me, and said, "Ready Mr. Henry? Let's go." I found the whole situation amusing. Here was such a confident little adventurer, humbled so quickly by a mother's public affection. Mothers had a way of doing that to their sons. You could love your mother and still want her to be more careful with treating you like her little boy in front of other people, at any age. As Andy and I headed out the door, there was something about that moment that just felt right—a mother's love, a son's strength. Both were important.

CHAPTER 7

As I watched little Andy march down the street with me towards Johnson's Pond, I could tell this was not the time to make jokes about his mother's hug good-bye. A cheap laugh did not provide enough value for the resistance it would cost, so I decided to take his mind off the moment and enjoy the day.

"So, Andy, do you know what kind of tree house you want to build?"

"Not a tree house, Mr. Henry—it's a fortress," he said with a determined voice.

"Sorry, fortress," I said apologetically. I was sure that little Andy would never know the difference.

"Yeah, I want to build a fortress big enough for me and George and up in a tree so you have to climb to get up to it," he said excitedly; his mood had obviously changed. "Then I want to only let people into the fortress that I say can come in."

"Are you going to let me in?"

"Sure Mr. Henry. I have to. You're helping me build it," he said as if this were just common sense.

This little boy seemed to have a master plan. If we followed it, things should be quite easy. I felt as though I should feel special to have already been invited to his tree house . . . I mean fortress.

I had never learned how to handle silence when I was with another person. I knew that too much talking was not always the best way of doing things, either, but it seemed to be my way. I wanted to keep the conversation going as we walked, so I asked

Andy another question. "Are you going to have a secret code to get in the fortress?"

Andy looked up at me with slight confusion. I smiled, thinking I had finally found something Andy hadn't thought about yet. I guess the adult was still smarter than the little boy after all.

Then he replied; almost condescendingly, "Well sure, Mr. Henry. Who wouldn't have a secret code?" For the briefest moment, I was about to say "*You,* Andy," but once again I saw no value in the comment just to prove a point.

I suppressed my amusement at this young man's way of looking at things. It made me wonder why so many things in my own life are so complicated. Maybe Andy's simple, matter-of-fact way could make things easier for me, if I could just learn how to use his technique maybe life would be easier

"Sure, I guess you're right. What's your secret code?"

"I can't tell you yet, Mr. Henry."

"Why not?" I questioned.

"George and me are still picking one. Don't worry, though. I know we'll have one before we finish the fortress."

"Okay then," I said as we rounded the corner. "We're here."

It hadn't been a long walk to Johnson's Pond, and the conversation between Andy and me had made the time go by even faster. Now we had to walk up the path to the Johnson house. It wasn't very far from the road, but the pathway was old and overgrown with weeds and crabgrass. The house wasn't in much better shape. I knew it was most likely over forty years old, with very little up keep. It had not yet been enveloped by suburban growth and may have even served as a kind of homestead property at one time. That was my best guess, based on the information my neighbors had passed on to me.

The house needed some fixing and cleanup around the yard. It was obvious just from looking at the siding that the paint was beginning to fall off and fade. I couldn't understand why the man had never switched over to the more common vinyl siding. It needed no paint and limited maintenance. Maybe he didn't have the cash.

Many older houses need some upgrading or extra maintenance. Johnson's house appeared to be no different. His house may even be worse than most. Not only did his house need painting but with a quick overview I could see shingles missing from his roof, rain spouts gone, a damaged garage door and so many other defects that indicated years of neglect. There was no sense imagining the problems I couldn't see. I was just glad it wasn't my house.

I could tell that there had been flower beds under the window areas at one time or another just by looking at the cheap landscaping blocks used to form the traditional flower bed areas. They were long forgotten and neglected; like the rest of the property. The plants, which may have once grown in abundance, now sat dead and brown. Pride of ownership and upkeep did not appear to be present in any fashion.

I had never met this man before so most of what I knew about old man Johnson consisted of more rumor than fact. Like many rumors repeated enough times, they had become truths in people's minds. Apparently, Johnson had been a widower for almost fifteen years, and it was never sure if his wife had died of natural or some other mysterious causes, "if you know what I mean," as one person had said to me. The wink after he said it told me he didn't know any more than I did. Anyway, no one was ever brave enough to challenge the old guy about this fact, so I believed I would never know for sure, since I wasn't going to ask him. I tried not to buy in to those kinds of rumors anyway. Sometimes, though, on a slow day, it was fun to wonder.

Thinking about all of these things stirred emotions and thoughts of my own. I knew that I would experience sadness if I lost my wife, so I had to believe another man would feel the same way. As these emotions ran through me, I found myself hoping that I wouldn't have to deal with the same loss anytime soon, or at the very least I would deal with it better than Johnson had. I know Marie would expect me to mourn, but she would also want me to get on with my life. I felt the same way about her, so why were these thoughts passing through my head? Strange the things that flashed through a person's mind at the oddest times. I decided it was a reaction to my current surroundings.

I wasn't an expert or anything but I knew a property this close to our residential area would be worth a small fortune. His house may not be worth much in the current condition but a developer wouldn't be interested in the house anyway. It was the land that would be important. Builders needed developers and developers needed land. Historically they paid well for prime land ready for the next big building boom. I was sure the old man knew that. That may be why he neglected his house upkeep. Of course who knew if money mattered to him at his age? How much did an old man need anyway? Maybe his property meant more to him than money. I had no way of knowing.

I had seen before how giving up your home full of memories was never easy. I remembered an old woman who had been forced off her farm where she had raised her children. She had lost her husband several years before and was getting too old to deal with the day-to-day issues of living on the farm, even though the land itself was rented out to other people. She was a friend of my parents, so they helped her and her family with the struggles of moving. It was a small way for them to offer support. The decision to move had not been hard for her children. They had all been away from the farm for some time and had gone on with their own lives. She had two boys and a daughter, and they had built new memories with their own families. It wasn't that they didn't care about their mother—quite the opposite. They told me that their childhood memories growing up on the farm were important to them—some of their best—but they were just memories. It had been a good way to grow up, but they didn't miss it.

Selling the farm was just a matter of business for the children. For the mother it had been the best part of her life. Giving it up was hard.

I came out of the fog of memories prompted by seeing this property and my attention returned to Andy as he spoke, "We're here, Mr. Henry."

I noticed that we were standing at Mr. Johnson's front door. I looked down at Andy by my side. He looked up at me with what appeared to be a sudden moment of trepidation and fear that I had not seen in this little boy before now. It made me wonder about my own wisdom of standing at old man Johnson's door. I didn't know what kind of a man he really was. How could I be sure he would react positively to our request? I was the adult, though, so I could not show the boy any uncertainty.

"Well, Andy, knock on the door."

"Okay, Mr. Henry," he said as he slowly stepped forward and tapped on the door.

"You better knock on the door harder or Mr. Johnson won't hear you." I didn't want to refer to him as old man Johnson in front of Andy.

Andy turned and pounded on the door in his young man's way. I figured if old man Johnson didn't hear that, then he was either in the bathroom, deaf, or dead. There was a rustling noise behind the door, like someone lifting himself off a La-Z-Boy recliner. I could hear the slapping noise of the footrest closing, and then I heard footsteps coming towards the door.

Johnson appeared like many people his age. He stood just less than six feet tall, with a protruding stomach. His skin had a leather-like quality, deeply lined and wrinkled. Most likely this was from spending too much time working outside in the sun without proper protection, except maybe a hat.

I looked at the man and wondered if older people weren't as concerned about their appearance as a younger person might be. The vanity of the new generation was responsible for many company fortunes. Looking at this man I decided that he had not contributed much to that part of industry.

Johnson's appearance was similar to his house—run down. I couldn't tell how old he was, but I guessed him to be in his mid to late sixties. Meeting new people the first time made me wonder what stories they had to tell. I figured this guy had some good ones.

His clothes, although clean, were simple. He wore a green work shirt and blue jeans with the pant cuffs rolled up, and his socks were white, which didn't match the rest of his outfit. He wore ordinary shoes, like clogs often worn around pool areas. The funniest part of his outfit was the outdated suspenders, which he wore to hold up his pants. I didn't even know where you bought those things anymore.

A cough and clearing of Johnson's throat brought my attention back to the front door. "Yes, what did you want?" The voice didn't sound gruff; more a raspy noise in nature; like the voice of a long-time smoker. This observation was confirmed quickly enough when I noticed the cigar he was holding in his right hand by his leg. I imagined he had been smoking it when we arrived.

I decided that since this project was Andy's idea, he should be the one to talk to Mr. Johnson first. I nudged him slightly to get his attention. When he looked up at me, I said to him, "This is Mr. Johnson. Tell him why we are here."

Andy took a big swallow and looked at Mr. Johnson while he worked up the courage to begin his presentation. The old man turned his attention to the boy as Andy began to speak.

"Hello, Mr. Johnson. My name is Andy Bell and this is my friend Mr. Henry. I want to build a fortress for me and my friend George so we can play by ourselves in it every day. Mr. Henry says he will help me, and I need help, because my Mom said I was too small to carry the boards. My mom also said I'm too young to use any kind of saw and hammer, so you see I need Mr. Henry's help. I want to build our fortress here near your pond. I want to build it in a tree so that it is above the ground."

His little boy's lungs finally ran out of air, as his fear had poured out in the form of words. Mr. Johnson took this pause as an opportunity to speak.

"So, you want to build a tree house on my land?"

"No, sir, a fortress," Andy said, regaining enough of his composure to correct the old man.

"What's the difference?"

"A tree house just sits in a tree. A fortress is a safe place to play and keep people out." Andy said this in a way that suggested Mr. Johnson should have known this.

Johnson looked up at me with an amused look on his face. I shrugged my shoulders. "I guess there's a difference," I said with a smile on my face.

I quickly removed my smile as Andy looked up at me. I didn't want him to think I wasn't taking him seriously.

"I see," continued Mr. Johnson. "So you want to build a *fortress* on my land then?"

"Yes, sir," said Andy.

"Why should I let you do that?" asked Mr. Johnson.

I was not sure if Johnson was just testing the boy or if he actually had a problem with Andy's request. When I looked down at Andy, I could see that he was pondering Johnson's question, trying to think of a good answer. I almost started to speak when it struck me that this was a great learning opportunity for the boy. I decided to stay quiet.

Andy's face lit up as he seemed to come up with a solution that would satisfy the old man.

"Because George and I will clean up your yard and we'll let you come into our fortress any time you want. If you know the secret code word to get in, that is." Once again Andy had come up with a simple answer that he was sure would work. Oh, if life could be as simple as this boy made it!

Mr. Johnson began to laugh. He put the cigar to his mouth, taking a long puff, pausing to evaluate Andy's offer. Andy looked up at him fully expecting a yes to his request, believing there could be no other answer.

"Well, boy," he said, "I don't need my yard cleaned up, and I'm too old to climb a tree to get in a fortress—even with the secret code."

Andy seemed to deflate at hearing this. Johnson appeared to ponder things for a moment longer, then added, "However, I had a place to play when I was your age that was much like a fortress, so I can understand why you want one. 'Course, mine was just a tree house."

Again, I couldn't tell if he was just making a small joke at Andy's expense. I still couldn't get a read on the old guy. If he was just teasing Andy, the boy had not taken it as a joke and didn't seem offended. I looked at the old man wondering if he had ever been Andy's age. Johnson didn't elaborate about his childhood tree house, and I was not sure I wanted to ask. I assumed it was just one of those life memories we all want to have.

"So, I think I might be able to help you out," he continued. "I have some rules, though, that you have to follow, or else I won't let you build it."

"Yes, sir," Andy said with excitement in his voice as he realized that his dream was going to happen. I figured he would agree to almost anything at this point.

"First thing, your friend here . . ." he looked up at me questioningly.

"Robert Henry," I finished his thought.

"Your friend, Mr. Henry, must be with you every time you are here until you are finished, or you have to come with some other adult. I don't want a couple of young lads having boards fall down on them, or falling from the tree when they tried to do too much."

"Okay," Andy said, nodding in agreement.

"This brings me to rule number two." He looked up at me. "You have to make sure that when you are finished, there is a strong and safe way to get into the tree house, uh, fortress. I don't want you to just scramble up tree branches each time you go in there."

I nodded at him and said, "I understand."

"Finally, he said, every time you come to use your fortress you have to let me know that you are here. You need to stop at my door to say hello and then stop to say good-bye." He again looked up at me to say, "I don't want kids just running around on my land whenever they want without me knowing about it!" I again acknowledged what he said with a nod.

Looking back at Andy, he asked, "Can you live with those rules, young man?"

Andy looked up at him; put a grin on his face then stuck his hand out towards the old man. "Yes sir, it's a deal."

Mr. Johnson and I chuckled at the young boy. The old man was most likely wondering where he had learned how to close a deal with a handshake just like I was. Mr. Johnson bent over take Andy's hand, shaking it to make the deal official.

"I may even know where you can build it," he said. He took a moment to clear his seemingly cluttered mind then pointed off in the direction of his tree line. He told us about an old oak tree on the far side of his property. "It's an old tree. Been there long before me, but it's quite safe and solid, with enough large branches to build a good platform for your fortress." I think Andy appreciated him referring to it as a fortress instead of a tree house.

"Sounds just right, doesn't it, Andy?"

Andy nodded so fast I thought his head might twist off his neck.

"What's the best way to get to this old tree, Mr. Johnson?" I asked.

"Well, just follow the tree line around the old pond until you come across a small open area full of cattails. You'll know it because there is a large rock, probably five feet high at the beginning of the open area. I don't know how it ever got there, but the rock is important, because when you see it just turn left walk about fifty feet and you'll see the tree I'm talking about. It should work well for you."

"Sounds simple enough," I said. I wasn't sure I really believed that. I just didn't want Andy to know I may get lost! "Is it all right if we took a walk out there now?"

"Sure, go ahead. If you can't find the tree just come back and I'll show you where it is." Johnson spoke in an amusing way that made me wonder if he wasn't now testing me a little bit. I know he didn't expect much out of Andy at this point. It was almost as if he was wondering if a "young guy" like me could understand simple directions any better than the boy could.

I felt I could pass the test so I told him "No problem. I'm sure we'll be fine."

"You ready to go, Andy?"

"Yes sir." He was clearly excited, but there was one other small bit of business to be done before we headed out.

"Okay, then, thank Mr. Johnson for his permission."

Andy stepped forward. Standing with all the dignity a young boy could muster, he thanked Mr. Johnson. I was pleased with the gratefulness he showed the old man. I could tell by looking at him that the old man was impressed as well.

"You're welcome. Have fun." I shook his hand then he nodded at me and with that turned to go back through the broken down screen door into the old house, which most likely served as *his* version of a fortress. How safe was he in a building like this one?

I put my hand on Andy's shoulder, steering him towards the old oak tree Johnson had spoken of and began walking in that direction.

CHAPTER 8

It didn't take long to walk the short distance to the area Johnson had told us about. There appeared to be an almost stagnant smell as we approached the tree. I figured it was just the standing water. Lots of things seemed stagnant to me lately so I just ignored it.

Then I saw the tree. It stood tall and seemed almost proud standing alone on the edge of the pond. I knew it was just a tree I was looking at, but for the briefest moment I could almost visualize Andy's fortress sitting majestically in the middle of the tree's outstretched branches. It should be a good building site. I began to imagine all the ways Andy and his friend would have fun in their new home. I was surprised by these thoughts. Why should it matter to me so much about Andy's fort? I barely knew the boy. Why should I feel any sense of pride when I had not yet done anything? Besides, I was only there to help out. It wasn't my project. Still why was it beginning to matter to me so much? Maybe my own childhood memories were beginning to come to life.

My childhood was long gone but it was as if someone had designed the tree years before just for the purpose of some day fulfilling this boy's dream. It was an old oak tree that reached for the sky and spread out with branches shaped like arms. It was a simple but welcoming sight. It was as if God had planted this tree many years ago just waiting for Andy's fortress.

Thinking back now, I was probably right about my childhood memories. It seemed that the feeling was more from something I had enjoyed as a young boy, probably not much older than Andy was right now. I couldn't really put my finger on it—childhood seemed a lifetime ago. It was just a feeling.

So many thoughts poured back when I looked at the boy. I had enjoyed my childhood. Why shouldn't he?

Seeing his excitement and then hearing him talk earlier about his plans for the fortress made me happy for him. I was also beginning to feel happiness for myself that he had chosen me to be a part of the experience. My participation was more a matter of luck than good management, but I had a fleeting thought that helping Andy build his fortress was helping me tear down mine. Maybe I wasn't as cynical as I tried to believe.

Child rearing was not always easy, but those small moments of laughter or joy in my own child's life made everything worth it. The work was hard, but the pay could be great! Just being a part of her life had made me richer. I saw the same joy in Andy as he looked up at the tree. It reminded me how the innocence of a child could bring freshness to a situation.

"Well we're here; what do you think? I asked already knowing what the answer would be. "Will it work?"

"You bet; it's perfect!" he said with a smile wide enough to back a truck into.

His excitement was contagious, and I found myself looking back at him with a smile of my own that was probably just as wide.

"Can you see your fortress sitting in this tree?"

"Sure, Mr. Henry; can't you?"

I almost laughed at Andy's answer; fair yet simple. "It's your fortress, Andy, so you have to tell me what you see."

Undaunted, he was quick to answer, "That's easy." Taking a deep breath again, he began to tell me what he saw. After about ten minutes of ideas and detailed descriptions, Andy began to run out of wind. I hadn't thought it possible! Andy had not lost steam, however; he was just gathering his strength to continue telling me how his fortress would look.

"And then over there we'll put a ladder so me and George can climb up." Pausing for a moment, deep in thought, he made one of those simplistic statements I had learned to expect. "I guess wo need a door too so we don't fall through the floor."

When he looked up at me and saw me smiling, he began to laugh. "Probably a good idea," I agreed.

I laughed too—as much in response to the moment as anything else. It was a good feeling, the first special moment shared between the two of us that we may never forget. These were the things I would come to appreciate as Andy's project moved along.

"When can we start Mr. Henry?"

"I think we can start next weekend after I get my Saturday morning chores done." Andy's face had a look of disappointment so I asked him. "When did you think we could start?"

"I thought we could get started today" he spoke with the total lack of experience.

"You have to remember that we need to gather a lot of things."

"Like what" Andy asked obviously forgetting the need for materials.

"Things like boards, nails, tools plus we have to measure everything so we can figure out the best way to build everything. Does that make sense?"

"Guess so" he agreed.

"That's how things work Andy. You want to build a good fortress don't you?"

"Yes sir" his words had a tone of acceptance, albeit a deflated one.

"Okay then let's head back home." I turned to walk back towards Johnson's house and back to the street. Andy turned to reluctantly follow me taking a final look at the tree that would become the home of his new fortress.

I believed the boy needed some encouragement and I didn't want to leave him with any kind of sadness so I spoke up by saying "Don't worry Andy. We'll be ready for next weekend and work will go quickly. Your fortress will be ready before spring is done."

This statement seemed to cheer the boy up even though he probably didn't even know what day spring ended and summer started. All that mattered to him was that his dream would come true

"That's great Mr. Henry" speaking once again with enthusiasm. "I can't wait to tell George."

"Your friend? I questioned.

"Yeah. He'll like the tree we picked."

"Sure was nice of Mr. Johnson to let you build on his land wasn't it?"

"Yes sir. He's a nice man."

I pondered a moment on my own impressions about the old man and decided to agree with the boy. "Yes he does seem like a nice man. Good thing for us right?"

"Yeah it sure is. I knew he would be though." Andy stated.

"You did, did you?" I questioned looking down at the boy.

"Uh Huh."

"How did you know that for sure? interested in his response.

"Because George said he would be."

"And how did your friend know this?"

"He met Mr. Johnson before and said he was actually a nice man."

This was the first time I had heard anything of this nature from the boy and was surprised by the connection of any kind with the old man.

"How come you didn't say anything before?"

"I don't know. I believed what George told me but I guess I wanted to see what Mr. Johnson was like for myself."

The boy continued to impress me with his combination of prudent simplicity and enthusiasm. I kept thinking; could life really be that simple?

Our conversation had taken us all the way back to George's house and looking down at my watch I was surprised to see that two hours in time had passed. We had obviously spent more time with Mr. Johnson as well as looking at the building site than I had expected. It was time for me to get home as well. Looking at George I said "Well we're home."

"Uh Huh" George's voice indicated something else was on his mind. Not one to let something he had to say go unsaid it didn't take long for me to discover what he was thinking about "When can we go next weekend?"

I paused for a moment; thinking about the upcoming week before responding "I'll get my chores done early Saturday morning and pick you up just after lunch. Okay?"

I was pretty sure by Andy's face that he was hoping for sooner but resigned himself to my schedule. I think he knew he needed me and couldn't force me to move any faster. I decided to give him one last ray of hope. "Don't worry Andy. I'll have everything ready in my truck including boards when I pick you up. Then we can start right away."

This statement seemed to bring hope back to the boy's dream. His face was once again full of smile. "Okay Mr. Henry. I'll see you then; I'll be ready when you get here. Thanks again." With that he ran up the stairs of the porch and into the house allowing the screen door to slam shut. It occurred to me that there had been no conversation about the money he had raised for his project or what he was bringing to the work site. Ironic I thought; feeling as though I had been tricked again. Nah I couldn't be that dumb; could I?

I found the next few days to be full of thought and planning. Andy's project was most likely simpler than I was making it out to be in my mind; but that's just the way I was. Friends of mine understood that I overanalyzed things. Many of them had made a point of telling me so. I knew they were right, because I had been analyzing things to death since I was a young man. I was doing it again now. For fun I would always say to them that maybe they were right, but I'd have to think about it! That often got a laugh, but just as often a quick shake of the head as though they couldn't figure me out. In a moment deep in thought I was positive that in many ways I was overanalyzing all aspects of my friendship with Andy, as well as the design of his fortress. Everything could be much simpler if I let it.

I didn't know it then but the truth was that the actual construction would turn out to be a simple process. It would only take Andy and me five weekends of working together to finish his new hiding place. It was a lifetime for Andy, of course; for me it was a weekend distraction. There would be some help provided along the way, but surprisingly it wouldn't come from his friend George. I would come to understand why as things moved along.

Of course I did have another job to do providing me with a living and making it possible to do whatever I wanted to do, but only on the weekends! Andy accepted my answer when I explained this to him, but I could tell that he didn't like it. Andy was too young to realize that I would be neglecting my own home life by working on this project with him. He was a young boy, so I didn't expect him to understand completely.

Marie had supported the idea of helping Andy right from the beginning; after I explained everything to her. I think she saw some kind of small purpose in my life, which made me happy, something that had been missing for some time. In the end she seemed happy for me, and I was grateful to her for that.

Her support often triggered more self-analysis for my analytical mind. For me, marriage was not just loving each other but liking each other too. I had learned that loving someone was easy, while liking them could be much harder. I felt fortunate, that our lives had developed into a friendship as much as a marriage. We had disagreed on many things, including how to raise our daughter, but most of the disagreements were over things that weren't really that important, like the altercation from the other day. Marie and I were able to talk most things out, but it hadn't always been that way. I had become tired of feeling like a salmon swimming upstream. They fight to get where they are going then die in the end. I didn't want to die young so I was choosing my fights more carefully; or at least tried to. Only the important ones mattered now. The rest were just annoyances. For now her support was all I needed.

I picked up Andy at his house the next weekend, as I had promised him.

I was greeted with an excited "Hi Mr. Henry."

I could see that Andy was sitting once again on the porch of his house waiting for me in anticipation. "HI Andy. How are you today?"

"Great. I'm ready to work. Can we go?"

"Sure in just a moment." I was going to knock on the door to let Andy's Mom know we were leaving when I glanced towards the living room window and saw her standing in plain site. She waved at me in acknowledgment and something told me she did not want to come to the front door. It was as though something was going on that she didn't want me to see. I don't know why that thought came to my mind but I accepted that she knew I was there and Andy was leaving. I waved back making an attempt to provide a smile of confidence so she wouldn't have to worry. Then I turned back to Andy.

"Sorry Andy but we'll have to stop at my house to pick up a few things. I wasn't able to get everything loaded this morning. I just ran out of time."

"That's okay Mr. Henry. I'll help so it will be easy."

"I'll take the help" I said. "Any help is good help."

We made our way to my garage and began loading some boards I had stored behind my backyard shed. Once that was done I grabbed some tools, nails, screws and some miscellaneous items I knew we would need before heading towards Johnson's Pond, ready for the day.

As we got closer to Johnson's land Andy pointed straight ahead and offered some navigation for me "There's a road Mr. Henry. Can we drive on it?"

I had noticed a dirt road the first day we were there that allowed us to drive within twenty feet of the tree. That was important, because I didn't want to carry anything farther than I had to. I had spoken to old man Johnson about using the road. He said he had no problem with us driving through the area, which was easier than carrying everything in from the street. I wanted Andy to feel a part of things right from the start so pretending to not know about the road I looked around as though I didn't see what he was talking about while asking "Where Andy? I don't see what you are talking about."

"Right there; in front of us" pointing once again at his discovery.

"Oh now I see what you are talking about" feigning a sense of importance to his instructions. "Yes I think that it might work. Should we try it?"

"Yeah let's use that road" Andy was now excited "It should get us close to the tree."

"Okay. That's where we'll go then" I responded as I turned onto the road; not more than a dirt trail; and moved closer to the tree.

Once we were backed up to the spot I chose to unload the materials we began the day's work mostly in silence. Simple instruction was the only communication needed for now. I think Andy was just happy we had started and would do anything he was told as long as his fortress was getting built.

As the day moved forward I decided to ask Andy about his friend George. I was unloading some tools and asked the question. "How come your friend George hasn't been around? Isn't this his fortress too?

"George wanted to be here to help," he apologized. "His family had to go away for a while, but he'll be back." Now that I think about it, he knew more at the time than he was letting on, but I was busy working on his fortress, so I hadn't really paid much attention to what he was saying. I was just trying to make conversation. I didn't really care if George was there or not, so I didn't press the situation except for saying "I'd like to meet him sometime."

"Oh you will. I swear" Andy said.

I didn't want the boy to feel cornered so I just left it there. Anyways I needed to focus on what I was doing since it could be easy for me to make mistakes. Enthusiasm for a project was great but I had to be sure to take my time when working on any plans. Most of my work was more functional than pretty, but I decided that was important. After all, it was a fortress.

Andy turned out to be a good worker. He was a small boy, so I had to be sure that he didn't try to do anything that would get him hurt. At the beginning, his own enthusiasm for this fortress made watching out for him a fulltime job. He was quick to listen, and I was able to create work for him that I knew he was capable of doing without risking any injury. I would have him hand me screws or nails, he would hold one end of a board while I sawed it, or he would bring me tools, such as a hammer. He just wanted to feel a sense of ownership that being a part of building the fortress would bring to him. He did not understand that, of course, but I did.

I would start a nail for him and let him hammer it in as best he could. I watched to make sure he didn't hurt himself. The satisfaction and pride on his face was nice to watch. Then, once in a while, he would hit the nail wrong, as we all do, and end up having to pull the bent nail out of the board.

Often I had to give him some help because he wasn't strong enough to remove the damaged nail by himself. He didn't appreciate this help at first, and I would hear a frustrated, "I can do it!" escape from his young boy's mouth. His determination was obvious, and I thought a couple of times that it might be best to just leave him alone rather than challenge his statement. That would be how he would learn. That's how I had learned, and I had not heard any curse words from him, so I was happy about that.

By the second day Andy began to realize that taking my help didn't mean that he couldn't do it, just that he needed some assistance to make things easier. I started to hear less "I can do it" and more "Can you help me, Mr. Henry?"

It was becoming obvious that getting his fortress built was more important to Andy than doing it all by himself. I knew many people who could learn from this little man. Too often we try to be heroes rather than the humble servants we should be. Middle-aged men—at least the smart ones—have discovered that being a hero can be fun but often doesn't get things done. Andy wanted to get it done. I was having fun.

It appeared to me that deep down, somehow he knew if we were able to get the building work done, then playing fortress hero would be his reward. He of course wouldn't be able to explain this to anyone, because he wasn't the analyzer I was. And he wasn't middle aged. Could he just be an old man inside a young man's body?

I enjoyed time to think just as much as I did talking; so watching Andy work and thinking about the experience itself actually brought me a certain enjoyment I didn't feel the need to explain to anyone else. It was something I shared with myself.

Old man Johnson showed real interest in our project as well. He came over to the work area on the first day of construction and was quite willing to offer feedback; maybe more than he needed to! Years before, I would have been annoyed with the "advice" he added to our conversation. It was my project and Andy's fortress. Did he have the right to tell us what to do just because it was on his land? I did listen, though, and I found a lot of things he had to say helped me to see a different way to do the work. As I said before I was not a naturally skilled carpenter, so sometimes I made far more elaborate plans than were necessary. Johnson's experience showed me simpler ways to accomplish the same things.

When I first saw the old man approaching us, I noticed how old he really looked. When I first met him I was more worried about making a good impression on him than what kind of impression he made on me. True, I had seen the wrinkles and outdated clothes, but I now saw something else. He moved with a determined stride that demonstrated signs of discomfort.

He walked slower than I would have expected, but then again, where did he have to go in a big hurry? I could tell by watching him that arthritis was a daily part of his life, something he had to learn to cope with. The cigar he was smoking was just like the one I saw him with the first time I met him. Hell maybe it was the same one!

As I watched him cross the field, the vision of this man made me wonder what I would be like when I grew older. I knew sore joints would be part of my life, because they had already begun a lifelong friendship with my body. I did know, however, that cigar smoking would never be something people would see me do, and God I hoped that I would dress a whole lot better than he did! Younger people would most likely point out to their friends how out of style I was, at least by their standards. That was what young people did, but that was still many years in the future, so I thought I had better come back to the present.

"Hello, Mr. Johnson," I said. "How are you today?"

"Just like any other old man, happy to see the sunrise. Don't worry about me. Every day is a new day . . . sorry, what was your first name again?"

"Robert." Noticing that he still didn't appear ready to offer his first name, I decided to lean in towards him to say, "Andy calls me, Mr. Henry, so please continue to let him call you Mr. Johnson, okay? Most young men lose that respect too soon as it is, don't you agree?"

He nodded at me as though he agreed wholeheartedly with my statement. He was from another generation, one that gave that kind of respect and which was even more disappointed with today's generation then I was. Then again, it was my generation who raised these children, so whose fault was it really?

"Hi, Andy," he said. "How's the work going?"

"We've just started, Mr. Johnson," the boy said. "But Mr. Henry says everything will be easy." He looked my way as if to confirm his statement as truth.

"Sounds good to me So, Mr. Henry knows what he's doing then?" He raised his eyes to me as if to say *you do know what you're doing, right?*

This would be the first opportunity to prove that I believed in the whole idea of the fort. I wanted to be sure I sounded confident.

"Well I guess we'll find out soon enough. But I can sure use any help you can give me."

My statement was offered as much as a courtesy as a request, but the old man was more than willing to add his two bits! He went on to tell me how to do everything right from the beginning. I didn't ignore the information he offered, but on the other hand I felt that I too knew a little something about carpentry.

I decided to take my own advice so I listened to his comments, used the good ones and discarded the rest. I began to laugh inside, because it occurred to me that Andy might be doing the same thing with me. Nah, he was still too young to know the difference, wasn't he?

As it turned out his help turned out to be more helpful than I thought; even though the tree fortress was not as big of a job as I had imagined. Johnson showed me I had to cut back three or four tree limbs and then how to level off a small area of the platform area before we began construction. I could see what he was talking about and understood right away what I had to do.

The old man had obviously done a lot of work with his hands, so when he showed me a small trick he had learned while working on a construction site when he was younger; I listened. I can't remember now what it was he told me, but it sure sounded like good advice back then, so I used it. Something said that the years he had spent working with his hands had taught him many more tradesman's tricks then I knew. Using his advice became important to the project.

Andy had provided his own input along the way as well, which I knew he would. I would have been surprised if he had just stood quiet without telling me what he thought would work. Patience was still not a word he knew how to understand, never mind spell. Then again, many grownups didn't seem to understand the concept either. My own work place demonstrated that much too often.

I spent the first day mostly listening to Andy and the old man telling me what steps I should take next and how. I wasn't used to having so many bosses, so I found myself practicing my own version of patience. Being the natural talker I was, I thought I did pretty well.

I noticed right away that Johnson was as much of a teller as a doer. I didn't think he was lazy or anything just that his best working days were behind him. Besides, at his age, why shouldn't he be able to stand there and tell me what should be done? After all I suppose he had the right to speak up after all it *was* his land.

"Well, that looks pretty good," Johnson stated, almost as though he didn't expect it. This was at the end of the day, after we had prepared the tree and built the platform base. "I think that's a good start. What do you think, Andy?"

"It looks great, Mr. Johnson. We still have to put the trap door in."

"That will be part of tomorrow's work," I said. "I think we've done enough for the day." I was tired, hungry, and ready to go home. Looking at my watch, I realized we had spent the whole Saturday working on Andy's fortress.

I was especially surprised that the old man had hung in all day long with us. Was there something in his past that made this project somehow a little bit special for him too? I was too tired to ask, and he wasn't offering any information, so I just left it alone.

I could see that Andy would be more than willing to keep working if I encouraged him. I also knew he would have no problem falling right to sleep tonight, which wouldn't be the case for me. I would find myself waking up in the middle of the night to go to the washroom or get a drink of water, only to remain awake for a couple of hours. Over time that kind of sleep wears you down, so if I said my day was finished, it was.

Johnson gave me a look that told me he knew what I was going through. He added, "Henry is right, Andy. You guys did a lot of work today. Leave some for tomorrow." I was grateful for his comments but also noticed that he had not included himself when he spoke of the day's work. I found that intriguing, since he had spent the whole day with us, offering his feedback. Maybe he thought smoking five cigars didn't count as work. The one good thing about his habit was that after that many cigars, at least I knew that he wasn't still smoking the same old cigar as the day I met him. I was also happy that we were outside so that the smell of cheap cigar hadn't permeated my clothes. An expensive one probably wouldn't have been any better, but I was pretty sure that would have been a luxury for the old man.

I thought about buying him a couple of good cigars as a small thank-you for allowing us on his land. I didn't have to like the smell to give them as a gift.

"Okay, Mr. Johnson," Andy said. "I guess Mom probably wants me home anyways," Andy said with a tone of resignation. He could tell arguing any more wouldn't help. So we packed up our tools and put everything back into my truck preparing to leave.

Andy and I said our good-byes to Mr. Johnson and watched him slowly amble back towards his house. I had offered him a ride to save him some discomfort, suspecting he didn't like to walk much. He thanked me but declined my offer, choosing to enjoy the last of his cigar on the way back to his house. He wasn't in a rush to get anywhere, so the walk might have given him a chance to enjoy the end of a warm day.

It didn't take us very long to drive back to Andy's home. He jumped out of my truck, gave me a big wave good-bye, and ran into the house. Most likely he was already telling his mother all about his day before the front door had even closed behind him. I smiled, imagining how his mother wouldn't get a word of her own into the conversation for several minutes while Andy regaled her with the day's adventure.

I turned around and drove to my house, looking forward to a great supper prepared by Marie and ready for a rest. My mind said I deserved it, and my body said hallelujah!

CHAPTER 9

Andy never looked back at Mr. Henry driving away because he couldn't wait to tell his mother about his day at the big construction site. He ran into the house, calling for his mother so he could tell her everything he could remember as soon as he entered.

"Mom!" he hollered. "Where are you, Mom? I want to tell you about my fortress!"

He hurried throughout the house looking for his mother until he finally found her in his bedroom, making the bed. When he opened the door, she turned towards him with a frown on her face. The look worried him.

"I thought I told you that you had to make your bed every day, Andy," she said in a chastising voice.

He was still so excited about the day that he tried to ignore what she was saying but before Andy could tell his story, his mother spoke again. "It's your responsibility to do this small chore, so why don't you just do it? I don't ask you to do very much, so start making your bed or else."

Andy was disheartened that his mother didn't want to listen to him, but he didn't know for sure what "or else" meant and he didn't want to find out. Afraid that she would stop him from going to the pond to build his fortress, he decided not to argue with her. Andy didn't know why his mother was in a bad mood, but he had seen it often enough to know that this was not the time to push his luck.

"Sorry, Mom," he said, dejected.

She could tell right away that she had hurt Andy's feelings. She shouldn't have snapped at him. It wasn't his fault that she was angry.

She'd had another fight with his father. There seemed to be more problems everyday between the two of them, and unfortunately her children often received some of the fallout. She didn't mean to hurt them, but it seemed to happen anyway. Besides, it was just an unmade bed. Was it more important than her son?

Laura attempted to recover the moment of Andy's excitement without actually apologizing—she believed that you shouldn't have to apologize to your young children for anything, something her own mother had taught her. "How did your day go, honey?"

"Fine; I'm really tired, Mom. I want to have a nap before supper. Is that okay?" It was his turn to block the conversation. If she didn't want to listen then he didn't want to talk.

She couldn't think of any other way to bring the conversation back to his day's activities, so she resigned herself to just saying yes to his question. The ironic part was that he would be climbing back into the very bed she had just made up.

"Sure, sweetie" she said, trying to offer some motherly comfort to her voice. "I'll call you when supper is ready." Laura then turned to leave the bedroom.

She felt ashamed about hurting Andy's feelings. But he was just a boy, so he wouldn't be able to understand the pressures she was under. How could he know anything at all about her problems? She thought that If Andy had been old enough to understand he would definitely be on her side. It would just be easier for her if their father wasn't around at all, but would that be better for her children? With that final thought, she closed the door and went down to the kitchen to start supper.

Andy did not fall asleep right away. It was his turn to think about his life without really understanding his feelings. He was feeling angry about the way his mother had treated him. Why did she make such a big deal about making his bed? She should have listened to what he had to say. Today had been a lot of fun and this was not the way he wanted it to end.

What he did want to end was the fighting his parents did. It seemed like his mother was always angry about something. They even fought about him and his sister. He didn't know what they had done wrong. Geez his bed shouldn't make her that angry.

He wanted to tell them he wasn't a kid you know and that he had talked to other kids his age about their own families. He knew that other families had problems too. He wanted to tell his parents that just because other kid's parents fought didn't mean they had to. Andy just wanted the fighting to stop.

Imagination was a good thing but it could get someone in trouble as well. It could be especially destructive when dealing with the bad things in life. Andy did not see that difference, and that's when his imagination would get him in trouble the most. Worrying more about his mother and father, he would go back to listening to his friends tell their story. There were times he shouldn't have.

They would tell him how their own parents fought so much that they finally just split up or divorced. Some kids said they didn't know what divorce meant just that their parents no longer lived together, and it hurt. He knew he didn't want that to happen to his parents. In the end that was all that mattered.

He didn't want to choose between his parents. What could be so bad that they couldn't get along? Then a thought came to him; maybe it really was his fault. Had he done something so terrible that his parents were forced to disagree about everything?

He knew that they fought about money and stuff, but what if they were really arguing about him when he wasn't there? Were there other things they were fighting about that he was not aware of? Why couldn't he be a better boy? These confusing thoughts ran through Andy's head as he lay in his bed. He hoped he was wrong but he said a small prayer to God and promised to make his bed the next time.

It was times like this when Andy missed George the most. He knew that George would have listened to him. He would have asked him questions about what was wrong. It would have been great if he could have been there today at the tree so they could have just shared the day's adventure. He knew George would be back soon, but it didn't mean he wasn't missing him now.

He began to think about how much he and Mr. Henry had gotten done this Saturday. He sensed a small smile when he thought about how great it would be to show George what they had accomplished.

When Andy saw George the last time he said he may have to be gone all summer and wouldn't be able to help. He hadn't told Mr. Henry anything about this because he didn't want him to think that George had to be there to help them. Anyway, he felt that Mr. Johnson would be of some help as well.

Mr. Johnson had seemed interested in what they were doing. Andy had also noticed a friendly nature hiding behind his gruff exterior. Maybe it was nothing, but Andy believed that Mr. Johnson was somehow more important to his fortress than he had thought. Or maybe he was wrong. It was just a small boy's fuzzy assessment. Time would always be the real test.

Andy had been happy with Mr. Henry's help today too with his building plans (in truth, Andy was actually more the helper than the builder, but he liked to think he was in charge.) He was contented when he thought about all this, because he knew the fortress was going to be good.

He was proud of what he was doing and he was sure that George would feel the same way. They would have so much fun in their new play world that it wouldn't matter if George helped build it or not. He would just have to show it to George when he was finished. All that really mattered was that it was built. Andy believed that the fortress was more than just a place to play; he just knew he would do important things there.

There was often something greater than any of us that people didn't always understand; or wanted to. Andy was one of those times when results could be surprising. God wants to help little boys grow into men, but often little boys are stronger than the men they become. Each situation calls for something different—a necessary strength to draw upon, a simple answer to a complicated problem, or just the belief of a young man's dream that anything is possible. Small boys often do a better job of listening to God than grown men do, because it is easier for them to believe in something they can't see. Maybe it was meant to be this way. A small boy like Andy, of course, wouldn't understand all of these things, at least not yet.

In Andy's case, his beliefs in himself, his fortress, and his friends would become more important with each passing day. He just didn't know it yet, but for now it didn't really matter. He had been asleep for twenty minutes dreaming about dragon slayers, castles, and fortress walls. His mind had even included his mother in his dreams. She was someone who he saved from the monsters of the night. The monsters were many, but in his dream he killed them all, making it safe for his mother to live happily ever after, just like he knew he would.

Nothing could stop him in his dreams. He and George always knew what they needed to do to save everyone. When they were together, no one could defeat them. They won every battle. It was strange, though, that his father was in none of his dreams.

History had shown us that dreams can build the world and sometimes even tear down the walls. Without dreams, what makes life worth living? Without dreams, why attempt something beyond your reach? Without dreams, how easy would it be to give up on life?

Even though he didn't know it, Andy's dreams were important. They were part of the past and a part of the future. They were a part of everything.

CHAPTER 10

The week had gone by quickly; maybe because of my anticipation of more fortress building. The project was beginning to take shape and I was happy with what had been accomplished to this point. We were able to get more work completed the last weekend on the boy's fortress than I had expected. Even old man Johnson seemed surprised at what we had done. It was easy to feel good about ourselves; maybe I was a better contractor than I thought!

I picked up Andy on the weekend the same time as I had before, so he was expecting me. I stepped up to ring the door bell and offer a hello to Andy's mom, Laura, when I heard a young boy running across the floor towards the door. I was hoping that the door opened to the inside so I wouldn't get hit in the face as Andy came rushing out to the front steps! Some of my friends would say that it could only improve my looks! For today, however I wanted my looks to stay the same.

"Hi, Mr. Henry," he said. "I'm ready."

"Okay Andy. I just want to say hello to your mom before we leave so she knows where you are."

"She knows, Mr. Henry. I told her you were coming so she knew that we were going to work on my fortress," Andy stated.

"That's fine, Andy but I would still like to say hello."

The young man seemed to be frustrated with my insistence on seeing his mother. "She's not home right now, Mr. Henry" he said in a cold small-boy voice. "She went to get groceries, and my grandpa is sleeping, so can't we just go?"

I looked at Andy, sizing up his statement and trying to decide how important challenging it would be. Andy would not lie to me—of that I was sure. There was something in his demeanor, however, that told me everything wasn't right. I took one last look at the front door then back to Andy, concluding that I would leave the situation alone and trust what he said. I listened as Andy jumped into the truck slamming the passenger door and I walked to the driver's side. I was going to say something to him about slamming the door but after looking through the window I decided to ignore that issue as well.

As I got into my truck, I did tell myself to speak with his mother another time to see what seemed to be making Andy feel so unsettled. I didn't want to pry into someone else's life, but I did want to know what I would be dealing with. I would find out in due time what could make such an optimistic young man so short in his reply.

For now I had my own problems. It was convenient that Andy obviously didn't want to talk. I started my vehicle and the silence allowed me to think about the things that were bothering me. I hadn't had a good week at work even though it went quick enough. There seemed to have been more pettiness and office politics than usual, and it was becoming more difficult not to be affected by the environment. Unfortunately, I would sometimes slip into the abyss of foolishness myself. I was not certain I had not created some of my own problems.

It was true that I thought I could rise above any soap opera scenario that developed in our office but it was becoming too hard to set everything aside and not fall into the trap myself. I just didn't seem to have the same energy be the bigger person anymore.

I think I was just fed up! Retirement was close enough to see, just not close enough to touch, and I was getting tired of taking orders from people that were younger than some of the shoes I owned! It was just one of those things I had to tolerate to get what I wanted.

I did find that the longer I stayed in a job I didn't really like, the harder it was becoming. I had always been responsible for the bulk of the family income, and I had no problem accepting that responsibility. It was just that sometimes the money did not seem worth the trouble. We needed what we had though, and Marie's income added to our comforts and I was grateful to have it working for us.

It was often said that a job is not really hard work if you find something you love doing. Most people have heard that message at one time or another. What a great philosophy! Although it is easy to agree with in theory, I had come to believe that the idea was full of holes. To begin with, most people took on jobs just to meet their obligations. They would find something that they had a skill for and would see a paycheck at the end of the week or month for their efforts. Many people had jobs with no skills at all. I know, because I worked with several of them! Workers were seldom happy with their jobs, seeing it as just something they had to do. It was reality.

I found many employees to be selfish people. Obtaining things just to have them had become an obsession with the "me generation." Credit had become an overused privilege that many people obtained with no sense of responsibility or accountability. People who got over their heads with irresponsible borrowing habits wouldn't actually admit it and they expected someone else to bail them out. Parents, grandparents, and even the more unpopular choice of bankruptcy had become easy avenues for younger people looking to solve problems they themselves had created. I didn't think that made for a better society.

All these thoughts were contributing to my bad mood. I worked hard, embraced responsibility, and performed my duties well. It didn't seem to matter. It felt as if I weren't going to get any further ahead than the lazy guy in the next office or the person down the hall from me, who spent more time hiding from his job than actually doing it. Frankly, it ticked me off. It was getting harder for me to be a cooperative staff member myself. Every day moved along slower and I couldn't wait to be done and gone from there. Many of my friends told me they felt the same way about their jobs.

This week had been especially annoying. I always told myself that I would not judge the generation behind me as I grew towards middle age. I was wrong. I found many of the younger people in my work environment to be not only selfish but self-centered as well. They didn't seem to care about doing a good job, as I did. I believed that my generation had been given less, which made us work for more. This younger generation was the opposite—they had been given more, which made it possible for them to work for less. It was something that I could handle most of the time, but this week was just one of those times when that particular attitude rubbed me the wrong way.

I was living in my own self-pity again, so I could not admit to myself that it was my generation that had created that attitude. Without the wealth we had accumulated, we could not have spoiled our children the way we had. In truth, why shouldn't they expect everything? Many children in my world had never really experienced the disappointment of not getting what they wanted.

I couldn't wait to leave home when I graduated high school, because the world was exciting to me. Not just the things I could buy, but the adventure of earning it myself. The sense of accomplishment was often a reward in itself, but many children today didn't see things that way. I suppose I understood. Would I have been so quick to leave home if I had everything I wanted, not just food and clothes, but televisions and cars and all other manner of luxury? Not to mention the free rent.

The best thing my parents ever gave me was nothing. I can just imagine my daughter rolling her eyes, as if she had heard that story before. I might have even told her the one about walking ten miles to school one way and twenty miles back home. I can even hear her saying "Yes Daddy, I know. You had a tougher time than I have." I don't think she was sympathetic.

Learning to set a goal and then finding my own way to reach it resulted in some of the happiest moments of my life. Working for something I wanted was often enjoyable, but it sure didn't mean that I always liked what I had to do to get it.

Deep down I knew I was generalizing. Many younger people used good judgment, taking on challenges with confidence and excitement. My own daughter, Annie, was a good example. Her mother and I gave her everything we could. We tried to do the best job we were capable of; which I suppose our own parents had done for us. I felt that she certainly had not missed out on much, even though we didn't always have the money to give her what she wanted. However, we always try to teach her that everything came with a responsibility, even if it was a gift. If she wanted something, she had to explain why and convince us of her need. We started this early in her life, and even though it might have seemed harsh to some people, it helped her develop skills that would serve her well as she grew older.

I felt Marie and I had taken a much more enlightened approach to teaching our child than our own parents had. The answer to everything when I was growing up was to obey, or expect a strong spanking. At the time it didn't bother me, because that was just the way it was. Every action had a consequence. Sometimes it was worth it, sometimes it wasn't. I wanted Annie to understand that. I wanted my child, and hopefully her friends, to know that we lived in a great country. It was a privilege to be appreciated.

I had defended these opinions many times before and frankly I was getting tired of it myself. I knew I sounded like a broken record and nothing seemed to ever change anyway. So why bother? My self-indulgent thoughts had temporarily made me forget the boy sitting beside me in my truck. Looking at him, I wondered if everything in my world was really that terrible. Andy had been more quiet than usual, so I wondered what was going on with him. Rather than add to Andy's unsettled poutiness, I decided to cheer him up. I figured I could use the cheering up myself.

"So you think we'll get lots done today, Andy?"

"I guess so."

I could tell that it was going to take more work to bring Andy around. Luckily, this was one job I wanted to do! His grin would be reward enough.

Then I remembered something from our last time together. "It was pretty funny last week when Mr. Johnson stepped into that puddle of water, wasn't it?" I began. "Especially since he was only wearing those silly Croc shoes." I laughed.

Andy began to smile a little bit breaking into laughter. "It sure was," he said. "When he pulled his foot out I think he had mud stuck between his toes."

"Are you sure it was just mud?"

"What do you mean?" Andy asked with a puzzled look on his face.

I looked over to his side of the truck and answered with a mischievous look in my eye, "Well, you know how we saw some dogs running around the other day?"

"Yeah I saw them too."

I then gave him a wink and offered a possibility he may not have thought about. "How do you know it wasn't dog poop?"

"Dog poop, you mean between his toes?"

"Did you check to be sure?" I asked. "Maybe you should have asked Mr. Johnson if you could smell his shoe just to be sure."

Andy looked at me for a moment then began to laugh. "Aw, you're just teasing me, Mr. Henry."

"Maybe I am. Maybe I'm not. I guess we'll never know for sure. You better be careful where you walk today or you might find out the hard way yourself."

I nudged Andy, letting him know that I really was just teasing him. I knew my joke was lame, but if it made Andy happy then it would make me happy too. He gave me the big smile I had come to expect from him, and I knew that everything would be okay after all. My week had gotten better already.

We were at our "job site" quickly enough, so we both jumped out of my truck ready to take on the work. It was amazing how easy it could be to make someone laugh or brighten his day, giving him a different outlook. It was equally amazing how making people laugh seemed an important part of my own life. Someone's laugh made me feel satisfied.

The way I had it figured humour could be a useful form of communication. When I was younger I often talked just for the sake of being a part of things. Eventually it occurred to me if I could just learn to shut up as I got older and speak less I might even be considered wise from time to time. It would be a nice goal to work toward, anyway. Shutting up was a goal many of my friends hoped I would achieve as well—just the close friends!

Today, however, I was happy that my humour had brightened my little friend's morning and I pushed aside any other thoughts leaving his smile a lasting memory.

Andy and I had just begun unloading the boards and tools when old man Johnson came shuffling towards us. He must have been looking out his front window, waiting for us to arrive so he could join us. His interest in Andy's project appeared to be growing as well, providing some sense of purpose for his own day.

He was wearing the same kind of clothes he always wore. I assumed they had been washed since our last visit, or at least I hoped so. The outdated suspenders replaced a belt and he was smoking his trademark cigar. Today he was wearing a hat with some kind of print on the visor. As he got closer, I could see that it had the name of a local golf course stitched across the front. This surprised me, because I couldn't imagine this old man as a golfer.

What was more important to me was what I saw in his other hand. It looked as if he had brought along two cups and a thermos. That meant coffee.

I had left the house this morning without having breakfast, which Marie always made for us on Saturdays. It had become a small tradition in our home that I looked forward to every weekend. I had slept in this morning and I did not want to disappoint Andy by being late, so I didn't take the time to eat breakfast or stop for coffee.

It was as though the old man somehow knew this. Starting my day with a coffee always made me feel better, so I was happy he had thought of this courtesy.

"Hello gentleman. How are you this morning?" Johnson said in a cheery voice. "I thought you might like a coffee, Henry, so I went down to the local coffee shop and picked up some for us. It's always cheaper if I take my own thermos." He then opened the container, poured me a cup full of hot black coffee, and handed it to me. I could already smell the wonderful aroma of good coffee and welcomed his gift.

I figured he just hadn't remembered my first name, so I corrected him, "Robert, and thanks Mr. Johnson. I could really use a coffee."

I called him Mr. Johnson because he had never told me his first name. It didn't appear that he was going to offer the information on this visit either. That was okay, because I felt that I should give him the same respect I enjoyed from Andy. I would continue to call him Mr. Johnson whenever I addressed him, unless he told me otherwise.

"I didn't know what you took in your coffee, so I brought some cream and sugar," he said as he reached into a brown bag to hand me some packs of sugar and small containers of cream from a local coffee house.

"Thanks," I said. "Just cream is all I need."

The old man looked at the small boy standing beside me. "I didn't know if you liked coffee as well, Andy," he joked, "so I brought you something else." He produced another small bag containing a chocolate covered donut, which he offered to the boy. Andy's eyes twinkled with anticipation as he took it from Mr. Johnson's hand.

"Thanks, Mr. Johnson. I love chocolate donuts."

"You're welcome, Andy. Figured you might"

I didn't know why, but it struck me as strange that the old guy could remember Andy's name so easily but seemed to forget the simple first name Robert. I pushed the thought to the back of my mind and turned my attention to the cup in my hand.

I enjoyed coffee so I was grateful for Johnson bringing it to the work site. I opened the cup lid, stirred some cream into the coffee, replaced the lid and took my first sip from the lid opening. The taste confirmed the coffee quality I had smelled earlier when he handed it to me. It tasted perfect.

I looked over at Andy, who had crawled on top of a rock sitting nearby content in munching away at his donut. He seemed to be getting happier by the bite.

"Looks like it should be a nice day," I opened the conversation.

"Should be," replied the old man. "It'll be a good day for work."

He said the last part as though it would be obvious that we would be doing the work, not him. The best I could hope for was some more of the same wisdom he had offered the last time. I think he was more than ready to offer that support.

I had always believed that I could learn at least one thing from even the dumbest person I met, so I was sure I could learn a lot from this man, as long as I took the time to listen. Something also told me he would have no problem passing his knowledge on to me, if I let him. He had certainly demonstrated that approach whenever he visited the job site.

Many people never gave it a second thought but I think the older we get the more we want to make a difference to other people. We want to leave something behind so others will remember us. Some people will have achieved great stature in their lifetime, but most remain ordinary people, like me, who will not be remembered for some grand event or accomplishment. Sometimes the most we can give to people is the advice of a mentor. It is up to the other person to decide what information best serves their own life.

With that in mind I turned back towards Mr. Johnson and asked him how long he had been retired.

"What makes you think I'm retired?"

I blushed a little with embarrassment, trying to save the moment, "Well, I just assumed at your age that you would have deserved to be retired."

"And what age is that?"

Seeing that there may be no graceful way out of this conversation I tried a different approach; "You know; the age where someone that has worked as hard as you have should be able to take the time to enjoy life."

I felt proud of myself for coming up with such an insightful answer. I just hoped he saw it the same way.

He looked at me as if he were trying to decide what I really meant by my statement; then appeared to choose to ignore it. "I never actually retired, Henry. It could be called more of a re-gearing."

"What do you mean," I questioned, trying to forgive the use of my last name again in his answer. I don't why it was bothering me but it did.

"Well, I worked in the construction field for most of my life, and when I finally got tired of going from jobsite to jobsite, I decided to quit and do something for myself."

I was right. I had surmised by the look of the man that he had been some kind of tradesman or something, but I still didn't understand what he meant about "re-gearing."

"So what did you do?"

"Well, it was actually quite easy," he said. "I wasn't a spring chicken anymore, but I thought I could still be useful, so rather than just roll over and die I started doing odd jobs for people."

"Like a handyman."

"Yeah, like a handyman. First I would build a fence for a friend, then maybe a deck for someone else, or even install some cupboards. At the beginning, I just worked at things I knew how to do, but it wasn't long before people started offering money to do the same things I had been doing for free. They would then ask me to work on something I hadn't tried before. I found that to be most interesting, because it gave me a chance to learn something I didn't already know. Re-gearing, you understand?"

"I'm beginning to," I answered, trying to sound confident.

"It really was quite simple. I didn't have to work full time—I didn't need the money."

I wondered what he meant by that. Was the answer as simple as it sounded, or was there more to it?

"So I just took on the jobs I wanted. Anytime I was being paid for my work, I made sure the customer paid me by the job, not by the hour. That way I could take my time, with no pressure of making mistakes. If I did something wrong I would re-do it until I got it right—no cost."

He stopped for a minute to take a sip of his coffee. This reminded me not to let my own coffee get cold, so I took a drink at the same time. For some reason I was dumb enough to take a gulp instead of a sip. I shouldn't have done that, since the coffee was still very hot.

I waited for my mouth to cool before asking him, "You kind of became a renovation contractor then?"

"I guess you could call it that. It was more than that, though. It was a new stage in my life."

I thought this was a strange thing for him to say, but he began to speak again before I could question his statement.

"Time came when I could work when I wanted to, choose what I wanted to do, and learn things I hadn't had time to learn before. It gave me a chance to spend more time at home with my wife and children, and best of all it gave me freedoms I never had before. I was shifting gears, see?"

This was the first time the old guy had mentioned his wife or family. I sensed he had said all he would about the subject, even though I would have loved to learn more. I had a feeling that there was something in his past that he wasn't ready to share with me yet. Maybe he never would.

I had asked the first question just to make conversation, but his answers had raised my interest. "Are you saying that by shifting gears you became happier?"

"Happier?" he pondered. "I don't know if I would say happier. If you mean did I find different joys in my life then I guess I would have to say yes. But happiness comes in many forms. We just have to be open to seeing it."

Was this gruff old man becoming more philosophical, or had I just underestimated him? I had judged him to be a blue-collar guy, not an intellectual, so I was a little surprised at the insights he was offering. Maybe he was just more comfortable talking with me now. We hadn't known each other that long. Up until now, we had only talked about the weather, building techniques, and other insignificant subjects. This was a small breakthrough in our new friendship. For a minute, I wondered if it was the coffee. Maybe there was some special ingredient in the cup that helped people talk. Had the old man slipped some booze or something else in? Those were silly thoughts of course but if he had, I certainly didn't need it—but it sure seemed to make it easier for him to share his thoughts with me.

I began to think that it would be a long time before this man would see me as a trusted friend. But now I felt he at least did not see me as an enemy but rather someone he would like to get to know. I felt the same. It could take awhile, but I guessed we would have plenty of time to get to know each other better. The fortress was long from finished and the old fellow seemed quite content to hang around and offer more advice. I was much more open to that idea now than I had been. Had he found another gear to shift into, or had I? I couldn't tell for sure, but as I looked over at Andy and noticed that he was becoming impatient, I found myself emptying the last of my cup. "I guess I better get to work before Andy fires me," I said.

"Well, we wouldn't want that to happen now, would we?" the old man said with a chuckle. "It can be hard to find a good job these days."

I had enjoyed talking to Johnson, but now it was time to turn my attention back to Andy. I was impressed that he had sat quiet for as long as he had. Although he was ready to work, he had not complained in any way. I couldn't decide if he had enjoyed listening to two old men talk or he just took a long time to eat his donut. Truth was I hadn't noticed how quiet he had been until now, so I thought I better get back to work before he ran out of patience.

I kept finding myself surprised and impressed with Andy. He showed patience young boys often didn't exhibit. Besides if he had heard something interesting I was sure it was from the old man. I was just the laborer. Johnson was the philosopher.

I jumped off the truck end gate, which I had been sitting on, ready to begin the day working on Andy's dream. The day would go by fast enough, and I wanted to get as much done as I could. Time seemed to be slipping away on me these days. Johnson had all the time in the world. I wondered what his philosophy on that subject would be, but I didn't want to get into another long conversation, so I didn't ask.

Talking with old man Johnson gave me a different way to look at things. He didn't seem like the doddering old man I had drawn a picture of in my mind. I wanted to give something back, so I made a mental note to myself. Next time I would bring the coffee.

CHAPTER 11

ndy appeared determined to make up for the hour I had lost talking with Mr. Johnson. He started by trying to unload some boards off my truck, which were much bigger than he was. It would have been humorous to step back and watch him try to do it himself, but I knew that he would get hurt if I did so I took the boards from him before he had a chance to pull them off the truck.

"In a hurry Andy?" I asked.

"I just want to get going, Mr. Henry."

"Okay, then, let's get going."

Andy seemed relieved that he didn't have to fight for the right to get on with the work. A small boy has lots of fight in him and is often ready to use it.

"What would you like to start with, Andy?"

"Let's build the walls, Mr. Henry. They should be next right?"

His assessment was correct, so I nodded to let him know that I agreed. Maybe he was a master carpenter after all.

"Any idea how we should do it?" I asked.

He gave me a puzzled look then turned towards the tree "I'm not sure. I never built walls before."

Once again a matter of fact statement that made sense. His simplistic look at everything provided me with a tinge of envy that life could not be as simple for me.

"What makes you think I have?" I teased.

My teasing received a crushed look from Andy that told me he was afraid that I really didn't know what to do.

"I'm just kidding" I confessed. I'm sure I can figure it out.

I think he concluded it would be better to bite his tongue than say anything. Besides he didn't have to speak because his response was a little boy's stare that screamed that he did not appreciate my sense of humor. No words were necessary.

I picked up my tool belt and tightened the buckle before saying "Andy please get my hammer from the back of the truck." He ran to my vehicle returning as quickly as possible looking afraid that any time wasted would be time lost. It was obvious he wanted those walls up.

"Okay; pick up those board over there and bring them to me. One at a time" I cautioned.

"These boards?"

"That's right." I had purposely chosen boards left off to the side I knew he could carry. I wanted him to be a part of things.

Struggling a bit, he was still just a small boy; Andy proudly presented me with the boards I had asked for. He started out with one at a time but began to carry two once he felt more confident.

"Okay I need some more nails and I'm going to need my level too. They're both in my truck; can you get them for me? The level is behind my seat."

"What's a level?" he asked.

I had forgotten for a moment who I was working with so I looked at him and said "We'll go get it together. Next time you will know what it looks like and you can get it yourself. Okay?"

"Sure. That's okay." So like the soldier he was he walked with me over to my truck and watched as I pulled the level from the cab of my truck.

"Can I carry it?"

"Sure, why not? I'll get the nails." I handed the level to him and grabbed a handful of nails all the time watching that the boy didn't bump my four foot long level. It was taller than he was. "Be careful Andy. Don't hit the truck."

"I won't." he shot back at me and continued walking.

With that we went back to the work area and began to design the grand walls Andy imagined. This was one time where I actually did know what I was doing so the work moved along at a steady pace.

The day turned out to be warm and comfortable, one of those days that made working outside fun. A small breeze blew across the pond, enough to keep the temperature just right. My muscles loosened up after about a half hour of carrying boards and equipment from the truck to the tree. The bending and kneeling on the ground as I framed up the walls was a bit more uncomfortable than I wanted to admit but I wasn't about to say anything. I knew I was an old man by Andy's standards, but I wasn't completely washed up.

As the day moved along I found the work to become easier so went into auto pilot as my mind drifted off to other things. One topic that stuck in my head was my conversation with the old man. Johnson's re-gearing theory was interesting to me, and I wondered if I would approach my retirement the same way. That was still a long time in coming, so I would learn what worked for me when my time came. I wasn't as old as Johnson, so I had lots of time to think everything out. Didn't I?

Still the idea of taking responsibility for changing my life rather than letting life make the choice for me was intriguing. Much of the context of retirement for me had been influenced by many older people who appeared to me to just sit around and watch the sunset. I realized there were times that watching a nice sunset especially with someone I cared about might be rewarding, but there had to be more.

I kept thinking that I didn't want to be one of the old men just "sitting on the bench feeding the birds" with nothing important in my life. That was probably why Johnson's theory appealed to me so much. Maybe there was still more to do in my lifetime than I had realized. I would just need to find it.

Days like this were also enjoyable for me and simple tasks certainly gave me time to do what I was best at—overanalyze! Marie kept telling me that retirement was a long ways away. Maybe she was right, but it sure felt like it was coming on faster than I wanted it to.

I became conscious of Andy standing beside me asking something.

I cleared my mind and focused on what he was saying "Sorry I didn't hear you. What did you say?"

"Is it time to use the level?" he questioned.

I had been so deep in thought that I hadn't noticed that two of the walls were fully framed ready to be put in place.

"You're a pretty smart carpenter" I smiled. "You're right it's just about time. First we have to brace the walls."

"What does that mean?"

I began to explain by telling him how we would take some two by fours to use as temporary bracing until we could put the wall in the proper position. It was easy to tell that my words were mostly lost on the boy so I decided to show him instead of explaining it.

"Okay now help me lift this section so I can move it over a bit on the floor."

Andy put every bit of muscle he had to lift the wall but I of course was doing all of the lifting. I just wanted him to enjoy seeing his fortress walls become reality.

"Now get me the level so I can make sure the wall is straight." Once again I saw no value in explaining anything so I simply completed the task then did the same thing with the next wall.

Both sections were properly squared and braced so I stepped back a bit with Andy to have a look at the work we had completed.

"What do you think?" I asked.

He looked at me with that innocent excitement and in his simple way answered "Great! What's next?

"Well the next two walls have to be built and put in place so we have the walls finished." I knew from past experience to put plywood on the framework before placing the walls up which was especially important on this project because there was no way I was going to attempt to hang from a tree while I finished a wall!

"Okay Mr. Henry. Let's do it!"

I was pretty sure it wouldn't be a good idea to tell him no so we continued with our work. The next two walls did not take much time to finish. I had taken the time to cut an opening for a window in offsetting walls before putting them in position. I could frame them later. I wasn't sure if I would do anything more than leave them open. I wanted the boys to have places to look from and of course they would need light. Andy told me he needed them so he could see anyone coming towards the fortress. I didn't ask him who he would watch out for.

Andy did his share of the work, but the young lad's enthusiasm outweighed his abilities. I had tried throughout the project to provide small tasks for him. Things I knew he could do on his own and if he couldn't I was always close by to avoid potential accidents. Protecting him from himself was almost a full time job in itself but Andy getting hurt was not something I wanted to explain to his mother.

"Do you have more nails, Mr. Henry?" Andy asked.

"Absolutely; just go to the back of the truck and get some from the bin. Bring me some too please."

I had placed a small box at the back of my truck to act as a stepping area to make it easier for Andy to get on the end gate of my truck and then crawl up into the box. I had also given him a small work belt when we began that I had taken out of a storage area in my garage. The old tool belt had certainly seen better days, but Andy wore it around his waist with the pride of a tradesman. I wasn't sure he would ever stop smiling when I told him that first day that it was his to keep.

It was something my Dad had given me and since Annie was a girl I didn't think she would ever need it. I suppose in a way I thought it should go to a boy. Besides I wasn't sure that his own father would ever give him anything like it.

It was his response to my gift that led me to adopt that opinion. Not only was he smiling but he also seemed more than surprised. "Boy my Dad doesn't have anything like this! I've never even seen one before."

He hadn't said too much about his father until then but his words gave me the feeling that he didn't expect much from him. I decided to just leave it alone but reminded myself to ask him more questions about his Dad another time. It occurred to me that I was becoming more interested the longer I knew the boy.

When I handed the tool belt to him I could tell immediately that he was such a small boy that I needed to use a screwdriver to make extra holes in the belt so it didn't fall off as he worked. It was funny to see him pull it up now and then, just to keep it around his waist. I had warned him not to put too many nails in the pouch. I didn't want to tell him the truth—that too much weight would force everything to fall to his ankles. Instead I made him think that real carpenters only kept a few nails at a time in their work belt so it made it easier to carry boards. The explanation wouldn't have made sense to me, but Andy believed it. That's all that mattered.

I watched as he gathered the nails from the box and moved to the back of the truck, retracing his path. Happy as usual, he jumped off the stepping area and ran over to me with a handful of nails.

"Here you go, Mr. Henry. Is that enough?"

"I think that will be enough for now. I'll get more when I need them."

Taking the nails from Andy, I placed them in my own tool belt then turned back to the fortress to visualize the next step in our project. I was beginning to feel this had become my project as much as it was Andy's. I couldn't deny that the feeling of building a fortress for a boy's childhood adventures made me feel good about what I was doing.

"You know something Andy; I never had anything like a fortress when I was your age."

"How come?'

Simple enough question; or so it seemed "Well I guess I didn't have anyone to help me."

"Like you; right Mr. Henry?"

I glanced down at the boy and chuckled "Yeah I guess so; no one like me."

"Didn't your Dad want to help?"

I flashed back to my own childhood memories thinking about his question. "Well I think he would have loved to have helped me build a place like this; he just never had the opportunity. He was gone." This fortress was stirring memories deep within my mind.

"What do you mean Mr. Henry? Where was your Dad?"

The memories of my father were very special to me and I wasn't sure it was something I could share with this young boy beside me but at times like this it was hard not to think about him. Wondering about Andy's Dad was really like with him probably contributed to my thoughts about my own father as well.

I decided to attempt to explain about my father to the young boy but wasn't positive in how to do it. I paused before speaking to him; then gathering my thoughts the best I could I spoke to Andy while I continued to work. I wanted it to sound more like a conversation than a lecture.

"Well Andy my Dad never lived very long. I was only a few years older than you when he died. So I didn't have much time to spend with him. Can you understand what I'm saying?"

"I think so." He still seemed a bit perplexed and although I was hesitant in carrying the conversation forward I felt that I didn't want to leave him confused.

I stopped and looked at the boy. "Do you know what it means for someone to die?"

"Oh sure; I had a turtle once that died. His name was Rocky. Mom said he went to heaven. That's where you go when you are good you know? That's what Mom says."

Deciding to stay with his simplistic understanding of death I continued by confirming his mother's statement. "That's right. Your Mom is right and my Dad was good so he went to heaven. Can you understand?"

"You think he's taking care of Rocky?"

I laughed and said "He might be doing just that. He loved all animals."

"I'm glad. Rocky was a good turtle. I miss him. Do you miss your Dad?"

"Every day Andy" I sighed "Every day." With that I turned my attention back to our work and continued with the task at hand. Although my hands were busy my mind was somewhere else thinking about Andy's questions and my Dad.

Andy brought me back to the moment with his next question; "What was he like Mr. Henry?"

"Who?" I asked.

"Your Dad" Andy said.

I thought about my answer for a moment before speaking. "He was a good man, someone I respected, but I think he didn't always get as much time as he had wanted to spend with me. He taught me many things, including some of my carpentry skills. He wasn't any better at it than I was" I glanced at the boy noticing that he wasn't giving me any argument about my skills. I was sure if it was an oversight from the boy or an opinion!

"What else?"

I wasn't sure why this boy was asking me all of the questions about my father but I found it easy to speak about him. "He was a fair man. I guess he was a simple man who didn't feel the need to be someone he wasn't to make new friends. He made it easy to respect him."

Andy and I kept working as we talked so neither of us was seeing any reaction from the other person. If we had been looking at each other the boy may have seen surprise on my face because not only was he asking me the questions he appeared to understand what I was saying as well even though some of my answers were very introspective.

"Did he ever spank you?" An odd question I thought; almost out of the blue making me wonder if there wasn't more to Andy's question than interest in my own father.

"Well I always tell people he was swift with discipline but it was just a part of growing up in our house. I didn't know any different. He used to always say that spanking me hurt him as much as it hurt me. I always wanted to argue the point but my ass could only take so much hurt from him!"

Andy looked over at me and laughed. I couldn't be sure it was because of my use of the word ass or the idea of my sore rear end.

"But in the end I guess I usually deserved the spankings. Knowing that didn't make it any easier to be spanked."

I paused for a moment as another wave of memories about my father came over me. Andy's questions made me remember more.

I remembered that I enjoyed the time I spent with him, and there were far more happy times than spankings. As well even though I was a young boy my father taught me three things most important to him. He always told me that respect, honesty, and accountability were important things for anyone to live by. He taught me that without those three things, no amount of money would ever replace what I didn't have. Sometimes I wondered if my father knew he would die while I was still young and felt the need to make sure I understood those three things. I tried to guide my life with those things in mind and never forgot them. I missed him and I hoped that he would have been proud of me. I would have liked to share the experience of my own fortress with him, but I couldn't. That time was gone.

I decided that it was time to turn the tables on Andy and find out more about him so I was the next to speak when I asked him "What about you Andy? Do you get spanked once in a while?"

I sensed for the briefest moment that the boy didn't want to answer. I was probably correct but he answered nonetheless "No my Dad has never spanked me."

"Really; are you that good of kid at home?"

Andy either didn't understand my attempt at poking fun at him; or just didn't care. Instead he ignored the question and answered by saying "No; Mom won't let him."

"What do you mean?" now intrigued by his answer.

"Well Dad tried to spank me a couple of times and Mom stepped in front of him and told him to not do it or hit her first."

Surprised my next question was straight to the point "What happened then?"

Andy was not being secretive but was hesitant in his response. "He almost hit my Mom but she just stared at him until he put his arm down. I don't know what I would have done if he had hit Mom." I suddenly realized that we had stopped working and were now looking at each other and I could sense sadness in his eyes that I hadn't seen before in this optimistic, energetic little boy. I was sorry that I had even asked the question. I was feeling uncomfortable with the conversation.

Before I could say anything else I heard a voice speak from behind me. It was Johnson again. He had left our work area after our morning coffee, returning to his house. Looking at my watch I calculated that the old man had been gone about four hours. He must have had some lunch by now, then a nap to get through the afternoon. I contemplated that men as old as him needed that extra rest. I swore to myself that I would never get as old as that. I would do whatever I had to avoid it—of that I was sure. Still; I was relieved to have him come back to the work site. It meant I didn't have to hear more about Andy's father.

"Afternoon boys," said the old man in his usual straightforward manner. Why waste any more words than that? It reminded me that my own father had been direct too. Not a bad way to be I suppose. It seemed to have worked for both of them. It was a skill I would be wise to master in my own life. *"Don't analyze everything to death"* I said to myself. *"My Dad had nothing to do with this man so quit comparing them; just enjoy his company."*

"Afternoon," I replied, trying to make my hello shorter than his. Johnson would never know the thoughts of my father that were going through my mind, so this small victory would mean nothing to him.

"Hello, Mr. Johnson," chirped up Andy; it was good to see the happy Andy again. "How do you like our walls? The fortress is just about done," he said. The young man's assessment was grander than the reality. There was some important work to complete. The roof would be next and I knew I would need some help with that.

I looked over to the old fellow, who was looking back at me with a twinkle in his eye. It appeared the same thought had just crossed his mind. He then looked back at the boy.

"Well, boy," Johnson began, "I think you might still want to put some kind of roof on your fortress, don't you think? How do you plan to do that?"

Andy looked back to the tree with another puzzled look on his face. It was obvious that he hadn't thought that far ahead. Why should he? He was still just a boy living in the moment. I guess this was one of the reasons that God had included me in Andy's fortress project.

I didn't want the boy to become discouraged, so I spoke up, "Don't worry, Andy. Mr. Johnson will help us." I had learned that the old man was more than willing to give advice—or, as he would see it, his wisdom—so now I would see if he would also be willing to put his money where his mouth was. I felt quite smug about my statement.

"Oh really," Johnson said, laughing. "You think so do you?"

"Well, it would be a good way to put your experience to good use," I offered diplomatically. "And I could sure use the help. The roof will be pretty hard for me to do by myself, don't you think?"

"I can help too, Mr. Henry!" Andy said with a tone of indignation.

"Of course, Andy; I hadn't forgotten about you," I replied. "I just meant that Mr. Johnson has probably built more roofs than we have, so his experience could help."

The answer seemed to make sense to Andy, so he nodded at me with approval. Then he looked towards old man Johnson. The look on Andy's face seemed to soften Johnson's heart. You never can tell with an old guy like him; for all I knew any change in his disposition could have been caused by gas! It didn't matter. Either way he appeared to be more comfortable and open to the idea then he had been a moment ago.

"Well," he said. I tried to anticipate his next sentence. "I guess it wouldn't hurt me to help out a bit. After all, the fortress *is* on my land."

Johnson glanced towards me. "Young guys can use any help they can get," he said, smiling.

I grinned back at him while throwing back a similar comment. "I think maybe old guys need help too. If you can't make it up the ladder to the tree, just let me know."

We laughed, knowing that each of us had taken a jab at the other. This strange-looking old man might have a good sense of humor after all. It was becoming clear to me that Johnson was having as hard a time saying no to Andy as I did. It was a young man's charm outweighing an old man's resistance—and it was fun to watch.

Andy had a large grin on his face as well—probably more from the knowledge that Mr. Johnson was going to help and the roof would be built. He didn't know that his two new friends were teasing each other. I took a sideways look at the boy, wondering if he was as innocent as he appeared. Had he orchestrated the whole situation? It couldn't have been too hard to get Johnson to join forces with us. Could young Andy have been the smartest one of us all?

Turning my attention back towards Johnson, I asked him when it would be a good time for him to help me with the roof.

"Anytime is good for me, Henry. I don't have much else to do anyways."

"Well I'll have to gather up some more materials before we get started, so how about next weekend?"

"Sure, I'll bring my own tools. Saturday morning okay for you guys?"

"Good for me," I said. "Is that okay with you, Andy?"

In a perfect world, he would rather have built the roof right now. Somehow, he did seem to understand that wasn't possible but he gave it a shot anyways.

"Can't we do it sooner?" He asked.

"No I don't think so" I replied. "I'll need Mr. Johnson's help and besides we still have some more work to finish up before we'll be ready for the roof, so next Saturday was the best we can hope for."

He nodded his head in agreement impressing me once again with his grand steps of maturity. Many boys his age would have pouted or argued with us. This child—and he was still just a child—took things in stride, moving on to the next challenge with a certain determination many men never had.

I would have enjoyed talking some more to Johnson, but I knew I better get the necessary work finished if I was going to be ready for the roof next Saturday. I also had some chores at home on my "to do" list that Marie had told me about, so I thought I had better pick up the pace.

Old man Johnson seemed content to hang around the job site for the rest of the afternoon, smoking his cigar as usual, ready to offer advice whenever he thought it was needed. Several times he even offered some advice that *wasn't* needed. Most of his comments were short and sweet so I took them in stride. Besides the wisdom of an old man came with the price of the occasional unwanted observation. Maybe I couldn't get one without the other—fair price to pay for something important.

Johnson was sitting on a tree stump not far from where we were working so that he could see what was going on yet remain far enough away not to get involved with the actual work. He was old enough to know that even though he had been enlisted in building the roof, he would not be sucked into anything more than that.

One thing that working with my hands also worked in my favor was that it gave me time to ponder things. Looking at Johnson made me wonder how many people thought he was just a doddering old man with nothing to offer. I wished I hadn't made that same judgment on our first visit, but I knew I had, so I promised myself not to make that mistake again. The more I came to know the man, the less true I knew my original judgment to be. I was beginning to discover that although he was more than a generation older than me, he was just as strong as I was. He was comfortable with who he was and did not need to prove himself to others anymore. If you didn't like him, he could live with that; it would make his life any better or worse—no hard feelings.

I was coming to realize that he did not impose his ideas on me; rather, he offered them as something I could consider if I wanted to. There had been real value to some of the comments. I didn't know how to use all the information, but there would be a time when the lessons would be important.

This had become more than just a construction project. It seemed to be opening doors for me, which had been closed for a long time.

True, I had grown up in a much different time, but was one little boy's dreams from years long ago much different from those of today's young lad? The memory of my father was just one door that could be opened through the connection with Andy and the old man. Some dreams I had shared with no-one.

Something crossed my mind. Had I spent much of my own life building my own fortress walls to keep people out? Were they too strong to tear down? They were there to protect me from the world, but the older I was becoming the more my walls were locking me in. Was that any different from anyone else? Geez was I becoming a philosopher myself?

Then there was the old man. When I glanced again at him it felt as though some mysterious door appeared to be opening for me. My wife would say it was part of life's energy. Maybe she was right. Still would this be a room of learning for me? His laid-back approach to life was definitely something I was beginning to admire and even envy. I always preached that I could learn at least one thing from every person I met; so what could I learn from this man?

Some comments that Johnson had made throughout the day told me that there was no doubt that life was not perfect for him either. He didn't say much and I didn't question him but I was sure that he had his own demons to deal with.

Looking at this new friend I decided that I wanted to take the time to find out what lessons he could teach me, what demons kept him awake at night and what angels protected him. I thought the journey could be interesting. For now however I would leave everything as it was. There would be lots of time to learn more about him.

The day had finished for Andy and me. We had continued our work at a steady enough pace to accomplish what was needed for the roof. My thoughts mixed with conversation had made the time go by fast enough. The walls had come together well; even better than I expected and we were prepared for the next step of construction the following Saturday. I packed up my tools and took one last look at the job we had done to this point. Andy was standing by my side doing the same thing. I wanted to think that both of us were proud in what we saw. It was coming together. His dream was becoming reality.

"Happy?" I asked Andy already knowing what his answer would be.

"Yeah! Looks pretty good doesn't it?"

"I think so."

"George is going to like it too" he said. "I can't wait to tell him what we have done so far?"

I had forgotten about his friend George so I made a comment. "Where is George anyways?"

"He's still out of town, but I talk to him every couple of days so I'll be able to let him know what we've done."

It appeared that was where the conversation would end so I left it there and didn't push the issue. I would probably meet this George soon enough.

Since the roof would be going on next week, the fortress would soon be finished. I felt good about that because then it would be a place for Andy and his friend George to hide out or just play in. I hoped they would have many days of fun to look forward to. As a matter of fact if George was anything like Andy I was sure of it.

Johnson had left at least an hour before. The balance of the afternoon had been spent quietly working. As I said Johnson had sat close by almost like a supervisor. We spoke only when one of us had a question or needed to offer some kind of input. It was not an uncomfortable silence, just one I was not used to with the man. It did make focusing on the work easier, and even when he didn't have something to say I think I appreciated him sitting there just in case I had missed something. Maybe Johnson was a help after all. Besides it seemed that when my mouth wasn't busy, my mind had been.

On the short ride to Andy's house, I looked over at the boy and noticed that he seemed more tired than I was. He had been quiet since we left the work site and was not his usual "chatty" self. There were times when it was easy to forget he was just a little boy, since he carried himself with the dignity of a young gentleman, but today had been a busy one for both of us. I had thought of things I had not given any thought to for many years. My mind had even drifted to thoughts of what could have been. Looking back could be painful as well as nostalgic. Thinking and remembering was often more tiring in some ways than the physical work itself.

For Andy, it was just the day of physical work that had tired him out. He was too young to have memories like mine, creating psychological walls around himself. Or was he? His earlier comments made me wonder. So when I thought of my past, Andy's present and Johnson's unknown it made me think that perhaps all three of us had more stories to tell. I couldn't know if there would be time to hear them all. I also didn't know at the time how much more of a story *I* would have to tell. For now I just knew that it had been a good day.

CHAPTER 12

George was waiting when Andy got home. He was sitting on the doorstep with a big smile on his face. He was so tired he hadn't seen him right away. Mr. Henry hadn't seen him either. George thought that the man appeared to be thinking of other things and simply hadn't noticed. *Maybe next time*, he thought.

"How's it going, Andy?"

"Great, I didn't know you were coming over."

"I wasn't sure myself. Can I come in?"

"Sure, let's go." Andy wasn't feeling tired anymore now that his friend was here.

As the boys ran through the house to Andy's room, he hollered a hello to his mom while informing her of George's presence. She acknowledged his hello, allowing him to continue on to his room with his friend. Andy found himself asking George why he hadn't been coming around more or why he had not been showing up to help with the fortress.

"Did you know that Mr. Henry has been asking about you?" Andy asked. The truth was he wanted to know as well. He didn't want to keep making excuses.

"Has he?" replied George.

"Yeah, and I don't know what I should tell him. I thought you were going to help me build our fortress."

George looked at his friend for a moment. "Well, Andy, I know that everything in your home isn't always great, but I've had my own problems lately. Stuff I can't tell you about. I'm sorry that I haven't been able to help. You'll just have to pass that message on to Mr. Henry. Anyway, I walked by the other day and it looks like you two are doing a good job without me."

"Mr. Henry has been great, and Mr. Johnson has helped some too; I think it's coming together great" Andy agreed. "It just isn't the same without you."

"I know, Andy. That's just the way it has to be."

The two young boys nodded to each other as if understanding some unspoken message. They were both so much older in spirit than they were in body.

Andy shrugged the idea off—it didn't matter anyway. He wasn't going to let anything spoil the time he would have with George. It was always great to see him. They were best friends.

They talked more about the fortress—what they were going to do and how much fun it would be. Andy had just about forgotten about some of the other stuff going on at home when George asked, "So what else is going on? Are your mom and dad still fighting, like you told me about?"

"Aw, they're always fighting. They treat me like a little kid. They think I don't know what is going on, but I hear them yell at each other. They think I'm stupid or something."

"They don't think you're stupid, Andy. I've seen it before in my own home. I'm sure they don't even know that you hear them. Don't worry about it. It's not your fight."

This made Andy feel better. If it was happening in other homes then maybe he wasn't alone. In the end, he decided that George was right. To Andy, his friend was so much smarter than him, so when George talked he listened. If George said not to worry, then he wouldn't worry.

He had other things to do. Andy needed to tell George more about their new fortress—how he was helping, how he got his new tool belt, and all of the other things that had happened. Even though they had already spent some of their visit talking about their new play home, Andy had so much more to add.

There were times he spoke faster than George could listen. They both laughed when that happened, and Andy would have to repeat himself. He didn't mind telling George twice. This was when they both spoke just like the friends they were and the children they should be. It was the sharing of innocence. Telling George all about his day made Andy feel happy. He noticed that George seemed happy too. That was just fine for both boys.

Robert Henry felt tired as he drove up to his house. He remembered how tired Andy; a young boy; appeared to look when he dropped him off so maybe he wasn't doing so bad after all for an "old man." Johnson hadn't appeared tired, but all he had done was talk. It was him who had done most of the work so it made sense that he should be tired. Still it wasn't that long ago when a day like this wouldn't have taken so much out of him. Age must be catching up after all.

Robert chuckled at this thought. Old age may be creeping up but it hadn't caught him yet. Mind you; being stronger than a young boy, no matter how full of energy, or a cigar puffing old man wasn't much of an accomplishment, was it? Still, a small victory was still a victory, right?

He gave everything one last thought; put on a big smile, remembered the great day he had, and walked through the door. He was glad to be home.

The first thing he saw was Marie sitting in the living room watching television. He was happy to see her take time for herself. She had not always done enough of that. Robert was beginning to better understand what it felt like to grow older; maybe Marie was experiencing the same things. Rest time was important.

"Hi, sweetie. How was your day?" he questioned.

Marie looked away from the television at Robert. "Not bad. It was busy as usual. How was yours?"

"Terrific," Robert said. "Andy's fortress is coming along great, and he seems happy with the results. The old man has been around more. He always has an opinion to offer, but I've come to like him. I find myself waiting for his input. Hell he may even know something I don't!"

"That's good, honey," Marie offered as she turned back to her television show.

Robert knew she didn't mean to dismiss him in that way, because by now he thought she understood how big this project had become to him. She was just preoccupied, he guessed.

Robert wondered why she couldn't show more interest in the things that were important to him. As busy people, they didn't take enough time to do the things they wanted to do. Maybe they believed they would make more time for each other when they got older—or retired! At least Robert hoped that was true. If it wasn't true then what were they working for?

With that thought in mind he sat down on the couch to watch television with her, even though he was not interested in what she was watching but content to do it anyway. She turned and gave him a small smile, adding to his happy day.

"What are you watching?"

"Oh nothing really; just some kind of home decorating show" she said without looking up. "You want something to eat?"

Marie appeared to get up as though to begin making a meal right away when Robert said "That's okay; I can wait. Let's just watch the rest of the show."

Robert thought he detected a small expression of gratitude from Marie; but it was probably just something he hoped she felt. He decided that life was often made up of too many big things, and the small things were left behind. They should be equally memorable for him, good or bad. This was one of those small moments.

When the show ended Marie asked him what he would like to eat for supper and offered a few suggestions. Once they agreed on the "menu" she got up and began to prepare the food.

It had been a busy day for Robert, so supper was going to taste good. He looked forward to being able to sit and talk with his wife with the television turned off. Things had been so busy with Andy and work that he was afraid he had neglected Marie. The kitchen table was a good place to share each other's day's events.

If he did neglect her; Robert thought; then Marie handled it well. Was it because she didn't feel neglected, or was it just something she was able to accept? Robert prayed for the first and hoped he would never test the second.

"Looks great, Marie; smells even better."

"Thanks," she said. It was a simple reply, but he could tell Marie appreciated the recognition. Everyone wants to feel appreciated, and Robert thought he owed it to her. She had earned it.

"I was telling you before how Andy's fortress is coming along." he said opening the conversation as they sat down to eat. "We've been working hard at it and it looks like we'll be done sooner than I thought. Andy is excited because he knows that he and his friends will be able to play out there soon."

"Does he have many friends Robert?" asked Marie.

"You know now that you mention it I'm not really sure" he pondered. "I know he has at least one close friend. He told me about a boy named George. Andy says he's his best friend."

"Have you met him?"

"No, as a matter of fact I haven't. He was supposed to be helping us with the fortress, but he has never showed up. I don't know why. Andy has hinted that George is busy with his own family. Who knows? Maybe he's just in Andy's imagination. I know he hasn't done any work," Robert said, laughing.

"I'm sure he's just another little boy like Andy who is just as excited about their new playhouse as he is. You can only guess why he hasn't shown up yet. Have you asked Andy directly?"

Sometimes Marie's answers were as simple as Andy's. It made it easier to provide an answer. "You're probably right. When I did ask Andy, he just told me that he hasn't seen him for a while. Like I said, he told me the boy is busy. I imagine he'll show up soon enough. It hasn't really made much of a difference. Everything is getting done plus, I'm not sure I would want to have to babysit two of them; and the old man. Still it's nice seeing how happy Andy is."

She looked at him questioningly cleared her throat then timidly began to speak. "Robert, can I ask you something?"

Robert could tell that they were no longer talking about Andy and the tone of her voice indicated that something was definitely on her mind.

"Of course," he replied. "What is it?"

"Do you ever wish we had a son?"

The question surprised him and he found himself holding a piece of roast chicken half way from the plate to his mouth. She had never asked him this before. Not knowing how to answer, he finished putting the meat into his mouth so that he could buy himself some time to gather his thoughts.

"What makes you ask that?"

"Well, you just seem so happy helping this Andy boy build his playhouse."

"Fortress."

"Whatever" she said ignoring the correction. "When you help him, do you ever wish Annie had been a boy or that we'd had a second child—a boy?"

"No, Marie. You know I love Annie and wouldn't trade her for anything."

"Of course I know that" she stated as though that was a given. "I guess what I really meant was, were you ever sorry that I wasn't able to have any more children?"

So that was the real mystery for her questions. Annie's delivery had been a tough one, causing many unexpected problems. As a result, she couldn't have any more children. It had made her sad for a long time, and in truth, it had made Robert sad as well. He wanted to hide his feelings, because it was important to him that Marie never felt any pressure over the issue. They had been given a beautiful, healthy daughter who would grow up to be a wonderful woman, and if that was their only gift, he could accept that. Robert thought she had as well. Maybe she hadn't.

"Marie," he began in a slow, deliberate tone, "Never think that I have been anything less than happy with the child we had together. She is one of the two great loves in my life. You are the other one. I have never felt that I was cheated out of anything or that I missed out on something because we never had a boy. Besides Annie was a handful herself. Another child, boy or girl might have pushed us over the edge."

Laughter filled the room as they remembered Annie's childhood antics, knowing that he was right in so many ways. She had been an inquisitive child who would question them to death until she got the answer she was looking for. She would play for hours by herself or with her friends at school with the same endless amount of energy. She enjoyed sports and was actually quite good at most of the games she tried. All of her activities kept them busy and gave them many snapshots of her childhood that they enjoyed together to this day. Memories could be that way—so long ago and yet so close.

"She was a handful, wasn't she?" said Marie, continuing to laugh.

"A handful?" he replied. "I know your hair is still natural, of course, but why do you think mine is so gray?"

She shot him a mischievous look, letting him know she was aware of his teasing. "I'd be happy with gray. That would mean both of your hairs would be the same color!"

They both laughed once again.

"You know, Marie, the reason I enjoy the project I am helping Andy with is not because I wanted a boy. It's just that it makes me feel like a boy again myself" he said. "It's great to see how excited he gets or how important such a simple project can be. There is so much ahead of this child, both good and bad. Right now, I'm just proud to be part of what should turn out to be a good memory in his life. I think old man Johnson feels the same way. Does that make sense?"

"Yes, honey, it does. Thank you," offered Marie.

The answer and Marie's response seemed to put her doubts aside. That was good enough for Robert, because like most people she had experienced too many of her own disappointments. He never wanted her to feel disappointed about children. She was a great mother and if they had kept a scorecard she was a better parent in many ways then he had been. At least that was his assessment of their parenting skills.

The conversation paused for a while as they continued eating their supper. Robert took this time to think about his daughter and the role each of them had played in her life. They both loved Annie, but he thought Marie had more patience than he did.

His lack of patience was never more apparent then the times she showed interest in someone. That was when he would continue to ask questions until he received the answers *he* was looking for! It was usually obvious that Annie did not always agree with his position or even understand it and many arguments between the two of them had ensued. But hey she was the teenager and he was the father so he was pretty sure he knew what he was talking about. He was not proud of it now but there were some times when his stubbornness embarrassed Annie and even appeared to scare her dates. At the time he liked it that way.

More patience probably would have made things easier for everyone. He chuckled knowing there were probably a couple of young men who don't drive by the house anymore because he scared the hell out of them! Some would say that was a father's job. Some would say he was an ass. Robert liked the first answer better.

Maybe he would be a terrific grandfather,—someday—given the opportunity. He believed he had learned enough from his own mistakes as a father and hoped to use the information wisely the next time as a grandfather. He even believed that his patience was getting better as he grew older or maybe he was just wearing out and didn't have time for impatience. Who knew for sure? He didn't have the time to figure it out or even want to try. None of it mattered as long as his daughter was happy. On that point both parents always agreed.

Robert continued to tell Marie about his day; about the boy and about the old man. She even seemed to find the stories entertaining, and laughter filled the room, so he continued to tell them. The description of old man Johnson was especially funny to her. Marie laughed when Robert told her about the white socks and suspenders. "You're teasing me again," she said.

"I swear on a stack of bibles," he promised, raising his hand while crossing himself.

She laughed some more, then said, "I'd love to see that someday."

"Be nice to Andy and there might be a time when he'll invite you to his fortress—if girls will be allowed. Or maybe you know someone who knows someone that can get you safely into the fortress," he joked offering Marie a humorous wink. "You never know. The old man may be around and you can see for yourself."

By this time both of them had cleared the table, washed the dishes, and were ready for dessert—his favorite part of the meal.

Marie and Robert moved back into the living room expecting to watch more television. Instead, they continued to talk, joke, and laugh.

It had been a great Sunday!

CHAPTER 13

The past two weekends had been busy ones. I was able to speak with Andy's Mom the last time I picked him up, and I even got a chance to meet his father briefly for the first time. I must admit it wasn't a highlight moment. He gave a grunt for a hello and wouldn't even shake my hand when I offered it to him. This convinced me that Andy had received his respectful ways from his mother.

There was something else I noticed about his dad that confirmed some of the rumors floating around the neighborhood. Deep down, I wished it were not true, but I could see that his father was giving far too much attention to a bottle of Jack Daniels he was carrying. Maybe that's why he didn't shake my hand? He didn't want to put the bottle down?

Laura looked at me with a sad embarrassment as her husband walked by us. "He's not feeling well today."

I didn't know what I should say in a situation like this. Since I had grown to like Andy, and wished the best for his mother, I tried to diffuse the awkwardness. "That's okay. You never know when someone can catch the flu."

Laura looked at me for a moment then choked out a small laugh. "If you're right, then he's been putting in a fulltime effort to get rid of the bug," she replied with obvious sarcasm. It was good to see she hadn't lost her sense of humor.

Andy came running past his dad and straight to the door. Maybe he was still too young to understand what was going on around him, or maybe too smart to let it ruin his day. I hoped for the latter, because I knew that I wasn't that smart. What I was seeing had already ruined part of my day, but I would never show that to Andy.

"Let's go, Mr. Henry. We'll finish my fortress today if Mr. Johnson is there to help us," Andy stated with distinct confidence. "Bye, Mom. See you later." He took the time to give his mother an obligatory hug good-bye so that he wouldn't be called back from the door. I noticed that he did not acknowledge his father. His dad offered a similar effort.

Wanting to ignore what was happening; I looked towards Laura and said, "Well, those are my marching orders. I better get going. The General has been this way ever since I was drafted!" Laura's laughter indicated that she had also served under "the General's" command.

"I wouldn't want to get you court marshaled." She shouted a simple good-bye to her little boy as he ran towards my truck. "Hope you finish today so you can get your life back," she added looking back at me.

"Oh, it hasn't been so bad," I replied. "It's actually been a lot of fun. It's been a bigger project than I expected, but I wouldn't have wanted to miss out on it."

"Well, thanks again, Mr. Henry. It has meant a lot to my boy. I'm very grateful."

Watching the situation with her husband in the background was spoiling more of my Sunday so I passed on my own good-bye, then headed to my truck before Andy began fidgeting, as he often did when he thought I was taking too long.

"Your mom is a real nice lady, isn't she?"

"Yeah, she's the best."

"I met your dad today too." I immediately regretted speaking about his father. I was just trying to keep the conversation going.

He gave me no response and it was painfully clear that this was not something Andy was willing to talk about. It was a similar response to the first time I had brought the subject of his father up. It seemed that he wasn't going to offer any effort to a conversation about his father so I just let the subject drop. We drove the balance of the short trip in silence.

We began unloading our tools and materials once we arrived at the job site preparing for the work ahead of us. Andy had updated me the week before about his friend George, explaining why he hadn't been around. I told him I understood, even though I wasn't certain I did. It wasn't a big deal anyway. As I had said to my wife, besides Johnson and our little carpenter, any more bodies would have just been in the way.

We talked when we needed something and stopped only briefly for refreshments; just as we had from the beginning. We had a rhythm going, and neither of us wanted to change that. Everyone appeared determined to see Andy's fortress come to fruition; not just the boy.

Interestingly enough; despite his comical appearance and cigar smoke blowing upwind of me plus an odor that suggested he had not showered for a couple of days, it still felt good working with the old man. His helpful pointers were becoming more important to me as we moved along which was good because he wasn't shy about giving advice! At one point I even turned to him and offered some advice of my own.

"I think it would be good to make a hole in the floor with some kind of trap door to let the boys crawl through."

"Don't think that's the best way to do it" he said without turning towards me.

"Why not?" I asked bristling a bit.

"Well what if the boys forget to put down the trap door one day? Think they may get hurt falling to the ground?" His tone sounded sarcastic.

"Got a better idea then?" I asked trying to ignore the sarcasm.

"Yeah; better one than you" he chuckled. "How about building a ladder up the tree and cut a door opening on the side of the wall right over there?"

I looked at where he was pointing and grudgingly said "Okay I can see how that might work too."

"Much safer don't you think?"

"Sure. I can live with it." I wasn't ready to concede that his idea was better than mine.

"Another thing I think we should do is cut bigger openings in all of the walls rather than the small holes you cut."

His comment puzzled me and annoyed me but all I asked was "What are you talking about?"

"The boys will find it too dark without bigger openings plus a fort should have openings all around it so they can see anything coming their way. Doesn't that make sense?"

I paused once again thinking about his question. I believed I could catch him off guard by asking him "Great idea. How will the roof stay up if we cut everything away?"

Johnson glanced at me with an amused look on his face making me feel like he thought I was as dumb as I looked.

"Where did you learn carpentry Henry?"

His question brought a flush to my face. I didn't have an answer for him.

He continued. "We don't cut everything away. Support posts will still be left in place and we built the roof properly so the headers will provide proper support. Basic carpentry, understand?" he said in a tone of voice often reserved for children.

I could tell that by now he was having some fun at my expense. I was positive his roof comment was meant to tell me that the roof would not have been built correctly if he hadn't been there to help.

Frustrated by his comments I snapped back "If this is all true then why didn't you say so the other day when I was putting the walls up? I know you saw me doing the work."

"Take it easy Henry." He said calmly; appearing to want to diffuse any frustration on my part that could spoil the good work we had done to this point. "You didn't ask and it *was* your project. Now it's mine too."

It was hard to argue with his logic. He was right I hadn't asked and his efforts to this point had surely made the fortress part of his life now and it *was* his land. Still didn't mean he couldn't have spoken up sooner. The old man hadn't seemed to have had any problem dishing out unsolicited advice before.

Grudgingly I was beginning to see that his construction plan *was* probably better than mine. I decided it was time to set my ego aside and do what was best for Andy. Probably didn't have a choice anyway.

"Alright old man; we'll do it your way." I was willing to agree but not willing to admit I was wrong.

Johnson smiled at me and said to me "Okay *young man*. Thanks for seeing it my way." I couldn't tell for sure but I sensed some condescension in his voice. I just let it pass.

Andy had been working off in a different part of the area and didn't appear to have heard our "conversation." I could tell he didn't understand why things were being changed so we told him it was just for his safety. In the end I don't think he really cared. It appeared to me that he just thought it would look cool. So we set to work doing it Johnson's way.

As we worked, I once again envisioned my own father working on a project like this. I think he would have enjoyed it. Probably would have done it Johnson's way too; I guessed. That thought brought a small smile to my face until another thought took the smile away.

When Andy was not close by I looked at the old man and said in a low voice "I am enjoying doing this work for Andy but I think his own father should be here. My Dad is long gone and we missed out on doing anything like this. I think he would have enjoyed it. I know I would have liked working with my father building a fort."

"I think you're right" he said. "Same thought has occurred to me."

"Why do you think he isn't here to help? I could tell when I saw him the other day that he appears to be a drinker but I don't think he's a drunk."

"We may never know Henry. By now even you should know everyone is responsible for themselves; can't change that."

"I know you're right. Still though I think Andy is missing out on something with his Dad not here to help him out. I know I would want to help a child of mine with a project like this."

"You told me you have a daughter didn't you?"

"That's right."

"Always do everything she wanted to do?"

"Well I sure as hell tried to be a part of the big things in her life. That's what a parent should do." I stated as a point of fact.

"Says you; each man's definition of involvement is different don't you think? Who has a right to set standards for someone else?"

I couldn't tell if Johnson was making generalizations or defending Andy's father. I didn't care either way.

"Still; you'd think he would want to be here."

"Do you actually know the man?"

"Well no. I guess not. But still . . ."

Johnson cut me off and said "Still what? How do you know what is going on in his life? I can agree that it would be nice for a father to spend time with his son but I can't make that decision for him. Can you?"

"No of course not" I shot back. "But if it was my son I would sure make sure that I helped him out."

"You're here aren't you? And Andy is not your son or mine. You made your own decision, let his father make his."

It was obvious I wasn't going to win this argument so I laughed and said "So who are you the great Guru of insight or something?"

Johnson must have been tiring of the conversation as well because he laughed before saying "No *sonny;* just a man who has lived longer than you and had to live with my own decisions. Age didn't make me smarter just more understanding."

I glanced at him thinking that his use of the word "sonny" was to remind me that I had not yet reached his level of enlightenment. Maybe he was right. One thing I knew for sure was that my respect for him was growing with each conversation. It was becoming clear that the old saying "can't tell a book by its cover" may be true with this odd fellow.

The afternoon was warm and comfortable once again so I was content enough to get back to work. The final shape of the fortress was coming together. I could tell just looking at the work we were doing that Johnson had been right. Damn; I thought happy with the results but annoyed with my own incompetence.

Andy had remained an active part of the process. Johnson and I were needed to complete the larger portions of the structure, but it was clear there was no way Andy would be prevented from doing his part. It was his fortress, and he was going to be a big part of its construction, no matter what. He would bring us nails, hold boards as we cut them and all of the usual things he had learned to do. I think it made him feel important.

There were a couple of times that Johnson or myself had to guide Andy to make sure he didn't get hurt but he seemed to take the direction well enough. Earlier on I had turned to the boy and said "Watch out Andy. Mr. Johnson and I have to cut this area out so I need you to step back a few feet okay?"

He looked at what we were working on before answering with a simple "Okay."

Once we finishing cutting a section of the wall out that we were working on Andy stepped back toward us.

"That looks pretty good" he said with excitement in his voice. "You guys really know what you're doing."

I looked over to Johnson and ignored his grin before saying "Well we try. But the idea was mostly Mr. Johnson's." I thought it best to give credit where credit was due. I didn't want another discussion about my skill level.

Johnson decided to become a part of the conversation and looked towards Andy before asking "Do you like the openings we made for you? You think they will work for you and your friend?"

I don't think Andy could believe that it was actually happening. His response emphasized his excitement once again when he said "Yeah; they're great. George and I will be able to see everything. I know he'll like them and I sure do! I never even thought about doing it that way."

"See I'm not the only one" I chuckled as I looked at the old man.

"Guess not" he said. "Course the boy still has more time to learn; how about you?"

His grin made it clear that he was once again just making a joke at my expense rather than taunting me. Frankly I enjoyed the banter. Laughter was a friend I had learned to enjoy. It was good to have a new friend to share it with.

"An old guy like you probably knows more about time than me. You're probably as smart as you can get; time is not on your side."

Andy was looking at both of us and joined us in our laughter. I don't think he knew what we were actually laughing about but I don't think it mattered. We were happy and so was he. All that really mattered to him was that as each hour went by he could see his fortress growing in size and shape. Soon he would be able to play in it. That would make any boy happy.

The day was almost over and we were all tired. We had worked hard and except for the design discussion most of the project had moved along smoothly enough. We had accomplished a lot in one day and I was happy with the result.

As we stood back near the truck I wondered what was going through each of our minds.

"Except for some minor finishing I think it looks pretty good; don't you think?"

Andy spoke before anyone had a chance to say anything else. "My fortress looks great! I'm going to have so much fun and George is going to love it too." He turned to us and added with a serious voice "You know both of you can come by anytime you like. I couldn't have built it without you."

We both acknowledged his invitation then Johnson added "So what do you think you boys are going to do with this grand place of yours?"

"Lot's of stuff" Andy exclaimed. "We already have a lot of ideas. It's going to be a lot of fun."

It seemed that Andy had a grand plan but was not yet ready to share the details. I glanced at Mr. Johnson and said "I just thought we were building a tree house but I guess it's actually a magic kingdom." I winked at him.

He looked back at me and joined in "Guess you're right. I guess it's a magic fortress. Hope I can find my sword; I think I'll need it if I leave my house. Who knows what will be coming on my land now."

"I think you're right. Do you have two swords?"

"I'll take a look. If I can't find another one I'll be sure to protect you. What do you think Andy; will we need swords to visit you here?"

The boy couldn't really tell that we were teasing him so his response was simple enough. "Don't worry George and me will be here. You'll be okay."

We began to laugh and when Andy looked at us wondering what was so funny I gathered myself before telling him "Thanks Andy. I think Mr. Johnson and I appreciate that. It's always good to have friends in a magic fortress when you need them most." I held back any further laughter or smile until he nodded and looked back at his fortress. The old man then got my attention by nudging my arm and gave me another wink of the eye so Andy couldn't see him. I think he was happy with his contribution as well.

Then for some reason it suddenly became quiet for the briefest moment as we all looked towards what we had built. Each of us appeared lost in our own thoughts. I couldn't be sure about Johnson's thoughts; I just hoped they were similar to mine. It was easy enough to read Andy's thoughts. The grin on his face told me that he couldn't have been happier. I imagined he had grand thoughts of dragon slayers and princesses to save. I believed he was thinking a lot about his friend George as well. He had spoken so often about his friend I just knew this fortress was meant for both of them.

I looked at the other man and said "you know I actually can't believe it's almost finished."

"I know what you mean. Who thought my old tree would grow a fortress!"

"All for a good cause I guess."

"I think you're right."

We looked towards the young boy but it appeared obvious he wasn't that interested in our comments. He was just focused on his new fortress. He had moved around to the back of the tree as though he needed to inspect the rest of our work.

Johnson took this opportunity to make a comment. "You know I'm actually glad you showed up with this boy. It's been a long time since kids have played on my property; probably since before my wife died. It feels good to see a kid's happiness back here again."

His voice sounded melancholy and I couldn't be sure if the happiness he was feeling was not interwoven with some sadness about his wife. I sensed there was more to the story than he would share today.

"I think I know what you mean" I said. "I never knew what I was in for when the boy walked up to my garage. I thought I was just giving him some bottles; but he was able to trick me into using my time, my boards, my nails and Lord knows what else" I chuckled. "But I'm glad he did."

I wasn't going to bring the issue up again about Andy's father and why he wasn't there to help. I just took the time to enjoy my own efforts.

"Who knows maybe he'll even name it after us."

Old man Johnson turned to me with a twinkle in his eye and said "I can't see that. Johnson Castle would sound great though wouldn't it?"

"Johnson Castle? Maybe it will be called Henry Land."

"Henry Land? Who in the hell would call it Henry Land? Even a boy as young as this one wouldn't name something as grand as his magic fortress a wimpy name as Henry Land. I think maybe you're in dreamland!"

It was clear that his challenge to my idea was said in a light hearted manner and who could tell for sure what was going through Andy's mind.

"I guess we'll just have to leave it up to the boys then" I stated. "We're probably just lucky that they'll let us visit no matter what they call it."

His laughter once again brightened my day. "Guess you're right" he said. "Still; I'm not sure that I would ever want to visit a place called Henry Land so I hope they do choose a good name; if they name it all."

That brought an end to the "great name debate" and Andy came around the corner finished with his inspection.

"Everything look okay?" I questioned.

"Yep" was his one word answer; spoken with the same excitement in his voice we had come to expect. Guess one word summed everything up. Life was so simple for a boy like him; lots of energy; lots of dreams.

I noticed Johnson's breathing was a bit more labored now than it had been at the start of the day. Maybe I didn't have the stamina of a young lad but I still had more energy than an old man; I thought. I smiled wondering what it was like to be *his* age.

Johnson looked at me and asked me what I was smiling at.

"Oh nothing" I said. "Just wondering what it would be like to be an old man . . . . like you" I grinned.

He grinned back and said to me "I'm sure you'll find out soon enough Henry. You're no spring chicken yourself!"

"Maybe not but I'm still a rooster; you're a stewing chicken."

Our friendly banter was becoming easier between the two of us. Sharing the experience of building Andy's fort appeared to have made both of us feel good.

"Stewing chicken huh? Keep talking feller and your goose might be cooked!" He laughed and I thought what a good way to bring a great day to an end.

"Guess we better get everything packed up then. Don't want to get hurt. How would I explain getting beat up by a crusty old man?"

Andy had been standing nearby appearing somewhat confused but still happy with the laughter going on between us. He probably thought he would never understand old people.

"Want to grab some of the tools and nails over there Andy and put them in the truck?"

"Don't forget the hammer over by the tree" added Johnson.

"Sure. I'll get them. Where do you want me to put them?"

"Same place as before." I stated. "Put everything in the back of my truck."

He turned and ran off towards the tree to pick things up and return them to where they belonged. I began to gather the larger items and do the same.

"I think I'll just sit here for awhile and let you two clean up" said Johnson. "After all an old bird like me shouldn't have to do all the work right?"

I glanced at him grinning once more and replied "You got that right. Besides how would I drag a fat guy like you back to your house?"

He looked at me and began to laugh but chose not to respond. That was okay with me too. It was one of the only times I got the last word in.

After we had cleaned everything up and put it back in the truck the three of us took a final look at what we had built. It was one of those things that just seem to happen. It wasn't like one of us said "hey look at the fortress." We just stood in silence near my truck looking at the tree lost in our own thoughts.

For me it felt like a small boy's dream had spilled over into my life. Looking back I felt richer for the experience but at the same time had no idea where things would lead from there and how much more my life would change. In the end it didn't matter because I would find out soon enough.

CHAPTER 14

"Well what do you think?" Andy said. "Isn't it the best?"

Andy had finally been able to get George out to see what he had built. It had taken almost a week longer than he had expected before the two boys could spare the time to join each other for the first visit to the fortress. Andy was excited about showing George, and it wouldn't have been a good idea to stand in front of him on this day, in case one of his shirt buttons popped off. He was so proud he was ready to burst!

George was equally excited about this event. He was older than Andy, but still a boy himself, so this was going to be a special place for him too. At the beginning, he had just seen it as a tree house, like so many others, but everything became much clearer to him as Andy steadfastly explained why it was a fortress. George then understood the importance of the place that lay before them.

"You bet, Andy," he exclaimed, unable to control his own excitement. "I wasn't sure you would finish it, but it sure means a lot to me that you did. It's great."

Finishing the fortress meant a lot to Andy too. Anyone looking at the two boys could tell how excited they were and only imagine how much fun they would have when they visited their fortress; it was written all over their faces; "Thanks George. Mr. Johnson and Mr. Henry helped a lot too. Isn't the tree something else?"

"The tree's great Andy. Looks like it was made special for our fortress" he said adding "How did you find it?"

"That was easy I told Mr. Johnson what I was doing and he told me about the tree. I just knew it was the right one as soon as I saw it. I guess he knew what I meant; Lucky huh?"

"Sure was."

"I always stop to see Mr. Johnson every time I come here. That was part of the deal. You have to do the same thing. I promised him."

"Okay that's fair enough. Is that why we stopped to seem him today?"

"Yeah; we have to make sure he knows we're here. That's what he told me to do; so I have to."

"He seems like a nice man" George stated.

"He's the best!" exclaimed Andy. "And his place is great too. It's fun to play out here; better than my house."

George made no response to Andy's statement. Instead he took a moment to think about meeting the man he spoke well of.

Today was the first time George had met Mr. Johnson. The boys had knocked on the owner's door then impatiently waited for the old man to come to the front of the house. It seemed to take forever but it was easy to hear him. He grunted loudly as he got out of his chair and coughed as he approached the door. George would understand the coughing once he saw him holding a cigar. Even as a boy he knew smoking wasn't good for you. Maybe it was just something old men did, thought George.

He then turned to Andy and asked "How old is Mr. Johnson?"

"I don't know; pretty old."

"Sure sounds like it." The boys looked at each other and grinned.

He waved at Andy as he approached and opened the screen door to let them in.

"Well hello, Andy. How are you today?" he had asked.

"I'm great, Mr. Johnson. I want you to meet George." Andy had a way of making every answer a direct statement. George liked that and he could tell Mr. Johnson liked it too.

"So this is the famous George," he said to Andy with a wry smile on his face. George was certain that he knew who he was because Andy had said he had told him they were coming. He must have been teasing them.

"Yes sir, Mr. Johnson. My name is George. It's real nice to finally meet you. Andy talks about you all of the time. Thanks for helping us with our fortress."

He winked at George's friend and said "Well you're welcome; anything for my friend Andy."

George noticed that Andy seemed happy about Mr. Johnson's comment. "I'm glad Andy has more friends than just me." The man gave George a puzzled look before the boy continued by saying "That way my ears get a rest sometimes."

Johnson looked at them both and let out a hearty laugh. "Well I can sure understand that problem. Andy has left my ears ringing a time or two as well."

Neither friend's comments hurt Andy's feelings at all; besides he didn't really understand what the problem was anyways; "Well, we better go, Mr. Johnson," Andy told him. "I want to show George the fortress."

"Of course," offered Mr. Johnson; "You better get going now. Thanks for stopping in to say hi."

"Thanks again, Mr. Johnson," said George.

"Yeah, thanks Mr. Johnson," added Andy. "We'll see you later."

"Okay boys. See you next time."

George heard Andy's voice and it brought his attention back to the fortress momentarily pushing thoughts of the old man from his mind.

"What you thinking about?" he asked.

"Nothing; Mr. Johnson seems like a nice man," George added repeating himself bringing the conversation back to Mr. Johnson. The two had been checking out the fortress for a while before either of them had spoken and that was the only thing George could think of to say.

"He sure is. I was a little bit scared when Mr. Henry and I first met him, but I like him now."

"Why were you scared?"

"I don't know. I guess he just seemed scary, that's all. Doesn't he scare you?"

George pondered the question. He knew a lot of older people who weren't very nice—and yes, even scary—but Mr. Johnson didn't seem like one of those people. "No, he's not scary. He does seem a little bit sad, though."

Andy didn't know why his friend would say something like that, and frankly it didn't matter. He trusted his older friend's judgment.

"Guess so. I never really noticed."

Changing the subject; and the mood; George asked "What else do you want to do today, Andy?"

"I don't know. What do you want to do?"

"I think we should paint our new fortress."

"Why?"

"Oh I don't know. I guess it could just use some color and it's something we can do together. Besides don't you think it would look better?"

Andy had never thought about doing anything like that, but it was a great idea. He had been so happy just to get it built that he had never even thought about painting his fortress. A light bulb turned on in Andy's head when he remembered that his grandfather still had some paint left over from last summer when he painted the backyard fence.

"That's a great idea! My grandfather has some paint from last summer. I know he'll let us have it."

"Good. What color is it?"

The boy gave his friend a perplexed look, realizing he didn't know. Andy tried to imagine what his grandfather's fence looked like so he could remember what color it was.

"I don't know," said Andy. "I'll have to look at our fence when I get home. Then I can tell you for sure. Is that okay?"

"Oh sure," said George nonchalantly. He didn't want to pressure his friend in any manner. "We'll do it tomorrow. The color doesn't matter anyway just so long as it is painted. Why don't we play with the swords?"

Andy had forgotten about those. They weren't real swords, of course, just toys made of plastic that his dad had given him. It was one of the few times he remembered his father doing something nice for him. It must have been his birthday or something, he couldn't remember. He just knew they were fun to play with so he had brought them along.

"Okay; that'll be fun. Let's pretend we're knights. My grandfather told me about the old days where knights saved people and worked for a king. I want to work for a king."

"Sure. Can I be the king?"

Andy looked at his friend and said "No; we both have to be knights. There is only one king and knights fight together. That's the best part."

"Okay if you say so. Let's fight for the king!" George and Andy picked up their swords and began to fight the battles.

Before the afternoon had gone by the boys had slain more dragons, captured more enemies, and saved more damsels in distress than any knight could have done in a lifetime! They knew they were the winners, because their imaginations could tell them that they were the only ones left on the battlefield. They were also the most tired.

If someone were to examine the day they would know that it had gone by fast and it had been fun, but it was time to head home. While walking home, the boys talked about the day's adventures. It had been another great day, a day of friendship and memories to be shared for a lifetime. The memories would fade as they grew older, but they would never be completely forgotten. That's the great thing about memories: you can call on them whenever you want, and they will come to you when you need them the most.

Since these boys had just begun their lifetime, more adventures were still to come, memories stored away, more days like this one they would remember forever.

The visit with the old man had been an important event as well. It had been clear that Johnson's first meeting with George was pleasant enough but for some reason seemed to stir up old memories for the man. The boys had clearly been in a hurry to get out to the tree, but it had been a lonely morning, so he had taken more time asking the boys questions than they probably wanted him to. Most of them were simple enough, things to keep the conversation going. Both boys were polite and mustered as much patience as they could, but Johnson could tell he was right—they did want to get out to the tree. They had just stopped in to say hello. He just hadn't made it that simple for them.

The longer the old man talked to the boys, the more he felt there was something odd about George. It was as if he had seen this boy before—where he couldn't remember, but there was something familiar about him.

Maybe he reminded them of his own children. He was finding more time to think about them lately and he often wondered if he had done everything he could; or should; have for his kids. George didn't look like any of his children at that age; neither did Andy for that matter so what seemed so familiar? What triggered these thoughts? Why did watching the two boys talk to him seem comfortable? It almost felt like a special calmness surrounded them.

Johnson had pushed the rambling thoughts out of his mind figuring they were just an old man's forgotten feelings of fatherhood. It didn't matter anyway he thought; they weren't his kids' right?

He had said his goodbyes and released the boys from more agonizing conversation. As they had moved out the door and began to run towards the tree Johnson was left smiling, watching the boys head towards their new play home. Suddenly a tinge of regret made him wish it was one of his own sons running towards something he had helped build. But it wasn't so he took his sadness and uncertainties back to his comfortable chair; re-lit his cigar and sat down to read the paper.

The birds could be heard outside; the sun shone through the window and his dog was stretched out comfortably on the floor but he noticed none of these things. He just couldn't stop thinking he knew George from somewhere; but where?

CHAPTER 15

It had been a busy summer. Between work, home projects that I had been putting off while spending time with Andy, combined with travel to family weddings on Marie's side, there had been little time to rest. We did get some holidaying in, but it was only for a week, so by the time I began to unwind the trip was over and it was time to get back to work.

As much as I hated to admit it to myself, things would have been easier for me ten years ago. Was I losing steam? Friends my age were telling me similar stories, so I knew it wasn't a problem only I was experiencing. I guess there is a time when even someone like me who always thought I was invincible had to accept that things had changed. I don't know who said that time stands still for no one, but I was feeling that not only did it not stand still, but it was speeding up!

I had always thought I had a good sense of humor, so I was still able to find some amusement in what was happening to my body. I had adopted some new policies, for example, the twenty-five-cent rule. One day; while standing in line for a coffee reaching into my pocket for cash I dropped some money to the floor; pausing for just a moment before a stranger behind me spoke up.

"Excuse me sir; you dropped some of your money."

"Yeah I know; just trying to decide if I should pick it up." The man had given me a puzzled look so I continued; "You see at my age I adopted the twenty-five cent rule."

"What's that?" asked the man.

"Well if I drop a quarter on the ground I then have to decide whether it was worth bending down to pick it up that day." I was frugal—actually, I was cheap—so I was still bending down for the quarters, but dimes were becoming less important.

The man appeared to understand what I meant by letting out a laugh. "Well how do you feel about today? Looks like you drop a ten dollar bill."

"Oh I feel good today. Ten dollars is very much worth bending down for. Now I'm just trying to stoop down and keep the groaning to a minimum. I don't want you to think I was fat and old, now, do I?"

The stranger in the coffee shop looked at me, laughed and said; "I think I'll just leave that one alone."

I returned his laugh before adding "Besides I'm at the front of the line. Thanks for helping an old man save a few dollars today" pretending to use a walker up to the counter where the clerk waited to take my order.

"Anytime old timer" he said with a grin.

That's why humor was such an important part of my life. It made growing older more fun; even with a stranger in a coffee shop. I paid for my coffee; turned to leave; nodded goodbye to the stranger and left feeling happy about the day. After all not only had I had a humorous encounter-I still had my ten dollars!

Humor was important at home too since Marie chose to have a few laughs at my expense. She teased me occasionally about my newfound limitations and pointed out how much I had changed.

One of her favorites was "Is that grey hair I see or a shine on the back of your head?"

Bald jokes never bothered me; it was something I couldn't do anything about anyways. I attempted to throw it back to her one time by countering with my own joke. "I can't be sure" I said; "I don't know what grey looks like; I never see it in your hair; what does that cost again?"

Although she took it in stride my words had appeared to sting Marie a bit more than hers had done to me. She had not replied and after a moment of uncomfortable silence. I tried to lighten the mood.

"Besides the hair on my head is the least of my worries. It's the hair in my ears that bothers me the most."

Poking fun at myself made the transition back to humor easier. I could be sure of that by Marie's next comment.

"It worries me too; she said with a twinkle in her eyes; "I think it's making it harder for you to hear me!"

"Huh?" I feigned deafness. "What did you say?"

"Funny; real funny" Marie stated choosing to accept my joke as a winning volley in the war of ages. Since I felt I was getting older faster than I wanted to I figured I had won the battle but was probably losing the war!

This kind of joking made for some fun, because both of us had never really taken our vanity seriously. Marie had been a pretty girl who had grown into an attractive woman and like many husbands I was more attracted to her inner beauty anyway.

Sure, she spent more time now preparing to go out and could be a bit self-conscious if she felt something wasn't just right, but overall, health was more important to her than vanity. The changes she had made in our diet and lifestyle made me feel like my health was very important to her too. I thought maybe she just wanted to keep me around for my sense of humor; but I believed she would probably be the first to say it wasn't *that* good!"

These were the kinds of the thoughts; and more; filling my mind during the past summer. I wondered if this self-reflection had come about because of the Andy Bell project. As much as I had enjoyed working with him and Mr. Johnson, I found I was more tired than usual at the end of each day. My middle-aged mind was telling me I could do these things, while my middle-aged body was saying, "Wanna bet?"

There were days when I fought reality and days when I just accepted it. I was learning to enjoy different things in my life, as well as think about the good things I had done before. Whenever I thought about the fortress sitting in the tree on the old man's property and the little boys enjoying it, I knew that was one of the small wins in my life.

I often took a moment to remind myself of the work we did, the laughter we had shared and the stories I had told about the project. My stories could be grand, so I hoped none of the people who heard me tell them would actually check out the work for themselves. How would I explain the truth then, vandals?

One day deep in thought while I worked in the front yard I even discovered myself muttering "Shit; I'm begin to reflect on my reflections! I better find something else to do before someone wonders what I'm thinking about." So I did.

I had visited old man Johnson a couple of times through the summer. He had invited me into his house the first time for a coffee, which I quickly accepted. I was glad to see him again and I hoped he felt the same. When I walked into his house I was taken aback by the state of the room. I was expecting a mess, with clutter all over the place and some dirty dishes in the sink. Instead, what I found was an organized and uncluttered home. Oh sure, some things were out of order—a coat thrown on the couch, dust on top of some of the furniture, and a newspaper lying on the floor—but those were minor details. After all, he was an old man living on his own in an old house that needed some fixing up. The fact that it was clean, to me, was quite an accomplishment.

I was also surprised by the dog lying near the back door. The whole time I had worked with Johnson, he never once mentioned that he had a dog or brought him outside. I suppose a dog made sense for a lonely old man. Pets made for good friends. They loved you unconditionally, looked to you for their meals, and gave you a responsibility that kept you active.

Before he served me the coffee, I was already saying, "Hey, I didn't know you had a dog."

"Yeah he's been with me twelve years now. Got him a couple years after my wife died. I found the house pretty lonely after she was gone. The kids weren't here, and they only visited once in a while, so when a friend asked me if I could take a dog off his hands, I jumped at it. I never asked him why he needed to give him away. As a kid I had a great dog, so I figured another one couldn't hurt." Then, with a look of amusement he reflected, "Funny thing, though. The friend who gave me the dog is dead. Makes you wonder if he knew something I didn't; huh?"

For some reason Johnson saw some humor in his comment, so I joined him with a laugh and offered my own thought. "Maybe the dog did too. Who would feed him?"

He laughed again. "True. He's like an alarm clock he never lets me forget when it's mealtime; this way both of us get fed the same time, just different food!"

"Well, that's good to hear. If you ate the same thing then you might just be a crazy old man eating dog food." I immediately regretted blurting out this statement and hoped he would take it as a joke. I thought he might.

I was right. He laughed while saying, "You can't be sure of that. You don't know how good my cooking is."

"That's true enough" I said with a grin. "Maybe the dog food would taste better; who knows?"

"Well if you're lucky you might find out someday."

"Is that a promise, a challenge or a threat?"

"You'll know after the first bite" he chuckled.

I laughed. "Not sure I want to put it to a test".

After taking a sip of coffee; and teasing him about how bad the coffee tasted never mind a meal I asked if he had seen Andy lately.

"Oh him, and his friend George come by every so often. I spoke with them a few times, but now they just give me a big wave and head out to their fortress; How about you?"

"Well, Andy did stop in to see me a couple of times when he saw me working in the yard or my garage. All he talked about was how much fun he was having in his new tree house. He still insists on calling it a fortress, so I just agree with him."

After hearing George's name, it occurred to me that I had not yet met Andy's friend.

"You've met George? Spoke to him, did you?"

"Yeah, Andy introduced him to me. Then I spoke to both of them a few times when they came to play."

"What's he like?"

"Just like any other young boy, I suppose. He is definitely different from Andy, though."

"How?"

"Well, he is older by two to three years—that's for sure—but there is something else about him. Something I can't put my finger on. It just seems that he is wise beyond his youthfulness," Johnson said with an odd look on his face. "Sounds stupid but he talks about things that I wouldn't expect little boys to know about."

I found this statement interesting, so I asked him what kind of things he was talking about.

"I don't know," he answered. "Just things about life that guys like you and me might talk about—you know grownup things. Then the next minute I see him for the little boy he is, playing with Andy, laughing, running, and having a carefree good time like little boys should. Funny thing though it's almost like I've met him before somewhere. Just can't remember where."

I told him I understood, even though I really didn't. I just wanted it to seem as if I were as smart or insightful as he was.

"Strange thing, though," he said. "Now that I think of it, I've seen Andy lots of times; just by himself but I've only seen George when Andy is with him. I wonder why?"

"He's Andy's friend so since Andy knows you he probably figures that he should only be here when his friend is here. I know Andy told me once that George has to spend a lot of time with his family so maybe he just doesn't have as much time to play as Andy does. Who knows for sure right?"

It appeared that he didn't have a better answer, and I sure didn't know of anything else I could add so we left it at that.

I was surprised myself by the kind of insight this old man seemed to have. I didn't expect him to be sensitive enough to see something like that in anyone, never mind George. I could only hope I had that ability myself someday. It made me respect him even more.

I could also tell that he was beginning to feel uncomfortable with this part of our conversation, maybe because he didn't have an answer of his own; so since my coffee had cooled, I took a large sip and decided to ask about something else I had noticed.

"I see that Andy's little fortress has a different color to it," I said with a mischievous look in my eye. "Know anything about that?"

Johnson chuckled again. "The boys had shown up knocking on my door one day, wondering if I had any paint brushes. When asked why they needed paint brushes, I was told they were going to paint their fortress."

He took a drink from his broken handled cup and went on to say "I even felt like they thought it was something that should be obvious to me. Maybe they figured painting was the next step and it was going to happen with or without me and I should understand that."

"They seemed quite serious so I didn't crack a smile, laugh or anything but I didn't want to seem stupid so I asked them some questions. I started by asking Andy where he had found some paint?"

"What did he tell you?"

He paused for a moment like he was organizing his thoughts; trying to remember then continued "Andy told me his grandfather had given him the paint but he didn't have any old paint brushes; however, he said he thought I would have some. I told him as it just so happened I did have a couple of brushes they could use. That made them pretty happy. I told them to wait while I went to my shop in the back where I grabbed some paint brushes plus old rags I thought they could use. I watched as they walked towards the fortress struggling with their cans of paint and the things I had given them. You couldn't have found two happier boys for sure that day" Johnson said.

When he finished telling me the story, I looked at him and stated, "Strong looking color."

With a loud laugh, he said, "Sure is. I wasn't sure that blue would look good, but they seemed happy with it, so who was I to argue? He told me that his grandfather had painted their fence that color. Why I don't know."

"It is an unusual color for a fence," I agreed. Since I knew what Andy's house looked like, I added, "Maybe his grandfather thought it would match some of the colors on his house. Who knows? There might have been a sale on blue that day. You know how cheap crazy old men can be."

He looked at me for a moment, noticing my grin then decided to take his own shot. "I know what you mean. Sometimes I think us old guys were crazy to keep you young guys around."

We chuckled at our simple jokes and drank the rest of our coffee. He offered me a second cup, which I accepted because I enjoyed spending time talking with him.

Once my coffee was freshened up, I continued, "I see they didn't paint the roof."

"No, I wouldn't let them," Johnson said. "It's too high off the ground and much too dangerous."

"I agree with you about that. Plus, Andy would be determined enough to try. Why not call it a two-tone building?" I said.

"Be careful or the boys will try to talk you into painting the roof for them—and they might win," he said in his usual tongue-in-cheek manner.

"Well good luck with that! I would be more concerned about me falling off of the roof than the boys. Their bones would heal. Mine might not."

Johnson chuckled from time to time as we continued to discuss the shortfalls old age can bring to each man, swapping stories to prove our point. His examples seemed funnier than mine because I had not yet experienced them, but when I made a comment about his "old man knowledge" he told me not to worry; it would come to me soon enough; *if* I was smart enough he added. I didn't want to say it, but I promised myself that a lot of the stories he was telling would never happen to me.

I took an opportunity to add a serious moment to our conversation. "You know what; sometimes I do wonder what is going to happen to me as I get older. I know there is more information now with better health care and awareness which should make things easier for me; but I wonder what it's all going to look like when I need it and who's going to be there to look after me. You ever wonder about that?"

I wasn't in prime physical condition, but I was certainly a lot better off than the old man sitting across the table from me. I didn't chew on a cigar like it was candy either so I figured if I was worried he must be scared.

"I suppose; sometimes. I don't give it much thought though. I figure things will happen the way they should and I can't do much about it."

I knew I didn't agree with him about that. I mean exercise and diet can certainly help people as they get older. Of course knowing and doing are two different things. I was a good example of that.

"Don't you think though that things may not be as good as we want when the time comes?"

"Not really sure what you mean but let me ask you something; are they ever?"

"Are they ever what?" I asked.

"Are things ever the way we want or expect them to be? Do you know of senior citizens who always said they would never go into an extended care lodge or home?

"Sure. Lots of people say that."

"How many of them are now living there?"

"I see your point; but since people are living longer they don't really have a choice right?"

"Okay. How about the guy who says just let me die if I'm living on a machine; do you think he really believes that if it really happens?"

"I don't know for sure because I've never had to make that kind of decision for anyone."

"Exactly; so no one truly knows the answer until the time comes. Like I said things will happen the way they are meant to and I'll deal with them when I have to."

"I don't want to sound like I'm arguing with you or anything but isn't that just avoiding the truths?"

"Not for me. It just means that I know God will give me what I can handle and thinking about it too much does me no good." This was the first time I had heard him mention anything about God and I was surprised. I just assumed he was an atheist!

He smiled at me again and added "Plus as you seem happy to often remind me; I'm an old man so I don't have time to spend on things I may not be able to change. At my age I could be gone any second." He pulled his finger across his neck making a throat sound indicating it could be over anytime.

"Geez; that sounds like a dying chicken" I chuckled. "Maybe even a stewing hen."

The laughter brought an end to the somber part of this conversation and we looked for other things to talk about. He was easy to talk with. I still had many doubts about life, death, health and the future but I figured for now if an old man could be optimistic than I should give it a try as well. What could I lose?

We spent time talking that afternoon about a variety of things. It was comforting that the conversation was not just about Andy or his fortress. Our friendship had begun through Andy's need for help, but it appeared to be growing stronger on its own terms.

It was obvious to me that we had so many more common things to talk about than I would have expected; things such as children, the pros and cons of today's politics, the changing world, how great things used to be, and how good they could still be were some of the topics of discussion.

One topic was about today's youth. In the end Johnson and I even agreed about the younger generations; at least somewhat. He admitted to me that he was as scared as anyone else! When I questioned him about his meaning his comments were straight forward.

"They'll be taking care of us in our time of need, and I'm worried because they don't seem to have the same commitment to taking care of older people; including parents; that we do. What will happen when we need them?" Luckily he had an opinion about that too and continued before I could respond.

"You know," he said "Most of the problems were created by your generation" deftly turning the tables towards me.

"What do you mean by that?"

"My generation raised kids to work hard, be respectful and make the most of their opportunities. You generation created many children with a selfish attitude and gave them too much without accountability."

It was difficult to dispute a statement like that when I thought back at my own daughter's childhood as well as her friends. They were certainly given more than I had been given at the same age.

"I suppose there is some truth to that argument," I stated "But we had more than my parents generation; wasn't it our responsibility to give our kids more?'

"That's an easy answer that sounds good but what did a lot of parents take away as they gave their children so many material things?"

I think he could tell I didn't have an immediate answer to his question.

"Pride, responsibility and accountability; that's what" he stated in a tone that made me feel that he thought that should be obvious to me.

Even though I agreed with his assessment I still became rankled at his comments and felt I needed to defend myself. "Well I'll tell you one thing; we may have spoiled our daughter more than we were; but we also taught her to appreciate what we gave her. We made sure she took care of her things and understood the value of the university degree we are paying for. She knows that it is her responsibility to do her best. That's all we ask of her."

"I'm sure your daughter does understand all of that Henry," he said in a calming voice. "I thought we were talking about a generation; not just your girl."

I collected myself and realized he was right. We were just having a philosophical conversation about generations today. It wasn't like we could solve all of the world's problems anyway.

"Still I think there are many good young people out there maybe we just don't look for them. It's easier to see the bad ones and easier for old guys like you to blame guys my age for the problems." I had a wry smile on my face so he didn't take it personally but I think he knew I thought I had caught him in moment of truth. My smile also appeared to lighten the mood as well.

"You could be right but old guys like me are the most worried; he said. "Like I told you before things will be the way they are meant to be I just pray that the good ones are the ones working in the old age homes when I get there!"

"You better pray a lot," I laughed, "because if I'm the one looking after an old fart like you who knows what kind of care you might get. My generation respects your generation but we also know how to work the machines. I might just turn yours off."

He laughed back at me and said "Well tough guy you might want to be sure to do it when I'm sleeping; because an old fart like me won't go without a fight! That's why we're living longer you know."

I added my own laughter taking a moment to wonder how we had gotten on the topic of generations in the first place. I guess it was hard to avoid since each generation judges the one before and after their own. I knew I didn't have all of the answers and I was pretty sure he didn't either. I was just happy that my daughter was one of the good ones; so I left it at that.

"Geez look at the time," I said looking at my watch. The day is almost gone and Marie will be expecting me for supper. I better get going; besides four cups of bad coffee is enough for me" I joked.

"Hey I was married for a long time. I know who the real boss is."

"Sadly true," I told him. "But I could have a lot worse bosses; so I'll be happy with this one. Thanks again for the hospitality."

"Anytime; I don't have anywhere to go anyways."

The tone of his voice made me wonder if his comment was a simple truth or a sadness he felt. I decided not to ask. I took a look at the old dog lying on the floor as I walked towards the door and marveled at how simple life was for him.

"Looks like your dog had a good afternoon. He must major in sleep or something."

Johnson looked back at his dog as he followed me to the door and added his own comment; "Yeah well nothing much bothers him. He's older than both of us so I guess the old dog figures life for him should just be about rest. There are days I wonder if he knows something I don't"

"I'm sure he does," I laughed. "Dogs are smarter than men right?"

"Maybe so" he chuckled.

Thanking him again I step out the door and began my walk back to my own home. I felt he had enjoyed having someone to talk to as much as I had enjoyed talking with him. It occurred to me that he probably didn't get a lot of visitors so my visit might have made the day go by faster for him. I guess I couldn't really know for sure; only imagine what he thought.

As I walked home I admitted to myself that the afternoon had been a pleasant one for me too. Not just because of the conversation but also the listening. It felt good to have someone who listened to my words and challenged me to think about what I was trying to say. I couldn't explain it; it was just one of those things that felt comfortable.

My thoughts of Johnson, his dog, and my visit were fresh in my mind as I took the final steps up my driveway and it occurred to me that even though we had talked all of the afternoon I still didn't know his dog's name, or for that matter why it was the first time I had actually seen the dog. He had mentioned his children but never told me anything about them. I knew his wife had passed away, but not how or why. Truth was I didn't know much more about the man now than I did before the visit. Strange how I could spend an afternoon of sharing and never really hear about some of the important things.

That moment of realization led me to think about Andy and his friend. George wasn't a dog, of course, but I hadn't met him yet either, and I didn't really know anything about him. Andy's description was sketchy at best and didn't help me fill in the blanks. Johnson's feedback about the boy had actually provided me with a better idea of what he was like. All I knew for sure was that he was important to Andy and for some reason he seemed important to me; I didn't know why. I opened the door to my house and as I stepped in I wondered when would the day come when I would meet the boy? What would he be like? Would I learn more about him from Johnson and finally did it really matter?

CHAPTER 16

There was no doubt for me that the seasons had changed when the new budget information was dropped on my desk. It was always one of the more unpleasant indicators for me that fall was here. More traditional things like raking leaves from the ground, storing lawn furniture and completing other fall time tasks also added merit to the fact that time was marching on, but somehow this year everything was different.

If it wasn't for the work before me I would have enjoyed the fall season more. Growing up it was one of my favorite seasons. Spring marked the beginning of growth and fall was the harvest; the reward for the work of the farm. I enjoyed the change in colors, the smell of burning leaves and even the crispness of the morning temperature.

Maybe what was different this year was that the challenge of wanting to do my job was becoming greater than the work itself. I had done the same thing for so long that I no longer enjoyed my role. I had realized that these feelings had been with me for sometime and as each year went by it was becoming harder to deny them. Still what was I suppose to do about it? I still had to work and make a living plus at my age what else could I do? It was thoughts like that which made doing my job harder.

For some reason, completing the year-end budget fell on my shoulders. It wasn't part of my job description, just something that I had adopted over the years. It wasn't a task I welcomed, but I had become good at doing it, so it made the most sense to pass it on to me. I knew from past years that procrastination only made it worse so I pushed thoughts of self pity from my mind and dived into the work before me, knowing the sooner I got started, the quicker it would be done. It only took me about twenty years to find that piece of wisdom!

I worked alone at my desk on the first day that I began working on the new budget since I had no one to help me. I briefly spoke with co-workers as they brought me more documents from the different departments, in the lunch room or as I passed someone in the hall; but that was the only contact I had with anyone outside my office.

If things were to be the same as past years I knew I would still have to look for much of the information I needed that had not been given to me. It was one of the more irritating parts of the job. I wouldn't be at that stage for awhile though so I continued to work quietly in my office cut off from most of the world outside my door.

Later in the day, I looked up from my desk attempting to rest my eyes for a brief moment and noticed the snow falling outside. I didn't know why I hadn't noticed it sooner. It couldn't be that late in the year, could it? Maybe winter had come early, or was the budget late in getting here? Was Christmas just around the corner? The sad truth I guess; was that the years felt like that they were now moving faster for me. Another birthday had passed, and I was beginning to feel the changes in my life more each day. Frankly, I found the changes annoying, and just like my job accepting them was becoming more difficult. Why was middle age being so difficult? Would old age be worse?

As I continued to stare at the whiteness of the fresh snowfall I realized that my work had become routine in nature allowing my mind to easily wander to thoughts of past and future. These thoughts brought me to an abrupt realization that middle age for me meant I would have to live well over one hundred years! That scared the hell out of me. This meant that even though I might be classed middle age, I was moving far too fast towards old age, and I didn't like it. One day I was at the top of the mountain and the next I was standing on a slippery slope, losing ground. Life sometimes felt like my job; I was going nowhere.

These thoughts were just plain depressing and made me wish I hadn't taken the time to indulge in such questions. I decided to set this foolishness aside and attempted to get back to work. After all, what could I do about it anyway?

I wish things would have ended with that conclusion however working with budget numbers was boring and having no one around to talk to made it tougher to not dwell on things. It didn't take long for me to drift back to my own world of insights. I had attempted to spend my adulthood building a life of comfort, full of small but important accomplishments. I had done that, hadn't I? I had a good family, including a great wife and daughter, so why did I have to judge myself so hard?

Why did it seem at my age that things were going downhill? Why couldn't the next twenty years be good ones? I didn't plan to live to be a hundred, so why not enjoy the healthy years I had left? I knew many people my age who were happy and active, didn't I? Why couldn't that be me, and why couldn't I think of anyone specific?

Oddly enough I had a conversation with old man Johnson about these things on one of my summer visits. The discussion had been expanded of course as many of our conversations were but in the end he didn't have any better answer than I did. He just said that's the way things were and I shouldn't think about it so much. Easy for him I thought.

Andy Bell came into my mind. We had talked about him from time to time as well and we both agreed that he was a little boy with nothing but dreams. What problems did he have? Johnson and I never brought up the issue of the boy's father. What we knew was sketchy at best and gossip at the worst; so we didn't speculate about it. I found myself wishing I were him. Wouldn't life be simple? I knew of course however; that things were never that simple.

The last time I had seen the boy, in the fall, he seemed somewhat sad. He had confessed to me about his family problems. He told me that he knew his dad was drinking more and his mom seemed sad all the time. I could tell that his understanding of that situation was more of a reaction than an intellectual assessment, but children were sensitive to unsettling situations.

Andy's comments gave the neighborhood rumors about his family more truth and even though it was a sad thing for a little boy how was it my problem right? What could I do for him anyway? My intellect told me the simple answer to that question: nothing. Still it seemed sad to me that he had he had to live with the problem. A child should not have to worry so much about the people who are responsible for him. The people he loved.

Andy's story was sad and far too common, but what business was it of mine? He wasn't my responsibility. I had my own problems. Was listening to him the only help I needed to offer him? Everything shouldn't be my problem.

I noticed that I was no longer working at my computer or looking at the budget documents. I had become so engrossed in my thoughts I had forgotten to perform the tasks before me. Maybe I was feeling sorry for myself, and frankly I decided that I wanted to wallow in self-pity rather than work on the stupid budget, so I bought myself more time by getting another coffee from the machine. That was another thing—our office coffee stank. I didn't even know why I bothered to drink it. I chuckled to myself, seeing that self-pity was definitely extending to every part of my life today.

My thoughts drifted back to Andy, his fortress, and the past year. Once I set the sad part of Andy's story to the side, I found that my thoughts cheered me up. The joy the fortress we had built had brought to the little boy. It was something I was proud to be a part of, and something Andy deserved. It was true that I couldn't do much for his family problems, but at least I had helped him achieve one of his dreams.

The more I thought about his fortress the more I thought about my life. It was ironic that Andy had wanted me to build a fortress with him. In so many ways, I had built many fortress walls in my own life, so I should be good at it. Walls took so many shapes and sizes that people could not identify many of them in their own lives. I was no different. Time had built the walls so I figured time could tear them down, as long as I lived long enough!

I attempted to get back to work once more, but for some reason more thoughts overwhelmed my mind. Thoughts were coming to me in a disjointed arrangement of memories and opinions. I remembered all the years I tried to be the strong one, the one who could be counted on by my family, my co-workers, and anyone else who needed me. I wanted to be the man my daughter looked up to and knew she could count on. So many times I wanted to say no to people but didn't. That was probably why I had said yes to Andy that first day, even though I originally found it to be a nuisance.

I wasn't all that strong, but I never wanted anyone to know. I had built walls to keep people from finding that out. My metaphor for the things that protected me in my life extended to my health issues as well. When anyone teased me about my age or asked me about my health, including my family, I would just laugh or pretend that everything was okay. I didn't want anyone to know how tired I really was or how much my body hurt, especially when I got up in the morning. *I was the strong one.* I didn't want anyone to see me getting older or weaker in any way. I had fooled them for a long time. I had fooled myself. My fortress walls were as strong as Andy's and no one was going to knock them down—that was a fact. I would find out I was wrong but that would be another day. Today was a work day.

It was just any other year, another boring budget that wasn't going to get done by itself, and people were counting on me. I thought to myself God I could use someone to talk to; but I knew that wasn't going to happen today so I poured back the last of the crappy coffee and turned back to the crappy work in front of me. What other choice did I have?

I sat back down at my desk and spent the rest of the day concentrating on the job I was being paid for. It made for a long, brain-draining day, a day I could mark off the calendar as one closer to retirement. Quitting time couldn't come fast enough but the day's end finally arrived. I gathered my briefcase, put on my coat and prepared to leave. There was one good thing about my job; I seldom had to take work home with me and since I had done the budget so many times days like this were no different. It would take a week or so but all of the work would be done at the office. I guess I should be grateful for that. The thoughts wouldn't brighten my spirits on the drive home; they would just make me feel older.

I reached the parking lot and swept the first signs of winter off my windows as I let my vehicle warm up before the drive home.

The snow had made the road slippery, which didn't help my sour mood, only reminded me of how unsafe the world could be. I was in a pessimistic state of mind. It had been a crappy day and it was going to get worse.

I walked into the house and was immediately greeted by Marie. This was not unusual, but the look on her face was.

After quick hellos, Marie began by saying, "Dr. Taylor called for you today."

"Oh, what did he want?" I asked, trying to remember the last time I had visited him. I had seen him for a regular checkup less than a month ago. Geez, was I getting so old that I couldn't remember such simple things?

"He said he needs to see you in his office as soon as possible." I could tell that Marie was troubled by the doctor's request, so I tried to minimize any concerns she might have. Even though I was in a crappy mood I didn't want to make her pay for it.

"Sure, why not. Taylor's not so bad, although I must admit, his last physical was much too physical for me, if you know what I mean," I said, laughing. Humor was still one of my best defensive tools.

Marie was not amused by my comments and continued with a worried voice, "It's not funny, Robert. Doctors don't just call you in to their office unless it is something serious."

"Don't worry so much, Marie. He probably thinks I'm too fat at my age and wants to put me on some kind of diet plan different from yours. I'm sure it's nothing." As I spoke the words, I could tell that I was worried as well. I couldn't remember ever being asked to return to the doctor after a general checkup.

The day's morose string of events as well as my overactive imagination began me thinking about an assortment of things; terrible scenarios that I didn't want to say out loud because I didn't want to add any extra worry on Marie. She was a worrier to begin with and needed no help from me so I continued to act as though it meant nothing.

"When does he want to see me?" I calmly asked.

"Thursday morning at nine," she said.

It was Tuesday, so I knew I could make arrangements at work tomorrow for the Thursday appointment.

"I should be able to make that. I'll call his office tomorrow."

"I already made the appointment," Marie said.

I was annoyed that she would make such an assumption, but I was also glad she cared enough for me to be that worried, so rather than begin an argument, I just offered a thank-you and went upstairs to change for supper.

With Marie out of the room, I again wondered what Dr. Taylor wanted to talk about. She was right—doctors didn't just call you in for nothing—so what was so important that he needed to see me that soon?

I reviewed the tests in my mind that he had done during my physical exam. Nothing unusual for a man my age, I thought. Blood tests, questions, and a general checkup were the only things he had put me through, same as any other time. It wasn't as if he had taken X-rays, done an EEG exam, or something extra like that, so what could have been triggering his request?

It was best not to keep Marie waiting too long for supper. I knew she would be more worried than she needed to be, especially when we still didn't really know anything yet. She was a strong, levelheaded woman and I knew she could handle a lot of stress, but this was different; this was the first time a doctor's request seemed mysterious. Who wouldn't be worried?

I wanted to keep my imagination under control hoping that it may also keep hers in check as well. The best way would be a quiet supper and an evening of television. She was putting everything on the table and I could smell the makings of a wonderful meal as I walked down the stairs. When I approached the kitchen I decided to make some conversation to distract her from whatever thoughts were already rambling through her mind.

"So what's for supper?" I tried to sound cheerful as I asked the question.

"Chicken, potatoes and a salad" she stated matter of factly.

I was never a big fan of salads and she knew that but instead of making it an issue I just added another question "Gravy to go with the chicken?"

"Yes." It appeared obvious her answers were going to be short and to the point. Opening up longer conversations was going to be a struggle. Instead I decided to "entertain" her with my own conversation. She always said I was a good talker.

"Well that's good. I enjoy your gravy; chicken would be nothing without it. Work was pretty boring," I added.

She continued to place the food on the table and provided no response so I continued to break the silence. "Budget time again; seems to come every year" I chuckled.

She offered me a small smile acknowledging my pathetic attempt at an ironic statement of truth.

"Same old things; numbers change a bit but the information stays the same. Becker is a pain in the ass again, but when isn't he?" Becker was my supervisor. Mostly left me alone to do my work but occasionally felt the need to prove his worth. Budget time was one of those times.

Marie finally decided to join the conversation albeit in a limited way. "Why? What did he do?"

Happy with any level of participation I answered "Nothing much; usual stuff. He came into my office for a minute to remind me about the budget deadline. I told him I was sure I could remember from last year when everything was due."

We were sitting at the table eating when Marie asked "What did he say?" before taking a bite of chicken.

"We've worked together so long he never really gave me an answer. He just nodded and said he just wanted to remind me. I told him thanks; I'll mark it on my day timer. I'm not sure he knew I was being sarcastic."

"Sometimes you say things you shouldn't" Marie admonished me.

Now that was the Marie I had come to know. Not really judgmental but clear in her message. My feelings weren't hurt because I thought her mind was no longer pre-occupied with the upcoming doctor visit. That was a good thing even if would just be for a little while.

"You're probably right; but too late to change now. Besides what are they going to do fire me?"

Her stern look made it clear she didn't find that funny either. Well I couldn't be funny all the time could I? After all I *did* write my own jokes. It was time to change direction.

"Great supper Marie: I like the roast chicken. Not crazy about the salad though; but I never am."

"It's good for you" she said.

"Can't argue with that; still not a fan." I tried to keep my tone conversational and not confrontational. She seemed to feel the same way because she provided no defensive reply.

The balance of the table conversation was mostly talk about Annie, how she was doing in school, when she would be home again; usual stuff. I think it helped keep our minds off the questions running through our minds.

After dessert I even helped to wash the dishes, which wasn't always something I did. There was definitely an unspoken shared concern as we worked together in the kitchen. I had lived with this woman long enough to sense most of her moods. I could tell she was worried but didn't really know what to say. I guess I felt the same way so I followed her lead choosing not to verbalize my fears, but I could tell they were there.

Idle comments filled the next few minutes as we worked clearing the table and washing the dishes.

"Put that pot over there" Marie said.

"Okay" I responded. "What about the plates; sink or dishwasher?"

"Dishwasher is full; I'll run it tonight. Just put them in the sink; we'll wash everything by hand."

Seemed simple enough instruction; I even felt a relief in her statement. It was as though this method of cleaning the dishes would eat up more of the time I didn't want to spend thinking about the doctor appointment.

"Putting me to work at hard labor tonight are you?" I teased my wife.

She glanced at me with a half hearted smile and replied "You my dear have no idea what hard labor is really like."

"Oh really?" I responded.

"Yeah; try doing this every night after work then complain to me."

There had been many times in the past when moments like this had begun as light hearted teasing and turned into moments of anger or frustration from a misplaced comment. I was determined not to make this one of those moments.

"Okay; okay. I give up" I laughed. "I may be in jail but the work isn't that hard!"

"Jail huh?" Marie grunted. "Looking for early release?"

I couldn't be sure yet if she was trying to be funny or defensive but decided to stay the course and take the high road.

"No not at all. Besides I figure jail isn't so bad when you have such a beautiful warden."

"Uh, Huh" she mumbled obviously suspicious of my blatantly weak attempt at flattery. She glanced at me only to see me with a grin on my face and cheeriness in my eyes. The grin served to produce a smile leading to a chuckle and quick slap with her wash cloth. The mood for the moment had changed for the better. My job was done and it appeared that my "jail" was safe and my "sentence" would be extended. Not a bad way to end a day of hard labor!

Between washing dishes, chatting and humor; my thoughts had gone back to Andy; maybe because of the earlier thoughts I had about his life when I was at the office. Maybe it was because I was thinking about his fortress and why it was so important to him.

As I stood at the sink I watched more snow fall through the kitchen window and I found myself wondering how his fortress walls would stand up to the winter. Had we built them strong enough? Would they support the challenge of a strong winter storm and would they still be there in springtime? I had to believe we had built the fortress walls strong enough to withstand any challenge. If we hadn't then what was all of the work for?

Once we were finished Marie moved from the kitchen to another room in our house where she spent her time reading. It was a place of her own that was quiet and allowed her some time for herself. I was left with my own thoughts.

As I moved into the living room to turn on the television the fear of my upcoming doctor's appointment reappeared; and not knowing what lay before me. I wondered how well my personal fortress would do in this situation. Maybe this would be my wintertime challenge. I had no idea what I was going to discover and I hoped no one would see the cracks of self doubt that were beginning to form in *my* walls. I had a feeling I would need a strong fortress, just like Andy's, maybe even stronger.

I knew from the past that not knowing only made things worse. Reality was often never as bad as imagination; for now imagination was all I had; I was worried that it would become a time when I would need all of the strength available to me.

Memories of family history, today's medical concerns and methods combined with snapshots in my mind of sick people shoved into hospital beds waiting to die; or worse living with no quality of life filled my brain. I could focus on nothing else and my imagination was once again getting the best of me. I doubted that I would get much sleep tonight.

I went to the fridge to grab a snack and as I looked to the side I could see my wife sitting in her chair deep in her own thoughts as she read her book and a wave of comfort came over me. I believed that I could face anything with her by my side. Maybe my own fortress was stronger than I gave it credit for. I would find out soon enough.

CHAPTER 17

The next day was overcast and snowing once again, an ugly day with no sense of hope. The weather reflected my feelings perfectly. I knew the thought was melodramatic, since at this point I didn't know anything. All I knew for sure was that my family doctor wanted to see me in his office. The unknown sat heavy on my mind and I was unable to get as much sleep as I wanted; or needed. My night of restlessness was shared by Marie. We didn't talk but I could tell by the rustling sounds that she was having a hard time embracing sleep as well.

We had eaten breakfast in silence, kissed each other goodbye and went on with our day. She had taken the time to remind me to take the necessary steps to arrange for Thursday's appointment. I assured her I was capable of making simple plans.

Marriage; no matter how good; still had moments of tension and annoyance; it was hard to avoid. This was one of them. I wanted to believe we were both making too much out of everything and wanted Marie to relax. Since it was obvious she wasn't going to I ignored any further comments and headed off to my job

Work was no different than any other day. Paperwork sat on my desk in the same pile I had left it in the day before and I performed my routine tasks just as I always did. I chose not to tell any of my co-workers about the upcoming appointment, because there really was nothing to tell. Even if there was, I wasn't sure how much I wanted to share with them. I decided to find out the facts first before I made any decisions. It was a novel approach for me.

I spoke to my supervisor Becker about taking Thursday off and he agreed with no apparent concern as to the reason. I was actually grateful for that because I did not want to have to explain anything to him either. The worst thing I could have happen to me right now was some kind of insincere compassion from someone I didn't respect much anyway.

Work had been no different; but I couldn't say the day itself was the same. Thoughts rambled through my mind like a train going nowhere.

Questions; so many questions; what if this appointment is more than just a routine visit? I had been to the doctor many times; why did this time feel different? What could be happening that made me worry so much? Was worry more my enemy than whatever the doctor had to tell me? Did most men my age worry about their health this much or was it just my active imagination reacting to the situation? Why; why; why?

So many questions not enough answers; well any answers that carried any real value. My answers were just guesses; still the end of the day couldn't come fast enough and I was exhausted; not from my job but all of the "thinking" going through my mind.

I finished up my day, cleaned up my desk and left for home. The evening went much as the night before. Marie and I did little talking to each other not because we were angry; probably just because we didn't really know what to say. At this point what could we really talk about? We were both concerned; of that I was sure of; most likely because this had never happened before and the unknown was making it harder.

We ate our supper, shared some small talk while avoiding the real question on both of our minds; what would the doctor tell me tomorrow? To an outsider our worry and thoughts would most likely appear as a melodramatic reaction to a simple problem. Maybe it was; I couldn't speak for Marie but I sensed that she too "just had a feeling something was wrong"; something a person can't explain but just as real as any truth that would be told.

My gloomy imagination had made me feel over-exhausted. It was time for bed and as tired as I was I still couldn't rest. Sleep did not come any easier than the night before and morning couldn't come soon enough for me; I just wanted to know

The bad weather, tiredness and my bad mood carried into Thursday morning as I prepared for my doctor's appointment. Marie wanted to stay home from work and go with me, but I assured her that it would be a simple problem with a simple solution, so she didn't have to take time off for me.

I was still trying to be gallant but the look of worry on her face created some fear in my own heart despite my attempt at chivalry. I wasn't going to let her feel worse though, so I did my best to hide my feelings. I attempted to lighten the mood, but that didn't seem to work very well either. She knew what I was doing, and although I think she appreciated the effort I don't believe it made anything easier for her. I guess she knew my characteristics as easily as I knew hers after years of marriage. She could tell when I used humor to hide concern.

Besides; worry was one of Marie's strengths; she was good at it and I think she even found worry a comfortable friend. Me; I hated worry even though I could engage the feeling as easily as she could so I tried to dismiss any negative thoughts from my mind and confidently encouraged her not to be concerned. My efforts were most likely fruitless but she finally went off to her job and I headed to my appointment. I didn't want to be late.

I arrived at the medical center with plenty of time to spare and greeted the receptionist.

"Good morning Julie." I had learned her name over years of visiting this office. She was a pleasant, friendly person; maybe a bit plump; married with three children and had worked in this office since she was twenty-three. I had discovered most of the information about her family as well as schooling, hobbies and such just by talking to her during the long waiting periods of a doctor's office. Somehow I seemed to always have to wait at least and hour for a doctor even if I was the first appointment. It was annoying but part of the process.

"Good morning Robert." The familiarity of first names had also developed over time. I liked it that way.

"How are you doing today?"

"Can't say; your office called *me* in so you tell me."

"The doctor won't be very long" she said in her practiced receptionist voice. We both knew I was in for a long wait.

"How are the kids doing?"

"They are driving me nuts!" she jumped in with a smile on her face. "The girls want new clothes for some dance at school (she had twin daughters) and my son's hockey has me and my husband running all over the country. We hardly get to see each other which can have some drawbacks; if you know what I mean."

My smile told her that I did understand what she meant. I was happy we could have this kind of friendly banter; it made the waiting easier. "Well I used to. Maybe you want to fill me just as a reminder" I teased her.

"Don't think so" she chuckled. "We do have some medical books you could look at that can explain everything."

"No thanks. Probably couldn't identify everything anyways." If Marie had been with me I know she would have given me a look of scorn because she never found my jokes about sex funny. I think she actually found them demeaning. With that in mind I decided to change the subject.

"Snow came early this year didn't it?" I opened with a standard question.

"I don't think so. Seems like the same time as last year."

"Really I thought it was early. Maybe time just going by faster. It seems like winter was just here; now it's back."

"The first snowfall is usually not too bad" Julie said; "Just a reminder that more will be on the way.

"Isn't that the truth!" I glanced at the clock behind her and noticed people coming in the front door so I looked back at her and said "I guess I'll just wait over here until the doctor is in."

"Sounds good; I'll call you as soon as he's available."

"Okay thanks. It's always nice seeing you."

"You too" she replied as she turned her attention to the next patient approaching her desk. With that I grabbed a magazine, sat down in a waiting room chair and awaited my appointment with destiny.

Waiting in a doctor's offices was one of the things I hated the most in life. I didn't think anyone else in the room was too thrilled either. With a quick glance I could see a mother with her child who obviously had the flu or something. I could tell by his sniffles and the way he clung to his mother as though her love would protect him and make him feel better. Another man to the left had what appeared to be a cast on his leg with crutches nearby so his reason for being there seemed obvious. A room full of maladies and stories. Some of the people may have even wondered why I was there. I wished that I could tell them. Time dragged on until I finally heard Julie call my name.

"Mr. Henry?" she called in a questioning voice as though she was searching for me in a crowded room. She always called me by my surname when the doctor was ready to see me. Professional courtesy I suppose; I never bothered to ask.

"Right here" I said quickly so that she didn't overlook me and move on to the next patient.

I tossed the magazine I had been reading on the nearby table and followed her down the hallway to the doctor's office. I entered the room; Julie said goodbye and closed the door. Another fifteen minutes went by before the door opened once more and in walked Dr. Taylor.

He was like most family doctors; at least by my standards. He was friendly, had average medical skills and ran a strong medical business. One thing I did like about him the most was that he was a straight shooter. Taylor had always told me the truth without pretending something was less or more serious than it was. He would just explain what he knew and then offer treatment solutions. After almost twenty years as his patient, this was something I appreciated about him.

I had never been summoned to his office for such a consultation before so I hoped Dr. Taylor continued his pattern of straightforwardness, because I needed to hear the truth now more than ever. I admit I was more than a little scared and my imagination was cranking up for another round of what ifs.

When he entered the room and saw me waiting in front of his desk he offered a quick good morning as he passed by. I returned the courtesy to him automatically. The doctor then sat in his chair, studying my file. He closed it, and he pushed it to the side of his desk.

He looked up at me. "We have a problem, Robert."

Thank God for this man, I thought. No messing around, no beating around the bush, no pretending. I was going to find out what he knew and what | needed to do. I know I was hoping for the best and dreading the worst.

"Well, I have a feeling I have more of a problem today than you do," I joked.

Dr. Taylor was used to me by now and had learned to appreciate my dry sense of humor. He joined me in a small chuckle.

"Yes, I suppose you're right" he responded; "but there is something we do need to talk about." I waited for him to continue, hoping that my imagination did not match my reality. "Based on your last physical exam, as well as the problems you had described to me before, it appears you may have prostate cancer."

It felt like the floor came up to hit me in the head. I guessed that there was something wrong, but cancer was not a word I was prepared for. There was a history of heart attacks, death by car accident, and even a suicide in my family background, but cancer was not something in my history. Even my imagination hadn't considered that possibility.

"Cancer?" I responded in almost a stunned tone of voice.

"Yes, that's right, but the news isn't all bad."

Thoughts raced through my mind as I wondered what could possibly make the news better. Was he going to tell me that I had cancer, but don't worry, my tonsils were fine? Or was he going to give me the great news that my miserable hemorrhoid problem was never coming back? My mind was full of sarcastic remarks that I couldn't say. Instead, I looked at him and said, "Okay, that's good. You've given me the bad news. What's the good news?"

"We will have to do more tests, but if it is prostate cancer—and I think it is—we have caught it early enough so treatment will be possible. Many men your age have this form of cancer and have gone on to live long, happy lives after successful medical treatments." His confident tone almost made me believe what he was saying. Lord knows I wanted him to be right but I wondered about the men who weren't so fortunate.

"Well that's good to know." I was still stunned by the news and was only half listening to what he was saying, but I did hear him say *more tests Monday*. I nodded in agreement as he told me that his office assistant would make the appointments, and call me to let me know what time to be there. I could tell he had been through this before, so I trusted his judgment, at least for now.

I gathered myself for the moment and began to ask him some of the questions swirling around in my head. "What does this mean, Doctor? Will I have to take some form of chemotherapy? Will I have to quit work? How bad is prostate cancer? What can I expect?" I had blurted out the words and I wasn't even waiting for the answers.

So many questions were flooding my brain that it was overwhelming. I felt helpless. I was a middle-aged man who should have been enjoying this time in life, and now I had to deal with a problem like this. It didn't seem fair. Sure, I had heard of many men my age with this problem—maybe even knew about a couple— but no one so close to me that I felt comfortable asking him any questions. Right now, Dr. Taylor was all I had.

"I know you have a lot of questions Robert—and believe me, we'll get all of them answered for you—but first we have to do more tests to confirm the problem. Then we can proceed with treatment. You need more tests before we can answer the questions and start treatment."

He leaned forward towards me. "I won't try to kid you Robert. If it is cancer it will be hard. No disease of this nature can be dismissed as something insignificant and it needs proper treatment but try not to worry too much."

Yeah, like that's going to happen, I thought.

"Plus even if you do have cancer, this is a very treatable kind. Cancer treatments have come a long way in the last couple of decades, and I see no reason why you can't beat this."

I hoped he was right and I appreciated that he hadn't said *we* could beat this together, because there was no *we*, just me. It was me that would have to fight this disease, not him or anyone else. I fought off the first wave of self-pity.

Then it hit me. How was I going to tell Marie?

I knew how she would react. Marie was the worrier in our family. She was a strong woman who could handle many problems, but this was a big one. I was feeling guilty about putting her through the worry of not knowing sooner, never mind what would happen if it proved to be true. Looking back the fair thing would have been to let her come with me so she could hear the news from the doctor first hand. But then who knows maybe Taylor was wrong.

Who was I kidding? I knew deep down that he was right. He was just covering his ass by sending me for more tests. All they would do was just offer more proof. I hadn't been feeling well for some time—that's what brought me to him in the first place. I had tried not to make a big deal about it, but something told me I had better look into the problem. That was most likely what had given my imagination so much to work with. So how would I tell her what the problem was without blowing it out of proportion?

So many emotions were flowing through my mind. Oddly, one of them was *relief*. I was relieved that things were out in the open. More tests or not, I knew what it was. Now I could deal with the problem without fighting the ghost of the unknown. I trusted the doctor's diagnosis. The real question was: what now?

I broke the moment of silence by saying "I know Marie will want to know what is going on and how long I'll have to wait for test results. What can I tell her?"

"You can tell her that everything is done in house, so we should have the results of Monday's tests by Thursday, no later than Friday. Can we set up another appointment for then?" His question was simple enough but I didn't think he understood how scared I was. Even though I knew that he was right I felt like it should seem more complicated than just booking an appointment for a haircut or something. After all who knew what the results were going to be?

I knew the man had more compassion than that, but for the moment my brain was only attempting to process his information, not his bedside manner. Besides how could I fight a disease until I knew for sure what I was fighting?

"Of course; what time?"

"I'll make an appointment for Friday morning at ten with my assistant. Will that work for you?"

How could I say no? He had just told me that I might have cancer. What was I supposed to say, *I'm busy. How about next month*? I agreed with the appointment time, telling him I would be there.

"Ten will be fine. I'll book the time off. Should I bring Marie?"

"That's not a bad idea. She doesn't have to be here for Monday's tests but I can review everything with both of you at the Friday appointment. So see if she can make it."

"I think the statement is more like *just try and stop her!*" attempting to supply a smile to go along with my words but I wasn't sure if I was able to accomplish that yet. I was trying my best to keep my thoughts on the task at hand and that was gathering some more information to answer the questions I knew I would be asked to answer at home. I didn't know what I would be able to remember but I thought I better try.

I asked Dr. Taylor a few more questions, which he answered in the usual direct manner. However, there were a couple of moments when he seemed to be guarded while giving his answers. He said he wanted to be careful and not worry me more than he had to before the extra tests were completed. It was, after all, the wise thing to do, so I decided I would leave things where they were. I did have a couple more things I wanted to know however.

"That's all fine and good" I said. "I can understand what you are saying but tell me something; if it is prostrate cancer what are my odds?"

"Statistics in this type of cancer at this stage are in your favor. As I said there are many more treatments available to us that weren't around only a few years ago. The best thing to do now is some reading. I'll have Julie provide you with some pamphlets before you leave. It'll give you a place to start."

With that he stood up bringing an end to my office appointment. He stated he would have to go because he had another patient waiting for him—he always did—and since my mind had once again become numb I followed his lead, preparing to leave. Taylor put his hand on my shoulder in a lame attempt to make me feel more comfortable about the news. I appreciated the effort.

"It's okay Robert. Everything will be okay. I have had lots of experience with cancer treatment, so I know this is beatable. It will be hard not to worry but I find information to help. Get on the internet and read the pamphlets we give you. The more you know the better prepared you'll be." Leaning on his desk, he scribbled some words on a piece of paper and handed it to me. "Here are some web pages that you can start with. They'll provide you with some basic information that should answer many questions and hopefully take some of the worry away."

His confident calmness let me believe that everything *would* be okay. I knew from listening to other people talk about cancer that I was facing a challenge that wouldn't be easy, but for the first time since I came into his office, I believed it was one I would conquer. I just prayed that I was right.

I said my goodbyes and accepted the information Julie handed to me. She must have known what to expect because she had it all ready for me as I walked to her desk. Her professionalism made it difficult to tell if she had any concern or hope for me. She was just doing her job; for me it was my life.

Marie was not home when I walked in. She wouldn't be home for another four hours. That was a good thing, because I needed some time to digest the morning events. Normally, upon arriving home, I would have turned on the television within fifteen minutes, if only for some form of background noise. For the first time, I didn't want television to dull my senses. There was a lot to think about.

Cancer; the word itself sounded so sinister. What would the disease be like? How hard would it be to beat? Would I be able to beat it? How much pain would I experience? Will I need surgery? Then I thought of things like; do I have my will in order? Would Marie and Annie be well taken care of? Do I know; God forbid; how I want to be buried? It amazed me what comes to a man's mind when he is faced with a life changing decision.

I knew I was being self-absorbed; maybe even feeling sorry for myself. I was positive that there were thousands of people all over the country going through the same problems. Many men my age had fought prostate cancer and come out victorious: I could believe that to be true but not reassuring. This was *my* life, and *I* would be the one that had to fight the disease. *I* would be the one who would have to explain it to my wife. How was I supposed to do that? Hell; I couldn't even believe it myself.

Feeling sorry for myself was not going to make things better but it was hard not to. I had worked hard and lived a responsible life. I was a good person; so why me? I just couldn't believe it. What did I ever do wrong to deserve this kind of setback in my life? Self-pity was so easy to indulge,

I gathered the information I had been given and began to look it over, and I tried to do my best to understand what the pamphlets were saying. I could digest the material maybe even begin to accept the facts of the disease, but cancer? The thought still scared me.

In the end though I wasn't as scared of dying as not living; I just prayed that I hadn't left my life too late. Had I done enough? I couldn't help thinking "my God" had I waited too long to enjoy the things I had worked for? I hoped that I hadn't wasted my life; I had so much left to do.

It was easy to see; even to me that I was becoming over dramatic again with all of my thoughts, and what was the point? There wasn't even an audience to enjoy the performance! I pulled myself together and dived headlong into the information the doctor had given me. I was determined to concentrate on what I was reading so I could answer questions. I wanted to be as prepared as I could be when Marie came home so that I could give her a reason not to worry. That most likely wouldn't happen, but information was power, or so I have been told, and if Marie had some of the facts then she would have some power of her own to face the challenge ahead. I knew it wouldn't be easy; for either of us.

My wife and I had been together a long time, and I knew her well. She was a pragmatic and supportive person who kept many of her emotions trapped in her heart. She was also a caring, compassionate person. She would understand the challenge that lay before us and would stand side by side with me. I loved her for that.

I also knew that she could make things harder on herself by trying to carry too much of the burden alone. She trapped emotions in her heart and too often she would keep her thoughts and feelings to herself when I believed that sharing them would make it easier for both of us. I hoped this time it would be different.

The walls Marie had built around herself were every bit as strong as my own. This time we might have to tear down some of the walls to share the burden of the disease and the excitement of the victory. That might prove to be a challenge itself. I hoped information would help; so I spent the rest of my time reading, understanding and digesting the material I had been given. I would be prepared.

Marie walked in the door and I gathered myself and prepared to answer the questions I knew she would have for me; she took no time at all to get to the point. No Hello or small talk chatter this afternoon. Today she walked in and the first words she uttered were "Did you get to the doctor on time? Why did he call you in? What did he say? Is it bad?" she said, blurting out questions like a machine gun.

"Whoa," I said, holding my hand up. "I can only answer one question at a time."

She gave me an impatient look but I think she was so worried about everything that she wasn't even mad at me for cutting her off; that was a first! She just wanted to know.

"Yes, I got to the doctor on time. He had some news for me and wants to do some more tests. Is it bad? I guess it depends on a person's perspective," I said with my attempt at lightheartedness. It didn't work.

"What do you mean? What's wrong?"

"Well now, remember that Dr. Taylor said he still wanted to do more tests to confirm everything—" I cautioned.

"Just tell me what it is," Marie said in a frustrated voice.

"Okay, now promise me that you won't get excited." Her body language told me that she was way past excited, well on her way to agitated, so I continued, "He thinks I have prostate cancer."

"Oh my God," Marie whispered as she fell back onto a kitchen chair. "I need to sit down." I guessed she hadn't expected that answer anymore than I had.

"You said you wanted to know,"

"Yes of course" she said trying to gather herself.

"Marie, it might not be as bad as it sounds," I said, trying to sound confidant and re-assuring. "Dr. Taylor said we have caught it early and it is very treatable. I've been reading some information he gave me, and according to what it says in the pamphlets, many, if not most men beat this form of cancer. At least that's what I'm being told. I don't think the news is as bad as it sounds."

"Okay; well it sounds bad."

"Of course it does honey; but like I said everything I read today states that this form of cancer *is* treatable and beatable. I have to believe that."

She appeared to ignore what I was saying and simply said "Let me see." She reached for the pamphlets I had pointed to lying on the countertop and began glancing through the information. Marie never had been able to believe what I told her. I had learned she didn't think I was stupid or anything or that it had anything to do with trust; she just had to see it for herself. She couldn't believe it till she saw it; a trait that could be annoying for me but necessary for her.

I had decided to make a small meal for tonight so it would be one less thing for my wife to be concerned about so I handed her the rest of the sheets I had printed off and spent the next twenty minutes finishing supper while Marie pored over the information in front of her. I couldn't tell by her body language whether she believed any of it or even understood it any more than I did. She finally stopped when I asked her to set the table.

I attempted to put on a brave front as we sat eating at the kitchen table. Marie had appeared to have regained some of her self-control by this time and did the same. The food wasn't great, but it didn't matter; we weren't that hungry anyways. There were uncomfortable moments of silence but we chose not to waste any time on small talk. The day's news was our only item of conversation.

"When does Dr. Taylor want you to come back in?" Marie asked.

"Monday; he says he will have the results by the end of next week."

"That's good; it's better to know as soon as possible" Marie said, sounding relieved that we weren't wasting any time taking the next step. That was the pragmatic part of her. Then the emotional side of her peeked out just a little bit. "What are we going to do if it is cancer, Robert? What will we tell Annie?"

I wanted to be strong and pragmatic myself so I answered her by saying "If it is cancer—and I have to assume it is—then we'll trust what we are told. We'll look at the options and move forward, just like we always have." What else could I say? She knew that was true, but hearing it didn't make it any easier for her. "As far as Annie goes, I don't want to tell her anything until we know for sure. No sense worrying our daughter for nothing, right?"

I had never wanted to burden my little girl with news like this. I didn't want her to see me as anything other than invincible, even if I had accepted the fact that she was no longer a child. She was every bit as strong as her mother, so when the time came, I could tell her anything and I believed she would understand what lay before us; but for now there was no advantage in telling her. Knowing her, she would be a great source of support, one that I would assuredly need but this fact wouldn't make telling her any easier so I wouldn't tell her until I had too.

Marie glanced back at me and said "I agree. Why tell her bad news until we know for sure; that makes the best sense right?"

"Right" I nodded in agreement. I didn't know what else to say so I added "Why don't we stop talking for a bit and finish our supper?"

She nodded and we nibbled away at our meal lost in our own thoughts as the first shock of the report began to subside a little. It was true we still had many more questions, but the information from the doctor's office gave us a good starting point and we would gather more answers as we went along.

With our meal eaten we engaged in more conversation. We were both optimistic people so after an hour or so of talking, I began to feel that beating this was not only possible but probable. Marie spoke with a similar confidence. I hoped we were right and not just throwing more walls up to protect each other.

After cleaning the table and washing the dishes I said "Would you like some dessert?" Marie looked at me with a mock astonishment on her face. I didn't often make the meals and maybe she couldn't remember the last time I had gone to so much trouble. I don't think it mattered to her if dessert tasted good or not. Just the idea was astonishing.

"A meal and dessert? You went all out" her tone was one of playful sarcasm. Luckily she chose not to point out that supper was made up of sandwiches, cheese and pickles; hardly the work of a chef. To her it was probably just the thought that counted. Besides, how hard was it to dish out ice cream?

Looking back at her I chuckled and said "Guess this may be more surprising than any other news."

A small smile formed on her face, the first one all day and she said, "Never thought I would see it happen." I wondered if she just meant the meal.

Her smile warmed my heart and I was glad to see some lightheartedness break through. We needed it; this had been a hard day for both of us. News like this was never something you expected and certainly never looked forward to telling someone so humor was a good medicine; maybe the best kind for a day like this.

The evening moved quickly into darkness and Marie had gone up to bed before me; exhausted. I knew she had gone to work and I was certain she had worried most of the day just like me; then come home to the news that her husband had cancer. Who wouldn't be exhausted! She had handled the news as best she could but now it was time for rest. I could see that on her face as she kissed me goodnight and I wished her a good night's sleep.

I still wasn't ready to go to sleep so I waited a bit longer before heading off to bed. Even after I finally walked up the stairs and fell into bed my mind was still full of questions. There were so many more thoughts and fears left to deal with that I was beginning to find myself exhausted just by contemplating the work that lay ahead of me. I assumed that some of the questions would be answered next week after the tests came back and many of the other issues were more logistical in nature; those things would take care of themselves. It wasn't the tasks I was afraid of it was the possibility of failure.

Reading about cancer had helped a bit but fearing cancer was more challenging. It was only one day, and I was already tired from the fight that lay before me. What the hell would happen if—no make that when—I had to fight the actual disease? Where would my strength come for that battle?

I looked across the bed to see Marie quietly sleeping and wondering what dreams—or nightmares—she may be having. It also gave me a moment of strength knowing that this woman was on my team. I wouldn't have to fight the battle alone. That thought albeit helpful did not alleviate the worry that was taking over my mind. I couldn't shake the concerns and it wasn't making it easier.

By now, I knew sleep was more important than anything else. I still had a job to do next day and I needed the rest. Exhaustion was present but I wasn't sure if I would be able to fall asleep right away. I knew I had better try. I would have plenty of time to deal with everything; or would I? I couldn't shake that thought from my mind as I drifted off to sleep.

CHAPTER 18

I was proven right. Sleep had not come to me easily the first night; even with the exhaustion that overwhelmed me. Years of marriage made me believe that Marie's sleep was as restless as mine. She was sleeping when I finally drifted off but I felt obligated to ask anyway.

"Morning Sweetie" I said to her as she walked from the bathroom. "How did you sleep?"

"Probably about the same as you; not well."

I guess years of marriage made her as intuitive as me. "Yeah; well I guess it would be hard for anyone to sleep after yesterday's news."

"That's for sure. What were you dreaming about?"

"What do you mean?" I questioned with a puzzled look.

"I was watching you and you were mumbling something; I couldn't make out the words; then for some reason you started swinging just like a boxer would."

"Geez I didn't hit you or anything did I?"

"Almost but I'm good at dodging" she said smiling.

I laughed and when she asked me what I was laughing at I told her "Could you imagine what kind of questions we would have been asked if you had entered the doctor's office with a black eye?"

She laughed with me and said "I'd just tell them the truth; my husband did it."

"Well I hope you would have told them the whole story so they would understand."

"Why? That wouldn't make them feel sorry for me now would it? A good story is better than the truth anyways." Her mischievous grin proved obvious to me that she was teasing and frankly the light banter made me feel a bit better. Anything was better than the other feelings I had been experiencing.

"Well if anyone can tell a story" I grinned back at her without having to finish the sentence.

"*ME?*" she exclaimed with a tone of disbelief "How about you? You're the big story teller not me."

It was going to be hard to defend the point since it was true; I could be a good story teller but I wasn't willing to accept defeat just quite yet.

"Well when you're good at something you need to use it" I bragged a little before adding. "I have noticed that you must be taking lessons too because your B.S.; uh I mean story telling seems to be getting better too."

She gave one final laugh; hugged me and said "I've learned from the best. How can I go wrong?"

I hugged her back and began my morning routine while she through on a housecoat and went downstairs to prepare a small breakfast as she always did. Although the joking had not made everything go away it had done a little bit to lighten the load; at least for the moment.

I could hear Marie call me to breakfast just as I was finishing dressing so the timing was perfect. After we ate I offered to put the dishes in the dishwasher while she went back upstairs to finish drying her hair and get ready for work. It had become such a normal routine for us we could have done it in our sleep. This morning however it was a comfortable routine that I could appreciate more than ever.

I always left for work before Marie did so when I was finished in the kitchen I gathered my coat and prepared to leave.

"Goodbye" I hollered back up the stairs "I'll call you later."

"Call me later" she called back.

Sometimes I wondered if she responded more to the sound rather than the words I spoke. I decided to let it slide and responded with a simple "Okay" then walked out to my car. The "day after" had begun.

The next few days proved to be almost excruciating. Not knowing was killing me; I couldn't help chuckle at the pun even though it wasn't funny. We still did not know anything more than we already did and we had not told Annie anything just as we had agreed. The two of us had attempted to go about our days in a usual manner. This, however, was not a usual problem.

There was nothing else so important in our lives at that moment, and even though we made attempts to talk about other things the discussion continued to return to my condition. Much of what we knew to this point was pure conjecture based on information we were able to access. We had spent most of Saturday and Sunday on the Internet searching for more answers. What we found was the usual medical terminology, testimonials, symptom descriptions, and other basic information, which helped us to better understand what we were up against. At least that's what I tried to tell myself.

I'd be lying if I said I understood everything. Marie was no better off than me, but I think between the both of us we were able to glean enough data to believe that this *was* beatable. Marie was leaning over my shoulder trying to read an article I had pulled up on a web site then pointed to a paragraph and said "According to this Robert prostate cancer is very treatable just like the doctor said. If it's treatable it should be beatable right?"

My only response was a simple "Guess so."

My reply apparently irked her because her next statement was harsher; "Well if you aren't going to have a positive attitude about this fight then why not just plan the funeral now!"

Marie could be cute when she got mad. This wasn't one of those times. I could tell it wasn't time to push her buttons; someone would get hurt and it would probably be me.

"It's not that honey" maybe charm would work, "Of course I want to fight. I've just never had a fight like this before. Don't plan the funeral yet though and for god sakes don't spend all the money on a new boyfriend!"

I always teased Marie like that and her smile indicated she knew I was teasing her now.

"Okay buddy" she grinned at me "then you better start fighting because I'm sure I could find someone to take your place pretty fast." Her humor was welcome and her challenge was just what I needed.

"No one could replace me lady" I laughed. "What's the saying when you have the best there's no reason to look at the rest?"

She continued to tease me "Hey the only reason I took you in the first place was because I was busy and I wasn't paying attention. Lucky thing my selection worked out" she smiled. "Well for the most part!"

Her parting shot left me wondering what part she thought worked out; but sometimes not knowing could be the best answer.

The banter between us broke some of the tension and we began to work together again as husband and wife against our current enemy; cancer. Sometimes it seemed liked Marie and I spent useless time bickering. I suppose most couples did; but I enjoyed it more when we were on the same side. It felt right and gave me the hope I needed.

The next week came too fast, and at the same time not fast enough. I completed all the tests Monday, and true to Dr. Taylor's word, I was sitting in his office Friday morning waiting for the test results.

Marie insisted on going along with me this time. I had tried to point out that the doctor was expecting her to be there with me but she just brushed me off. She said that it would affect her just as much as me, because she would be the one to help me every step of the way. She said she needed to know the information so she knew what to do. I shrugged in agreement plus even though I didn't want to admit it; in truth I was glad she was there with me. It wasn't as though I could have stopped her anyways, even if I had wanted to.

Dr. Taylor entered his office offering good-morning acknowledgments to both of us. He took a few minutes more to exchange pleasantries with my wife. I think he wanted to make the moment less stressful for her by taking her mind off the news. Of course that would never happen but his "bedside manner" that he had not used on me before; kicked in to prepare both of us for the news—good or bad. Maybe he just didn't want to tell us.

After a few more minutes of what I would describe as useless conversation considering what was before me I looked directly at him and asked "So what's the story? What are we looking at?"

He turned to the test results in my file, taking a moment to flip through the pages then closed the file before looking up at me. "I reviewed all your tests yesterday, Robert. I was right; it's cancer."

"Well that's not a surprise is it? I hoped you would have a different result to report but I guess that was too much to wish for. I can't deny that maybe I would have liked it better if you had eased into it a bit more. Maybe tell me there was a possibility of cancer but hey did you see the big game last night? Then give me the news." Marie looked at me with an obvious look of annoyance at my lame attempt at humor. She always said I talked too much but she wouldn't verbally chastise me in public; it wasn't her style. Besides she didn't have to use words; her look spoke volumes.

"I'm sorry. I wish it was something else, but it is definitely prostate cancer I have found that in these situations it is better to be straight forward and upfront; it makes it easier for everyone."

Maybe easier for you I thought but was smart enough to offer no reply.

Marie had prepared herself for the message. I think; just like me; she hoped for the best and expected the worst so before I even had a chance to open my mouth again she began to speak. "We appreciate the directness Doctor. It does make it easier if we know what we are up against" she offered "So what can we do about it?"

"Well as I mentioned to Robert on his first visit, this is a very common and treatable form of cancer. Statistics show that one in six men will develop prostate cancer in his lifetime. The good news is that treatment success rates exceed ninety percent."

The last part of his sentence was encouraging.

"I know we read about that" she said "And we did see some of the information on treatment but frankly we don't understand much of it and have no idea what needs to be done. So what's next?" Her question was an impatient restatement of her previous question. I knew this from experience but if the doctor picked up on it he chose to ignore it and carried on with his answer.

"Well one of the most common forms of treatment is radiation. I think this will be the best form of treatment for Robert."

The word *radiation* seemed almost as bad as the word *cancer*, but I decided to not interrupt the doctor with my fears.

"He'll have to see some other medical staff, such as Dr. Rivers, an oncologist, and Dr. Bryan, who is a pathologist first before any treatments."

"Why?" was the only question I could think of.

Turning back to my wife he said "They will do more tests to confirm my diagnosis and decide on a method of treatment. If there is an alternative to radiation then we'll consider it. For now however I'll need their input. They are specialists in this field and will also work with Robert through the whole process. They're good doctors. You'll like them."

I was becoming annoyed that he was doing all of the talking to Marie, practically ignoring me; even when I was the one asking the question. Wasn't I the one who was sick? I tried to believe that Marie needed the information and attention more than I did. Besides; I told myself; she would likely absorb more than I would. She was the better listener. Still though I thought it would be great if I could be a part of the solution as well as the problem. Feeling sorry for myself was becoming easier and easier.

No one in the room appeared to notice me sulking in my chair and since the only way I was going to get attention was to speak I decided to assert myself.

"What can we expect and how soon do we get started?" I questioned. There I thought; if they could be pragmatic than so could I. No one was going to leave me out of the loop. Strange isn't it how strong a person could be even when they felt helpless?

I paused; waiting for an answer; even one I didn't want to hear. It was true that I wasn't excited about rushing into some kind of radiation treatment or whatever someone had planned for me but there were certain times to let things happen as they should or had to. Insight was also becoming a part of my new life with cancer. My "insight" was also telling me that not only did I have to accept the truths of my disease but I also recognized that it was equally important to empower Marie with some of the responsibility. Taking her out of the loop would hurt both of us so I set my ego aside for the moment, kept quiet and waited for her say "Robert's right. When do we get started?"

"We start right away," he said. "We'll get him into the hospital next week for the tests then after I review the results and consult the specialists we'll move forward with a treatment schedule. I know we have your family's health care plan information on file, so don't worry about any of those details."

That was comforting information because I hadn't even thought about that. I didn't always like my job but I was grateful we had the benefit plan; especially now.

My thoughts went back to Annie. Oh God, now that we know for sure what we are facing how would we tell her about this? It was something we wouldn't be able to avoid any longer. I cleared my thoughts and decided I would worry about that after we left his office.

"I'll give you this information outlining some of the side effects," he said, pulling a sheet from his file and handing it to Marie. "It will also list some things to avoid during treatment."

"Thank you, Doctor" said Marie. "As I mentioned we were able to obtain some information off the Internet, but this will help."

That wasn't good enough for me so I had to ask "What kind of side effects?"

"Read the information first. Write down any questions that you have and I can answer them for you at our next meeting."

That was a great way to side step the question I thought but decided to leave things where they were "Okay" I nodded. "We'll read the information." What else could I say?

Of course I couldn't not say something . . . that just wouldn't be me "The only real side effect I'm concerned about is will I still be a man after radiation treatment."

He could tell I was joking by the smirk on my face.

"As much of a man as you were before," he said, grinning back at me.

My feeble attempt at humor appeared to relieve some of the tension in the room even for my wife because I heard her add "Geez I was hoping for something better."

Leave it to my wife to put me in my place but when I looked at her I remembered how much I liked her sense of humor. They began to laugh and all I could do was laugh with them.

"Well, honey, this may be all the man you can handle."

She looked at me then back at the doctor; began to say something; thought better of it; shook her head and smiled. I grinned back.

A small part of the somber mood had been lifted and for that I was grateful. The seriousness of the situation did not elude me but at least now the knowledge of reality made it possible to take a step forward.

"The first step comes immediately" he said.

Taylor obviously had more to tell us, so we spent the next few minutes listening to him. "I am going to give you some more information to read to go along with what you already have, some contact names, a letter for your work in case you need one and I want to schedule appointment times so once I have all of the information you can begin treatment immediately."

It occurred to me that he seemed to be in an awful hurry for a man who indicated that this was a beatable disease. Maybe I was just over-thinking again.

After he finished speaking we gathered everything from his desk and prepared to leave, but before we reached the door he spoke one more time.

"I know that everyone will try to tell you this, but please try not to worry. You really do have a treatable cancer. Catching it early is crucial and I believe we have and I have seen enough cases to know you'll beat this. In fact, I'm counting on it. I don't plan to retire for twelve more years, and I need the billable hours!"

Marie and I gave a lighthearted laugh at his comments. His humor and positive approach was exactly what we needed in that moment: even if his joke was somewhat lame.

"I'll do my best to help you out" I replied "Just make sure you do *your* best!"

"You got it" he said. Then he shook my hand and opened the door so we could re-enter the world outside.

I asked Marie not to let Annie know anything about my health until we had a chance to speak with her in person. She would be coming over for Sunday dinner, so I said we could tell her then. Marie agreed that would be the best way. We could have simply called her but that would have been a tough way for a child to hear this kind of news.

Tired of all the reading material, I decided Saturday night to put aside all the books, sheets of paper, pictures, and anything else we had accumulated on the subject to think about something else. I felt we had a basic understanding of what lay ahead of us and we both needed a night out.

I looked over to Marie and said "Why don't we take a break?"

She must have felt the same as I did because she looked up at me and nodded.

"Why don't I take you out for a nice supper? Maybe Romeros?" It would have been in bad humor to make some comment about it being my last supper, so I didn't. I was sick not stupid!

"I like Romeros" she said. "Just give me a half hour to get ready."

"Sure. I'll be waiting." Truth was I needed the half hour just to have some time for myself. There was so much to think about it was overwhelming. Maybe a pleasant evening out around other people would be just the ticket.

We arrived at the restaurant about an hour later. The distance to the restaurant wasn't far but Marie had underestimated the amount of time required to get ready so we were eating a bit later than I expected. I didn't mind. We parked the car, walked in through the front door and asked for a table. Once we settled in the waiter asked if we wanted a drink.

"I don't know" I said glancing at Marie "I wonder if I'm suppose to or not?"

Always on the cautious side her reply was a simple "I don't think you should."

"Well I wasn't told I couldn't."

She knew that we often enjoyed a glass of wine when we went out for a meal but it was obvious by her stare that this would not be one of those times. Her words confirmed it. She looked at the waiter; ignored me and said "Just bring us coffee please."

He looked at me and the best I could offer was a shrug and a half hearted "She's the boss; coffee it is." The waiter nodded then turned to bring us our drinks and menus.

The rest of the evening was not eventful. It appeared that both of us were content to leave any talk of cancer at home for the night. I think we were both quite tired; I know I was. Instead we made idle chatter. Talked a bit about looking forward to seeing Annie the next day and ironically never even discussed how to handle telling her the news. Maybe deep down I just believed the words would come as I needed them. Besides; that was tomorrow. Today had been overwhelming so for tonight I just wanted to forget about what lay ahead of us. I wasn't trying to avoid the truths; just needed to give my brain a rest

By the time we left the restaurant, drove home and prepared for bed it was obvious both of us were ready for sleep. I often watched some television or read a book before going to bed but on this night we kissed each other goodnight, turned out the lights and drifted off to our dreams. We were tired and sleep was a welcome friend.

Sunday started out normal enough, with breakfast and a trip to church service. Nothing was said, but I think Marie was asking God for support. I knew I was. The service seemed more personal today, likely due to the recent news. If I ever needed God before, I needed him more than ever now. It could have been the church or my state of mind, but somehow I felt he was there with me this day. I knew he was there, listening to our hearts.

Driving home in silence was somewhat unsettling for me, since I was such a talker. It felt as though I had used up all of my idle chatter the night before at the restaurant. Small talk just wasn't coming easy this morning.

I think Marie and I had so much on our minds that we weren't letting our hearts talk. Or maybe the silence meant that we *were* talking with our hearts since what lay before us would be a challenge for the whole family and it was their fight as much as mine. Not speaking might also mean that both of us understood the magnitude of the situation and useless verbiage on a somber Sunday morning was unnecessary. Or maybe we just had nothing to say. In the end the reasons didn't matter to me; it only mattered that she was there with me. Her presence spoke volumes.

When we walked into the house Marie hung up her coat and without looking back said "Annie will be home soon so I'll get lunch started. Why don't you go into the living room and rest for a while. Maybe watch some television."

She was probably just being kind but her statement annoyed me. I wasn't so old or fragile that I needed to be treated like a cancer patient yet, was I? After all, I wasn't dying.

"I can help if you want me to do something" I replied.

"No I'm fine; just go into the living room."

I couldn't be sure if she didn't want my help, didn't need it or just wanted to be left alone. I decided to let the moment pass without making it an issue and went into the living room to watch some sports on television. Maybe I still wanted to be seen as strong and I didn't want to milk her pity but what the heck why not take advantage of it while I could?

It didn't take long for the smell of Marie's cooking to drift into the room. I often bragged about her cooking. It was one of the things I loved about her. Just by looking at me probably made it easy for people to believe that I enjoyed her cooking so I wondered if I would lose weight with this illness and how much? Will it make me look sick to others? Tough way to diet isn't it? I pondered.

It also occurred to me how stupid some of my thoughts could be. Geez why did I keep letting my brain over think everything? Was I really that scared? I gave my head a shake and focused once again on the wonderful feeling of Marie's kitchen warmth. The familiar aromas made things feel right.

"Your girl is going to be happy with dinner" I hollered into the kitchen "especially after eating college cafeteria food for so long. There was nothing like a home-cooked meal for a student. It smells great; what are we having?"

I hoped she knew that it was easy enough for me to figure it out on my own but she gave me a simple answer just the same "Roast beef, gravy, mashed potatoes, vegetables; all the usual things; nothing special." She had ignored my compliment; which she usually did and had offered a humble answer. Truth was this meal would be an important one because after today the truth would be out and Annie would be included in my struggle whether she wanted to be or not. I couldn't tell if Marie felt the same way or not but for me nothing would ever be the same as today's meal; it couldn't be. God how easy melodrama came to me!

Before I could add anything to the conversation or expand on my analysis I heard the front door open and Annie came through the door like a windstorm of happiness. College suited her well, and it showed. We had talked to her about living at home while she went to college; which she did for the first year; then she had told us she wanted more independence. She had said that she wanted to have the full college experience.

Just looking at her made me think she must be enjoying the experience to the maximum because every time I saw her she appeared so happy. Just looking at her gave me second thoughts about telling her the bad news, but I knew Marie would not allow that. She gave both her mother and me a big hug and kiss. I looked forward to the Sundays when we got to see our daughter. Her fun-loving personality was one of the reasons I enjoyed her so much. She never failed to brighten my day.

"Have a good week, sweetie?"

"Just the best, Dad! My classes were great this week and my professor loved my paper. I aced it."

I didn't know what paper she was speaking of and frankly I didn't care. As long as things were going well for her, I was happy. She went on to tell us about her friends, what she had done the past week, and even a party she had gone to the night before. My father radar perked up at this, but her story seemed harmless enough, so I sat back to listen, refreshed by her enthusiasm for life.

She finished by saying "It was a lot of fun. I got to meet some new people and even got to do some dancing."

"With boys?" I teased.

"Yes Dad. There were boys. I *am* old enough to date you know?"

"Don't I get to meet them first?" I said with a light hearted banter.

This subject had become a dance of my own between me and my daughter and she danced even better than I did!

"No Dad; you only get to meet them when I'm married with two children."

"You only plan on having two children?" I countered. "I thought maybe three or four would make me a good grandfather."

"Sure. Then you can stay at my place and change the diapers" she laughed.

"Don't count on it girlie" I grinned "Besides why don't we wait until you find someone who *wants* to marry you before we worry about grandchildren?"

Marie had just walked into the living room; heard the ongoing conversation and decided to add her two bits worth to our teasing "Don't worry about our daughter Robert; there will be *lots* of men who will want to marry her. The question is will there be one worth marrying; right honey?"

"Thanks Mom! It's nice to know someone believes in me" she said while putting her arm around her mother and looking at me with mock indignation.

I raised my arms above my head and laughed while saying "Okay, Okay I surrender! I can't beat both of you so I'll just shut up and give up."

Both of my girls looked at each other then back at me as if to say "That'll be the day." They didn't say the words but the message was clear. It was good to have Annie home; if just for the day.

She turned and stepped into the kitchen to help her mother finish preparing for lunch. I watched as she sneaked little bits of cheese from the plate she placed it on the table. Marie never liked when anyone did that; Annie knew that. My daughter saw me looking at her nibbling the cheese and gave me a smile. She put her finger to her lips, sealing the secret between us. I smiled back and nodded to acknowledge the conspiracy. Then, before I knew it, lunch was ready, so I joined Marie and Annie at the table. I said a small prayer of thanks (without mentioning anything about my health) and we began to enjoy the meal Marie had prepared.

Annie had carried most of the conversation at the table, while my wife and I just sat there, happy to listen. I realized that perhaps she had some of her dad's gift of gab after all—maybe too much.

"Dinner's good Mom" she mumbled while forcing a warm bun into her mouth.

"Thanks honey" her mother replied with a patented humble acknowledgement.

Not wanting to let an opportunity to tease my daughter slip by; especially having being defeated so easily earlier in the day I added my own comment "It's hard to tell Annie. Maybe you should try to breathe between bites."

"Very funny Dad; Looks to me like you could do some breathing exercises of your own" she said while poking my stomach with her finger. "I'm surprised you haven't passed out from not breathing at all . . . just eating!"

I began to respond when Marie began to laugh. I could tell then by watching the two of them laugh that I wasn't going to win this battle either. My teasing had backfired! It didn't matter though because their laughter at my expense was always worth it. This family laughter was one of the things that made a Sunday special for me. I was just saddened that I would soon have to change the mood.

When we were finished eating and the dishes were cleared the three of us had moved into the living room. I looked across the room at Marie, knowing that I could no longer avoid telling our daughter the bad news. She nodded at me and I got Annie's attention by interrupting one of her stories. She paused and turned towards me listening to my words.

"It's nice having you home" I said "We always enjoy your company."

"Well who wouldn't?" she countered in the same light hearted manner of before.

I could see she was prepared for a smartass response and appeared puzzled by my simple statement "But we have to tell you something, Annie."

She looked at me suspiciously. I think she could tell right away that something was wrong and the seriousness of my voice got her attention and made her question sound apprehensive.

"What is it, Daddy?"

I took one look at my little girl and wondered how I should start. I figured the beginning was the only way. "Well honey I had not wanted to say anything before but I haven't been feeling very well lately so I recently went to see the doctor."

"What do you mean? What's wrong?" she said in the same matter of fact manner of her mother.

I figured she needed me to be just as direct so I ploughed right in with my answer "Well he took some tests and discovered that I have prostrate cancer."

"Cancer?"

She was frightened by the word. I could detect that response immediately so I tried to minimize the fear by adding "That's right, but don't worry he says it is treatable and I'll probably be okay." I immediately regretted using the word "probably" instead of just telling her I would be okay. It was a subtle distinction but Annie was a master of subtly. I knew we had to tell her about my illness but I didn't want to overburden her with worry.

Marie stepped in to save the day by saying "It's not as bad as it sounds Annie. We were told that cancer treatment has come a long way and everything we have read so far confirms that message." She smiled at her daughter before adding "Your Dad is strong so I know things will work out."

Although grateful for my wife's assessment I could tell by looking at my daughter's face that she still wasn't convinced.

"Tell me more" she said. "How did this happen?"

"I guess it's just one of those things" then added It's probably just genetics."

"Genetics! Well that doesn't make me feel any better" she exclaimed.

I didn't want to respond in a cross manner or react with a tone of annoyance; after all we had been talking about this for a few days; she was hearing it for the first time so I spoke to her as calmly as I could. "I'm not a doctor Annie so I really can't give you a better answer. I wish I could but I just haven't got one." A wave of sadness came over me knowing that my daughter was confused and worried, not to mention angry about this news; and there was nothing I could do about it. Emotions were hard to control; especially someone else's.

Marie spoke once again by adding her own opinion "Your father and I never really asked the doctor how he got cancer because that really doesn't matter now. What matters is that he has it and we have to help him beat it. Can you do that?"

Annie looked at her mother and said the only thing she thought she could "Of course I can. You know you can count on me. I just need to know more, that's all."

"I understand that" I said. "And we'll tell you everything we can but you may have to do some of the research about cancer yourself if you want to know more because your mother will be busy taking me to my treatments."

"What kind of treatments?" she asked.

I suddenly laughed when I realized that I didn't know myself.

Both women looked at me puzzled at my laughter then Annie asked me "What's so funny?"

"I was so surprised at the news myself that I forgot to ask what treatments I was signed up for. All I know is that I'm supposed to start them next week. Boy I sure must trust that doctor. I hope he knows what he's doing because apparently I don't" chuckling again at my own realization.

The girls looked at me for a moment like I had fallen off the balance beam of sanity until Marie saw the irony of knowing so much and yet so little that she too began to chuckle. Annie smiled at me while speaking to me in a patronizing manner "Geez Dad if you don't even know what is going to happen then maybe you better make sure Mom or I hold your hand when you get to the *big* hospital. You may get lost."

"Ha-Ha" I scoffed at her joke. I was relieved that things were now in the open and our family was beginning to come together for the fight.

We spent most of the afternoon answering questions and Annie seemed to be handling the news even better than I was. Always the determined researcher she turned on our computer to find out more about prostrate cancer. Some of the information she discovered was different than what we had read and actually quite interesting; if I didn't have cancer myself I may have even found the learning experience intriguing. I was suddenly grateful that my college student daughter was good at researching topics. Her work that afternoon made some of what to expect clearer for all of us. It might even have made it less scary.

I began asking Annie some questions about the information she was finding on the internet. Her answers were mostly a regurgitation of what she was reading so we tried to analyze the information the best we could. It wasn't easy since none of us knew any more than what we were reading. I spent some of the time just looking over her shoulder reading directly from the websites she had discovered. Some of the information was redundant and there was no purpose in printing the article.

When I was finished I asked Marie if she had anything to add. She provided Annie with a few more details that I had forgotten. She also asked some of her own questions about the articles we were reading and offered the kind of support I had come to expect from her. Annie and Marie had a close relationship; naturally different from the one my daughter and I shared, so when Marie asked questions or spoke of potential concerns Annie listened. The same was true when Annie spoke. As I watched the two of them work together that afternoon I found myself thinking, with them in my corner how could I lose?

The three of us finally ran out of steam late in the afternoon. It was then that Annie looked at both of us with an appearance of love in her eyes. Without saying a word, she came over to my chair and sat down on my lap. She gave me a hug, and as I choked back my emotion, she looked directly into my eyes and said, "So what do we do now, Daddy?"

CHAPTER 19

Annie left late in the day to go back to her dorm and prepare for the next day's classes. As I sat alone in my chair the thought of her question puzzled me. What *was* I suppose to do now? I knew from Dr. Taylor's instructions that I would be scheduled in the next two weeks for some more tests, then preparation for treatment. Past that, I had no idea.

Her question gave me more pauses for reflection. As though I needed more to think about! I began to think about how many people that would soon be a part of my life: doctors, nurses, friends, family and others I was sure to meet as things moved along. They would become part of my everyday fight against this disease and if cancer was the enemy then these people would be my soldiers. I smiled when it occurred to me to call this group of people "Team Henry." They would be a part of my journey, and although I had no way yet of knowing how far I would travel this road and it was clear that the fight had just begun I wanted to think we would win the battle. With a great team would come a great victory; I had to believe that.

What do I do now? My daughter had asked such a simple question with such a complex answer. I could tell her what I *wanted* to do. I wanted to run away, but that wasn't going to help anything. Staying to fight was all I could do for now. That part was clear to me. To do that I would need to be a team player myself. I would have to listen to others; put my trust in people I did not know and follow instructions not always clear to me.

From what I had understood from the reading material there would be many times when I would feel lonely or depressed and to expect days when I would need other people's support. One article stated that a patient's support system combined with the necessary medical treatments could play a large factor in total recovery for a cancer patient. There was so much to digest and I was just learning the rules of the game; I could only hope that I would be a fast learner. What do I do now? *What in the hell do I do now?*

I brought my boss up to speed on Monday about what was happening and told him about the upcoming appointments. He passed on the obligatory apologies and support such as "I'm really sorry to hear that. You know I'll help you all I can." I appreciated the words but I could see by the veiled look of what appeared to be fear on his face that he was uncomfortable in speaking them.

His reaction stirred a memory of an article I had read on the weekend. I couldn't remember all that it said but the basics of the information was to expect that many people did not understand cancer and were scared to speak of it. Now I began to believe it was true; I was watching him fidget and he appeared to be lost for words. I knew it was unfair to keep him on the spot so I ended the conversation with a simple reply "Thanks. I would also appreciate it if we just kept this on a need to know basis for now if that's okay?"

"Of course; just tell me what you need."

"I'll let you know once I find out more information. I'm sure the hospital and doctors will tell me what to expect. I'll pass on any information I get when I get it. I can't be sure but I would think I will probably need to take some time off."

"Sure, sure; you just let me know how long and I'll arrange it with human resources."

One more thank you and I left his office feeling although the interaction had become a bit awkward maybe my boss had joined "Team Henry." More as a draft selection rather than volunteer but hey every bit helped.

The next thing I did was to include a couple of co-workers I knew I could trust with my news. I left the rest of the office staff in the dark. Experience had taught me that gossip would be more important to them than the truth ever could be, so let them guess. Besides so far they had no idea anything was wrong.

I told my friends I wanted to talk to them and asked both of them to go to a coffee shop with me at lunchtime. I even said I would pay.

"Must be important if you're offering to pay!" joked one of them.

"Important enough" I replied.

I saw them take a quick glance at each other understanding that I wasn't joking and wondering what could be that important. The banter ended there.

I wanted to tell both of them at the same time so I wouldn't have to repeat the story. The coffee shop was close by but the uncomfortable silence seemed to make the walk longer. I ordered the coffees; we had spent enough years working together for me to know how they liked their coffee; and took them back to the table where they sat waiting for me.

I took a moment to gather my thoughts; took a sip of my coffee and began to speak.

"I wanted to tell you guys something because I've worked with you a long time. I wish I didn't have anything to say but if I don't tell someone besides my family I think I'll go mad."

"What is it?"

I didn't want to waste words so I dived in. "I recently found out that I have cancer."

"Cancer?" one of them asked; "Are you sure?"

"I wish I could say no but unfortunately I can't. It's real."

I noticed that both of my friends had not touched their coffee then one of them spoke by saying "I don't know what to say?" I always appreciated his direct honesty.

"Me either" said the other one; pausing before asking "Is it treatable?"

"Actually yes it is; it's prostate cancer and the doctor says it's very treatable."

"That's good news."

"I guess so" I answered. "Better than no treatment at all I suppose."

Another awkward moment came between us. Finally I broke the silence "You guys better drink your coffee. You won't be able to get me to buy a second cup!" I laughed.

They joined me with laughter and all I could hear was a "That's for sure" and see heads nodding in agreement.

I spent the next few minutes answering questions and listening to supportive conversation from my friends.

"There is something I want to ask both of you to do for me though" I said interrupting the moment.

"Sure; of course."

"You know you can count on us. What is it?"

"Actually what I want you to do is nothing."

I could tell by the puzzled look on their faces that it was unclear to them what I meant. It wasn't completely clear to me either but I thought I needed to try to explain.

"You see the doctor said I should let people close to me know what's going on because they will see changes in my body and even my mood because of the cure as much as the disease. I told the boss because he had to know I would be taking time off; but you guys are the only two at work that I feel comfortable telling." I sensed they felt good about the trust I was putting in them. "But I don't want anyone else to know what's happening so can we keep this between the three of us?"

"Of course Robert; you can count on us."

"I know that's why I wanted to tell you guys."

"And you know you can talk to us whenever you want to . . . or need to."

"Thanks; I appreciate that." I had said what I wanted to say and everything was becoming more serious than one cup of coffee so I decided that it was time to get back to the world. I drank the last of my coffee and rose to leave. "Well time to go. You know the office will go to hell without us there."

"Two of us anyways" my friend joked. I don't think it occurred to them that depending on what happened his statement could be a self-prophesy.

The walk back to the office was just as quiet as it had been going to the coffee shop; but it didn't feel like an awkward silence. Information had helped my friends understand what was happening and helped me feel better about letting them know. It was an important step.

The world stops for no one and the winter was going by fast. My friends had delivered on their promise. They had been there when I needed them and had not spoken to anyone else at work about my illness. Things in the office had remained normal. I think some of the other workers wondered why I was missing so much time but my boss stayed as true to his word as my friends. If anyone was going to discover what was happening it wasn't going to be those three that would tell them.

I was grateful for their loyalty and compassion for my situation. There were enough things on my plate I didn't need to add office politics to the picture. At least that was the way I saw it. It was my life and I figured I had the right to keep things to myself.

Time as they say; marches on whether we are healthy or sick so it wasn't long before we were preparing for the holidays. The Christmas season was always a special time in our home but my cancer made this holiday different. Although it had not been an unhappy time; there was a somber feeling that had not been there in past years.

Others in my family had been made aware of my cancer fight and as much as everyone wanted to be festive it was obvious that my medical status was in my family's thoughts even as we tried to enjoy the visiting. It was a hard feeling to shake. Sometimes it was just a cautious look my way when someone told a bad joke or times when I was feeling overprotected. I didn't say anything out loud but there were a few moments when I almost screamed "I'm fine; leave me alone! I'm not dead yet!"

I think everyone meant well and I could appreciate the sentiment but I didn't want to feel helpless and I resisted the support. I didn't want to hurt anyone's feelings so rather than verbalize my frustration I would just make some excuse to go for a walk or just into another room. I don't know if I was fooling anyone but it made it easier for me.

Sometimes rather than leave I attempted to lighten the mood. Sometimes it worked, sometimes it didn't. My jokes weren't always well received. I could tell that Marie and Annie couldn't see what was funny but from time to time I could feel the weight of my problem pushing down on me and I was determined not to let it beat me so I reminded myself to continue on a positive path and never give up. Humor was one of the tools I tried to use to stay optimistic. It was easy to think that way most days, but there were other times, especially late at night, when I wasn't completely sure.

The radiation treatments had been going on for several weeks. It seemed like a lifetime. Everything was going just as Dr. Taylor had said they would. Radiation was no fun, but Marie and Annie had been great. They were truly remarkable women and all three of us had met several other nice people throughout the process. I had been poked, checked, and examined in ways I hoped I would never experience again. Cancer may not be as scary as it had been thirty years ago, but it was sure as hell just as uncomfortable now as ever.

Fortunately, the nice people I encountered made things easier for me. Some were compassionate people with kindness and patience, which I needed now more than ever. I learned that many medical people possessed compassion that went well beyond their job. I spent a lot of my time waiting, so I watched the hospital workers during those times as well as when I went through my treatment sessions. I soon learned how to separate the people who saw this as a job from those whose work meant more to them. It was the small things: the way they spoke to elderly people, treating them with dignity and respect, or the way they would take a moment from their day to say hello and ask how I was doing. These people did so many things to make having a disease like cancer easier to deal with. I was grateful for them.

There had been one oddity in my journey that still surprised me. It soon became apparent how uncomfortable many of my friends were when I was around them. They would avoid any conversation of any kind about my illness. I would get the occasional obligatory comment, meant to provide support, but nobody would actually sit down with me and let me pour my heart out. Whenever I tried, they would find a way to make a quick if not graceful exit. Their responses amazed me. I tried to think back to a time when I spoke with a friend about any major illness. I couldn't think of one, so maybe it wasn't so unusual.

When my wife was at work, Annie at school and my friends obviously uncomfortable about talking with me about cancer exercise became a refuge for my thoughts. It gave me a chance to think about things and yes maybe even time to speak to God. He always listened.

The doctor had suggested that it was important to use light exercise as part of the recovery program. My form of exercise was quite simple: walking. I would take at least one hour each day to go for a stroll around the neighborhood or walking paths that circled the subdivision. It became a daily routine that I learned to enjoy, and it made me more conscious of the beauty of life. Waves of nostalgia would come over me during these walks, but more importantly so would thoughts of hope. The walks became just as important as the support of my loved ones and medical staff.

It was on one of these walks that I approached old man Johnson's house. Spring had not arrived, and the air was cold. I made a decision to take a break from my walk to see if Mr. Johnson was home.

It had been some time since I had spoken to him, well before my diagnosis, so I thought it would be a good opportunity to say hello. I wasn't sure what I would talk to him about, but the other visits were friendly so I was sure this one would be as well.

Before I knocked on his door I remembered Andy's fortress. I looked in the direction of the tree where it stood and was astonished by what I saw. It was as though I were seeing it for the first time. It wasn't that the leaves were gone from the tree or that snow sat on the roof—in fact, nothing much had changed at all—but there was something different; something that gave me a feeling that this fortress was once again important.

I wondered what Andy and his friend George thought about while they played in their fortress. Were they acting out imaginary adventures? Did they slay the dragons Andy had talked about or save the princess? Did they share secrets that only they would ever know? Thinking back to my own childhood, I decided that they did all those things and more. I felt happy for them, and for the briefest moment my problem seemed to fade away.

Mr. Johnson came immediately to the door after hearing me knock. It was as though he were expecting me.

"Well, hello stranger," he said as he opened the door and shook my hand. "It's great to see you again. I thought you had gone away or something."

How close to the truth you are, I thought. "Great to see you too," I replied.

"Well, come on in. Have a cup of coffee."

I accepted his invitation and entered his front room. Not much had changed here either. Same old chair, same old dog, same old man. Still, Johnson seemed different. There was a spark in his eye that wasn't there before. I didn't know if I would find out why, but it was comforting to see it.

"So, how have you been?" Johnson asked as he placed a cup of coffee and cream in front of me. Pointing at the sugar on the table he added, "Just help your self."

"Not bad," I lied as I stirred cream in my coffee. He obviously forgot that I didn't use sugar.

Johnson gave me a sideways look as though he knew something was up but decided to leave it alone.

"That's good. What have you been up to?"

"The usual," I said. "Work keeps me busy. Always something to do at home and Marie helps me find something if things are too slow."

He laughed. "I remember those days. My wife always helped me stay busy—even when I didn't want to. I think she sat up nights making to-do lists just for me. Could never prove it, but I had suspicions."

I returned his laugh. After more small talk and another two cups of coffee, he suddenly looked at me and said, "I heard some news about you awhile ago."

"Really?"

"Yeah, I heard you had cancer."

I held my cup halfway to my mouth. All I could think was, *How in the hell would he know about that?* Did he have some kind of secret information source I didn't know about?

Taking a sip of coffee, I pondered my answer. He had been direct, so I decided to be just as direct. I set my cup down looked across the table and said, "That's right. How did you know?"

"That's not important" he said dismissing my question. "I still remember what it was like when my wife had cancer. No one to talk to made it harder to deal with."

"You're wife died of cancer?"

"Yes."

"What kind?"

"Does it matter?"

"No I guess not" I said. "You couldn't get people to talk to you either?"

"No."

"Why not?" I questioned amazed that his comments hit home so quickly.

"Well came to the conclusion that most people are scared and it makes them feel uncomfortable to talk to someone else about a disease they don't understand. Everyone probably knows someone who has had cancer or someone who knows someone who has had it and even though it is supposedly one of the leading causes of death people try to ignore the truth and avoid the topic." Then he continued. "I have found that most of us think we are invincible until we're not. That's the time when we find out what we can really handle right?"

"You sound quite profound" I said with a small grin on my face.

"You'd be surprised how enlightened a person gets when they are faced with something like cancer."

I thought for a moment about what he was saying then answered with a simple "I guess that's true."

"I don't think anyone is trying to be rude but after all who likes to talk about death? Could you talk much about cancer or death before you got sick?"

"No I suppose I didn't." I tried to remember if there were any times that I had confided in a friend that death scared me. Or that I didn't know what I would do if my wife or daughter died before me. I continued by saying "You know you're right. I was once invincible but I've sure lost that title."

He laughed and said "Buddy we were all invincible . . . . when we were young. I've lost that title as well. Now I just feel like the king of old, fat and tired!"

I joined him in laughter at his comments and couldn't keep from telling him "You may be the king but I think I'm the prince waiting for your throne. My wife would probably agree!"

"You'll make a great king someday."

"Thanks a lot" I said grinning at him.

I was finding it easy and comforting to talk with old man Johnson. His story was different than mine because he watched someone with cancer die instead of enduring it himself but I could tell from the conversation he could understand some of what I was going through. It was nice to know I wasn't alone.

I wanted to find out more so I asked "If no one wanted to talk to you then what did you do? How did you not feel alone?"

"Well I read a lot of information, probably like you have, so that I had a better idea of what I was in for. I spoke with some people at the hospital, counselors who mostly just listened. I think that was the best thing they could have done for me."

"Why do you say that?"

"When I was able to tell someone how I felt and how hard it was to watch my wife suffer with no power to do anything about it I felt less alone. They reminded me that the best I could do for my wife was to continue to be there, let her know she wasn't alone. One of the people I met at the hospital even told me that it was important to forgive myself."

"Forgive yourself? What do you mean?"

"I was her husband. I should have protected her and I didn't. At least that was what I thought. Then this woman at the hospital said something to me I'll never forget."

"What?"

"She looked me square in the eye and I heard her say. Arrogant son of a bitch aren't you?"

I didn't know what else to ask him so all I could say was "what did you tell her?"

"At first I was quite pissed off. I thought what in the hell do you know about me? How could you know what I was like? I even thought about walking out but I didn't." He shifted in his chair and leaned forward. "Instead I calmed down and replied with a simple "Excuse me?""

I waited for him to continue, wondering what she could possibly add to a comment such as that one.

"The woman ignored my cold stare and without turning away she quietly began to speak. A man your age Mr. Johnson must have figured out by now that you aren't God. Only God would have the power to protect someone from disease or death. There was no smile on her face so I could tell she wasn't trying to be funny."

"Then what?"

"Well at first I thought I had some religious nut sitting in front of me. Maybe I just didn't want to believe what she was saying. I thought I could put her in her place with her own words so speaking in a cold tone I said fine then why isn't your God saving my wife? Her next question floored me"

He had me hooked now; it was as if the room had become quiet and the only thing that mattered to me was his next words. "What was it?"

"She asked me what makes you think he isn't?"

I knew he could tell by the look on my face that I was puzzled because he answered my questioning eyes with a simple "Yeah I didn't understand it either."

I waited for a moment not wanting to speak because I was positive he had more to tell.

"Since I didn't understand what she meant all I could do was ask her to explain what she was talking about. She said she knew my wife was sick and would probably die soon but was it better to live on earth suffering or join God in heaven. Her next question was you do believe in heaven don't you Mr. Johnson?" He paused again and took a sip of coffee. "Well by now I felt I wasn't dealing with some ordinary counselor so I told her of course I do. My answer led to her last question then if heaven exists and God is the only one that can welcome her in then don't you think he might be a little more powerful than you?"

I still didn't completely understand so I asked Johnson what that meant.

"We talked some more. I asked her a lot of questions and what the woman was trying to tell me was that God did not make my wife sick and neither had I. It wasn't in my power to give someone cancer and it wasn't in my power to take it away so stop trying to do something I couldn't. The best I could do was to be there to offer supportive comfort. It was just a part of life and if I spent less time feeling angry or pity for myself I would be more useful to do the job I was meant to do, love my wife. God would take care of the rest."

"Did you believe that?" I asked.

"Honestly at first I didn't know what to think. It was so much easier thinking I was invincible and could change the outcome of things. Of course the more I thought about her words the more sense it made to me. I even began to think maybe she wasn't a religious nut."

Before I could change my mind I said to him "I think her technique was a bit unorthodox for a hospital counselor. Sounds like you should have been in a church."

"What makes you think I wasn't?" he said.

"Well your story . . . ."

"I said one of the people I met in the hospital. I didn't say she was a counselor."

"You made it sound like it was one of the counselors" I said defensively.

"Kind of easy to imagine things that aren't necessarily true isn't it? Do you think maybe some of your friends make big issues out of small ones?

"Yeah you're probably right" I conceded.

"You see cancer scares most people and death is only something they deal with when they have to. Most friends don't want to imagine someone leaving there life and many avoid the whole issue so they don't have to face the possibility. Make sense?"

I gave him a long look then said "When did you get so wise?"

He laughed then added "After that woman talked to me in the hospital."

"Who was she anyway a pastor or something?"

"No she was someone I met in the hospital chapel. Her husband was sick and dying and she was in the chapel for quiet prayer. I don't know how she knew about my wife but she did and her directness was the kick in the pants I needed. I'm not much of a religious person but I do believe there was a reason I wandered into that place that day. So when no-one else talked to me or I began to feel invincible again I remembered that day, that conversation and it humbles me. Still does. Then I ask God what I should do. He always talks to me."

I contemplated his story then listened while he added "You never know what you have until you lose it. It's an old saying but a true one. So enjoy it while you have it."

I was a bit floored by his whole story. I never took him for such an enlightened soul, but his statement hit home. "I can tell you that I have gained a new respect for what I have in my life, and if having cancer did one good thing it was to teach me that a day wasted is a day lost." I looked at him and continued "I think I forgot that ... or maybe never realized it. I am discovering that people and time were the real gifts in life, not money, not things, and certainly not the petty ideas so many people held on to in order to protect themselves from the world. Seems like such a simple idea when a person has to think about dying."

"Sadly most of us need that kind of possibility to wake us up. To make us understand that what we own is not as valuable as what we have to lose; ourselves." He raised his head to look me in the eyes and said "Maybe that's why people aren't comfortable talking to you. They can't understand something they can't see and it scares them. What do you think?"

"I think you have given me another way to look at things. Maybe *you* should be a counselor."

He laughed and said to me "what makes you think I'm not?"

I had no response so I simply joined him in laughter.

The old man and I continued to talk. He made me think that maybe it was okay to be scared. It was okay to know how serious the disease was, as long as I remembered how beatable it was. It was okay to let my guard down from time to time, especially around my family, so they would know how I felt. That kind of knowledge, he said, would make it easier for them to be supportive.

When I asked him what I should do about my experiences with my friends and how they seemed so uncomfortable around me his response was a bit surprising, "Forgive them" he said. "They are more scared than you are."

How could that be possible, I thought? *I* was the one with cancer.

I think he sensed I had a question because before I could ask him to explain, he continued by saying, "You have the advantage. For the most part, you know what you are up against. Cancer was real for me. It was real for my family, because they lived with me, and it was real for the medical world, because they saw it all the time. Friends who never had those experiences could never understand what I was going through. For many people, it was the fear that it could happen to them too. Looking at me only reminded people that cancer could be in the next room. No one wanted that, and avoiding that reality was easier than accepting it."

The more I listened to what he was saying the less heavy my load felt. It was the first time since my diagnosis that someone close to me understood so much of what I was going through. I was grateful for the time he spent sharing his experiences with me.

The afternoon had slipped away. It was almost dark, and Marie would be getting home soon. I thought I had better get on my way, so I gulped down the last of my coffee and picked up my coat, preparing to leave.

"Geez I didn't realize it had gotten so late. I better get home before my wife does. Thanks for the coffee and especially for the conversation. It really helped."

"No problem but before you leave, I have something for you," he said.

He opened a drawer in a cabinet and pulled something out. Walking towards me, he said, "This isn't much. It was my wife's. Something tells me she would want you to have it."

He then handed me a small, simple cross. I was dumbfounded. How could I accept the cross of this man's dead wife? It was obviously something that meant a lot to him, since he had kept it for so long.

"I can't take this," I found myself saying.

"How can you not?"

"Wouldn't you want to give it to one of your children?"

"They already have lots of things, including special items their mother left them. They don't need more. Besides, there is something special about that cross," he said.

What could be more special than the gift itself? I thought.

"That cross has been passed from cancer patient to cancer patient for fifty years. It was given to my wife by another patient when she got sick, and now I'm giving it to you. It represents faith, hope, belief, and strength. It lets us know that some things are not under our control. We are only given what we can handle, and I think you can handle this. So please accept it."

"I don't know what to say," I muttered. "Thank you."

"You're welcome. Now go home to your wife. I don't want either of us to get into trouble," he said with a wink and chuckle. "We'll see each other again."

I reached out to shake his hand. The old man took my arm then gave me a hug. I wasn't expecting it, and I was embarrassed. I wasn't used to someone showing me this kind of friendship. Then again maybe deep down this was the kind of support I was looking for. In the end the reason didn't matter. I just think the afternoon had become as important to him as it had been to me.

Both of us had shared old wounds and offered support to each other in the clumsy way men do. It never occurred to me that this man could know so much of what I was going through, that he could be so sensitive and be able to express it. Talking about his wife might have reminded him of the past and all the good moments, along with the bad. The visit helped both of us immensely. Not bad for an afternoon walk. Still I never would have expected such a response from such an odd looking man. I guess I had underestimated him.

Stepping through the door, I took one last look towards the fortress, put the gift in my pocket, and began the short trip home. For the first time since the word cancer had invaded my life, I felt healthy, felt invincible again, in a more educated manner. I understood that friends come to us in all sorts of ways. Finally, I realized that I had just left an important friend who had come into my life for a reason I could now understand. I needed him. Maybe God did answer silent prayers after all.

CHAPTER 20

Springtime had always been my favorite time of the year, and this spring would be even more special to me because I was getting healthier. It looked like I was beating cancer and I was feeling stronger everyday. It was a cliché but the flowers definitely smelled fresher.

The support I had received from my family was astonishing. Marie and Annie had been with me every step of the way, even during the times when I didn't want them to be with me, because it took them away from the things they needed to do. Any protests I made were ignored. The two most important ladies in my life were making me the most important man in theirs. I could not have loved them more for what they did for me.

I always believed that I had a small but strong family. I just never knew how strong until my fight with cancer. Quit was not a word any of us would speak, and cancer was a word to defeat. The positive attitude all three of us demonstrated carried me through some hard moments. Sure, there had been some emotional times as well—some tears, frustration, and anger at the world. Who wouldn't expect those things? It was clear from the beginning, however, that the glass was half full. We were determined to keep filling it up.

Mr. Johnson and I had begun to visit regularly, sometimes at my house so I could offer him the same hospitality he had offered me. Marie had met him by now, and although her first impressions were mixed, I assured her that he was a good person. The more she got to know him, the more she saw what I saw. She could see the positive support his friendship gave me, so that was good enough for her. Anything else just didn't matter.

Most of the time, however, I visited him in his home. I suppose it gave me a reason to go out and him a reason to visit.

I had even begun to spend more hours back at work. I had been right; gossip had spread rampant through the office. I was sitting at my desk one day when my friend/co-worker came up and sat down.

"Want to hear something funny?"

I could always use a good laugh so I offered a simple "Sure, why not?"

"I just heard a good story about why you were gone from work so much."

"Go on" I said. "You have my full attention."

"Well word is that you had drunk a glass of tequila with a worm in the bottom while visiting Mexico. The best part of the story is that this worm had been eating you up from the inside and that was why you missed work and lost weight."

The lost weight was obvious but I laughed at the explanation. "Wow that is a good story. Especially since I've never been to Mexico and hate Tequila! Where do people get this stuff?"

"Haven't a clue" he said joining me in my laughter.

"Who told you this?" I questioned.

"Well Betty on the second floor told me, but I think the story was being told to me after several times in the telling. You know what she can be like."

Since I agreed with his statement I continued by asking "Is there more to the story?"

"Not much really. Speculation is that you were in Mexico with a strange woman and came back early because you got sick. Now that part no one will believe."

"Why?"

"Because a guy like you was lucky enough to fool one woman into marrying him, there is no way you could trick another one into a date!"

I wanted to reply to his smart aleck statement but his laughter gave me no opportunity to respond. Instead I joined him in laughter. When we were done all I could add was "I only wish that wasn't true. Of course you're single right now aren't you?"

He had proven to be a good friend and the twinkle in my eyes told him I was teasing so he knew I had him and offered a lame answer "Yeah, well you got me there." He tried to take one last stab at shooting back by saying, "Still I would have a better chance in Mexico than you would?"

"You mean swallowing a worm?"

Having no quick answer to that statement he shrugged his shoulders conceding that he wasn't going to win this battle of words; still though it was a funny story.

"So many stories so little time" I offered as an ending to the conversation.

"Isn't that the truth?" my friend added. "Well see you later."

"You bet. Thanks for the update."

"Anytime, I'll let you know if I hear more. I can't believe anything will beat that one though."

I nodded in agreement and gave one final chuckle as he walked away.

When I told Marie the story later that night all she could do was laugh. The only thing she had to say to me was "There may be a time or two when I would call you a worm, but never think you would swallow one. Besides that you can have your phantom woman call me. I'll fill her in on what kind of fish a worm really catches. She'll probably just throw you back!"

"Ha-Ha" I said. "Real funny."

"I thought so" she shot back obviously proud of herself.

Laughter was becoming good for us and an important part of our day. It eased the tension and probably brought us closer together. Humor was still proving to be our friend.

There were times though when we had to simply ignore the gossip. It wasn't always funny and served no good purpose, Gossip never served any real purpose anyways and people often liked to tell stories rather than know the truth. Maybe that's what made it fun for the person providing the gossip. I didn't know and didn't care. This story however had been so ridiculous I just had to tell my wife about it. I even told Johnson about the story in it's entirety including Marie's feedback. I wasn't sure he was going to stop laughing.

My visits with my fortress friend were always warmly received and the subject matter during these visits with the old man varied greatly. Some days we talked about sports, some days were for politics, and some days were for cancer. A couple of times we hardly talked at all and just watched television. It was good to spend time with someone who I didn't have to explain things to or be guarded around. I think it took some pressure off Marie, for which I was grateful. He had become a good friend to have around. Maybe my company brought some life to his day as well. I hoped so anyways.

Something else that became a constant in my visits and offered a certain comfort was Johnson's dog. The dog was always there, no matter what we were doing, and I would often look at him wondering what it would be like to enjoy the world with such a simple, unhurried pace of life. I never did find out his name, and I always forgot to ask.

I did find it amusing to think that his life was simple because there was always someone there to feed him, care for him and take him for a bathroom walk. *Wait a minute*, I thought, *except for the bathroom stuff, isn't that pretty much what my last few months have been like?*

I commented one time about how my life had changed. I had told the old man what I thought of his dog's life and continued by saying, "You know my life seems to be moving at a simple pace too. Things don't bother me like they used to. I think I'm learning to enjoy life more."

"Funny how that happens isn't it?" he said.

"Well since you're so wise why don't you just tell me why?"

"Why do you think?" It was obvious he wanted me to find my own answer, but I wasn't ready to look that hard for it yet.

"Don't know" I said. "Maybe when I'm an old man like you I'll know the answer."

By now he and I had gotten to know each other well enough that he could tell I was joking so his answer to me was in a similar vein "Keep talking like that and you may never get a chance to become an old man! Even if you do you'll never be as smart as me."

I couldn't let him off the hook that easily so I shot back at him with a simple "Or as ugly I hope."

"You started out that way. How could it get any worse?"

I laughed because he seemed to always get the best of me. Maybe age did bring wisdom. "I surrender. I wave the white flag, you win!" I said.

He seemed satisfied with the victory, gave me a big smile and moved on to the next subject. I still didn't know exactly why I was enjoying life more, just grateful that I was.

As our conversations went on I learned more about Johnson each time we talked. He; of course learned more about me too. The distraction was good for me. It made my health problems only part of my life and not all of it.

I discovered that he had come from a rural background, much as I had. He had only finished grade ten before he left school to begin working in the construction field, and he made it clear that he was proud of his children for going so much further with their education. He credited his wife for that.

Throughout the time I listened to his stories I discovered sadness in the man. It was something he couldn't change but obviously it was something he wished he could. According to him his children had grown apart from him when he was younger mostly because of his time away working on various jobsites, and he admitted that he had not spent enough time with them when he was home. After the death of his wife, he had found it too difficult to let things go, and he became bitter. At first he pushed his children away rather than accept their help. As the bitterness was replaced with acceptance, he was able to make more of an effort in life. Fortunately, his children began to understand and were visiting him more often.

It sounded to me as if his children had grown up; they understood more about how he felt and now, most importantly, he had opened his heart to let them in. He said it had begun with small steps: a phone call, a short visit, a football game, anything that helped develop a string of communication. Common interests began to develop with his children, making it easier to share their time.

One time though when he was talking about his children he confided to me "It's true that my children do visit more often and I'm happy for that, but it's also obvious to me that there will always be a certain distance between us."

"What do you mean?" I questioned.

"I don't really know. Maybe there is still a small amount of resentment towards me, or maybe they just don't feel the closeness that I think they had with their mother."

"I don't think that's uncommon" I offered.

"Maybe" he said. "I hope that's the only reason."

"Well why don't you ask them?"

"Simple. I'm scared."

"Scared? Of what?"

"Of pushing them away again, I think I just want to enjoy their visits and not jeopardize what I have."

I found much of what he was saying to make sense, but was surprised at his unwillingness to be honest and straight forward with his kids. He always seemed to have no problem being that way with other people, including me. I decided to let it lie. Luckily he had more to add to the conversation that brought optimism to his life.

"One thing though that I am happy about is my grandchildren."

"Why's that?" I asked.

"It gives me a second chance to do better than I did with my kids. Sometimes it's easier to be a grandfather than it was a father. Less responsibility, more chance for fun."

I had heard that from many older people so it was easy to believe what he was saying. I wondered if would be the same for me whenever Annie had children. Of course I wanted her to get married first!

It was interesting to me that what appeared to have touched him the most was the reconnection with his grandchildren. As he said it had given him a chance to do a better job than the last time. He made it clear that he wasn't going to waste it.

I listened to what he had to say and all I could add was a simple "I think I can understand."

Like mine, his stories led me to think that his life had been a good one for the most part. His greatest loss was his wife, and when he spoke of her, I could tell that she had been an important person to him, someone he missed and someone who helped define the man he had become. Maybe I hadn't given Marie enough credit for the same accomplishment.

"I hope so" the old man said.

"Why?" This question seemed to be more and more on my lips each time I listened to what he had to say. I didn't mean for it to happen but in a way I think the man had become a bit of a mentor for me.

"I had preached to my family that it was up to each person to attract the things to our lives that we needed or wanted. We could also attract bad things. I believed that we were in charge of our own destinies—or at least I used to" he replied.

"You say you used to, don't you still believe it?"

"Yes of course. The difference is not so much the attraction of these things it's more what to do with them. That's the real accountability we hold. The less preaching I did the clearer it had become to me. I just want to pass that message onto my grandchildren."

"How do you plan to do that?" I asked him.

"By living my life rather than preaching to them how to live theirs; like I did my children. Maybe living it will be more of a lesson than preaching was."

"You seem to do a good job talking with me." I said. "I never feel like you're preaching."

"Thanks I appreciate that, but you're not one of my kids. A person can only be heard if someone wants to listen to him."

I paused for a moment surprised once again by his profound statements. The more I listened to the old man talk, the more my impressions of him changed. My own belief system was being challenged as well. I was beginning to think that maybe I wasn't so much in charge of my own destiny after all. Maybe I was just in charge of the gifts I was given.

As he talked something occurred to me that I hadn't thought of before. How could I have been so arrogant to believe I had the power to change the course of someone's life; even my own? The less I talked and the more I listened, I began to understand how large the universe was and how small I was in it. It seemed that the deeper I thought about things the easier it was to accept them. As a matter of fact the more I accepted things as they were the less I had to worry about them and the easier it was to live my life. My God I wasn't becoming profound as well was I? I chuckled to myself and thought Nah I'm a long way from being that smart.

The old man's insights were simple enough. He wasn't a spiritual scholar or anything like that. He was just an ordinary man, like me, doing the best he could. He had learned to accept, to adapt, and to move on, and I was learning those things by listening to him.

Cancer had made my life an open book for Johnson. I couldn't hide from him. He had seen it all before and could tell when I was feeling sad, when I was feeling happy, or when I was just feeling sorry for myself. He could also tell when I wasn't putting forth the proper effort. During those times he offered compassion but would not listen to any excuses. His favorite saying to me at those times was, "So suck it up!" His explanations and comments often proved to me that things weren't near as bad as I made them out to be. He kept me grounded.

"I guess no one is too old to learn something."

"Isn't that the truth!" he said with a certainty in his voice.

"You know that my illness, cancer; sure forces a person to stop and look at himself" I said. "But I think you already know that."

"Yes that's probably true and although I enjoy visiting with you Henry; (he still never used my first name) more than anything I want you to understand that no one person is alone in this world. We may think so but there are many people out there who can be a part of our joy or sadness if we let them. The trick is to find the ones who embrace life not shrink from it."

I felt as though I was hearing a message meant just for me. I still couldn't believe this un-educated, blue collar old man could spew forth such pearls of wisdom. "So when DID you become so smart?" I challenged him.

He looked at me with a wry smile and said "I was always smart, just not always smart enough to use it."

All the things going on in my life and it surprised me that it was his words that had forced me to re-evaluate the way I lived my life. This man, this stranger who had come into my life just when I needed him the most wouldn't let me hide from the truth, and so I learned to accept things I couldn't before. I had learned to set aside my anger and only fight the important battles. As cliché as it sounds, life seemed worth living again.

"One thing I can tell you is that cancer has given me a new appreciation for what I have, who I am, and what still lay before me."

"I'm not surprised" he said.

His demeanor made his statement appear quite true. "Even though I know I will beat this thing it still scared the hell out of me. Cancer made everything else seem less important."

"That's fine" he said. "Now though you have another challenge before you."

"What challenge?" I said to him with a puzzled look.

"Well we've spent much of our time over the last months talking about your illness and even though it is important to use this time to evaluate what is important to you I think it's time to put it behind you and move on. Frankly I'm getting tired of rehashing all of your feelings. Your family may be tired too."

I looked at the old man with a feeling of betrayal. I thought he understood the most because of his past history. He had certainly sounded supportive. What changed?

He continued. "Don't get me wrong Henry. I'll talk with you anytime about your experiences with cancer; it's just that I want you to start telling me what is next for you. What do you want to do? You've been given a second chance so now what?"

His words softened his message and gave me pause to think about his questions.

Johnson was a big part of awakening thoughts and messages in me never before considered. His manner was unapologetic, firm, and straightforward. It was as though he knew his own time would come soon enough, so he didn't want to waste it. I would have thought all older people looked at things that way, but it wasn't true. Thinking back, I remembered lots of people in my own life who were wasting the moments they had left. They were bitter and angry, and knowing what I now knew, it made me sad for them. This was just another moment where his direct challenge was forcing me not to drop too deeply in an analytical state of mind that would do nothing but cause me grief.

As much as I had experienced over the last few months, as much as I had learned and as much as I had shared, I was still in many ways self-absorbed. It wasn't that I only thought of myself, but I had definitely made myself priority number one. Other people had enabled me in that process. Cancer makes it easy for a person to wonder, *Why me?* An illness like this makes it easy for people close to you to want to do things for you and hard for you not to let them.

I gave his question some thought before replying "I don't really know. I enjoy our conversations as well but it never occurred to me what I want to do next. So far it just seemed like I wanted to take it day by day."

"That's a good start" Johnson nodded "But now the next stage of healing needs to begin. It is part of the natural progression. My wife never got a chance to do that. You do."

The sudden change in our conversation had frankly put me back on my heels. At the very least I was confused and at the most I was angry. I knew he meant well and I knew he was right; I just wasn't sure I was ready. He was once again pushing the envelope. Times like this I felt that maybe I was standing on quick sand rather than a wonderful beach.

"Okay. I hear you" was the best I could offer.

"I hope so. I wouldn't want to think I wasted all this time talking to you just to have my "wisdom" lost on a numb skull." He winked at me as he spoke the words and I knew he was mocking me about his wisdom. I smiled back appreciative of the kindness in his eyes. It took the sting out of his words and made the message easier to listen to.

I took a moment to reflect on what this old man had given me over the time I had known him. He probably understood me and how I felt about the recent events in my life more than anyone else I knew; even my family. Johnson acknowledged all of my emotions in one way or another but reminded me that there comes a time when I would need to open my heart to pass on the same compassion to someone else. The world was not just about me. It was full of people who needed others. I was soon to find out how true that was.

I remember the day when Johnson came to my door with his news. It was another warm spring day. I had spoken with Dr. Taylor just two days before, and he had informed me that my cancer treatments seemed to have worked. I was in remission. Relief came over me in a wave of emotion as I sat in his office. He cautioned me that I would have to continue to come in for regular checkups to monitor the results. He assured me that in most cases, at this stage the cancer would not come back, but nothing was ever certain. I understood what he was saying, but even his cautionary disclaimer wouldn't eliminate the emotions I felt.

Marie had wanted to come with me for support but I wouldn't let her. This was something I had wanted to face alone but once I received the news I couldn't wait to get home to tell Marie. This was good news and she deserved to hear it.

When I passed on the doctor's message Marie and Annie were just as ecstatic with the news as I had been. Tears came to Marie's eyes as she hugged me and thanked God for the recovery. I was once more reminded how hard this had been on her. It was my body that fought the battles, but she had fought the war. I couldn't think of anyone else I would have wanted by my side.

Marie said "I think this news requires a special night out." I agreed, so we made reservations at our favorite restaurant and treated ourselves to a great meal with wonderful companions— each other.

So two days had passed since the wonderful news and my family was still on an emotional high. Then my doorbell rang. I was the only one home, so I answered it myself. I hadn't spoken to Johnson for about a week so when I saw who it was I grinned and said, "Come on in. I've got great news."

"No, I can't," he said somberly. "I have some bad news."

I was momentarily annoyed that he could think his news was more important than mine. Of course, he didn't know about my news yet, so how could he judge? It was obvious something important was on his mind, so I questioned him, "What is it?"

"Andy Bell's dad is dead."

It hit me like a rock. His father was dead? How, why, who? So many questions flashed through my mind that I didn't know what to ask first.

"What?"

"He was killed in a drunk-driving incident late last night. He was coming home from a bar, three sheets to the wind, and apparently crossed a meridian down on Fourth Street, hitting another car on the other side of the road. He was pronounced dead on the scene, and the teenage girl driving the other vehicle died early this morning in hospital. Two families destroyed by one man."

I didn't know how he had learned all this information so quickly, but that seemed unimportant. His matter of fact way of speaking to me made it sound like a news report on the six o'clock news. Saying it any other way wouldn't have made a difference.

"I knew his dad was a drinker. I saw him a couple of times when I picked Andy up. He always had a bottle in his hand. Plus, the way his wife spoke, I could tell something wasn't right. But to be that stupid . . ." My voice drifted off, but Johnson knew what I meant. "I wonder how Andy is doing. Have you seen him?" I asked.

"No. I imagine it might be more important for him to be with his family now. The funeral is on Monday and I'm planning on going. You want to come?"

"Yes, of course," I said. I was almost back to full hours at work, and even though I would feel guilty missing another day, this was too important to ignore. Andy needed our support.

"Okay. The funeral is one o'clock at the Guardian Funeral Home, about two miles from here. I'll pick you up Monday at noon."

"Okay, I'll be ready."

I closed the door as the old man walked down the pathway towards the street. I was stunned by his news. I then remembered I had not told him about my own news. Somehow my good news didn't seem as important—*I* wasn't that important. It was Andy and his family I was more worried about now. He would need the support of a friend, and I hoped I was capable of offering that help. For now, I closed the door and retreated into my thoughts.

CHAPTER 21

M r. Johnson picked me up on time Monday, just as I expected. I hadn't heard any more details about the accident, and Johnson didn't know anything else either. I wanted to go to Andy's house to pass on my condolences to his mother and see how Andy was doing, but for some reason I just couldn't do it.

When we arrived at the funeral home, we found the parking lot almost full. Johnson was able to find an open spot, and after parking we quietly walked towards the door. It always seemed to me that young people—the obituary in the paper said he was thirty-three—drew a crowd to their funeral, possibly because there were more people their age still alive to mourn. Old people had more time on their hands to attend funerals; they just had fewer friends to come to their own. Sometimes I thought it was easier to die young, a martyr, than to grow old and be seen for the frail person we have become. However, in this case the man was no martyr, just a stupid person who left his family behind to suffer. I knew that was harsh, but it was the way I felt.

Johnson and I had agreed that since we wouldn't really know anyone, we would stay for the service and go to the gravesite but not attend the lunch they were offering later. I was comfortable with that. The service itself was like any other, simple, with some friends to say nice things. After what had happened I was surprised they could actually find anyone. I reminded myself that I was there for Andy, not to judge his father.

It soon became obvious the man had not been one of the churchgoers in our community. Everything was done at the funeral home, and there was no man of the cloth performing the service. I hoped he believed in God before he died, because his family would need that kind of faith. He could use it as well. When the service was over the funeral director made the gravesite and lunch announcements, and then we watched as the pallbearers moved the casket towards the door. I noted that it had been a closed casket service, probably because of the way he died.

It almost broke my heart to see little Andy and his mom follow the casket from the funeral home. I could tell he was doing his best to be brave. That was Andy, I thought. He was almost a year older than when I had first met him but still a young boy with an old man's soul. I pushed the thought to the back of my mind and moved from the funeral home with the rest of the mourners.

The cemetery was not much farther away, so it was a short drive. Johnson and I hadn't really spoken much. What was there to say? Everyone who was attending the gravesite service had moved from their vehicles to stand around the coffin. Mr. Johnson and I stood off to the side, out of the way.

I noticed a small boy standing only a few feet away from Andy and his younger sister. He appeared a couple of years older than Andy and was dressed in his Sunday best. Something seemed familiar about him, so I nudged Johnson to get his attention. When he turned towards me, I whispered, "Is that George standing over there?"

He looked in the direction I indicated, then turned back and whispered, "Yes."

I had not met George yet, mostly because of my treatment schedule, but I had occasionally seen him walking with Andy in the neighborhood. That's why he seemed so familiar to me, I guessed. I wanted to go over and introduce myself to the little boy, but I knew it wasn't the time or place.

Driving back to my house, Johnson and I spoke about the service and how Andy had handled the day. There really wasn't much to say and I sensed a couple of awkward moments. Even after all of my conversations with the old man about my own illness or possibility of death it was still difficult for me to talk about such things surrounding other people; I guess that was the feeling other people had around me; just like the old man had said. We both agreed that Andy's family had carried themselves well especially since it was an unforgiveable tragedy that could have been avoided.

It was the first time either of us had seen the little girl as well. I knew Andy had a sister from our conversations, and part of me was glad that she seemed to be so young that she would not understand the importance of the event. Growing up without her father was going to be tough on her. Then again, maybe she wouldn't miss what she didn't have. I could never know.

As I stepped from Johnson's truck, I invited him in for a cup of coffee or maybe even a drink. He thanked me but declined. I understood, because I wanted to be alone too. Death of any kind has a way of putting things into perspective. The most ironic part, I thought, was that no matter how much death ended things for someone, the world never stopped for anyone. People still had to go on with their day. They had to work, play, pay bills, and do whatever else their life routine included. My cancer scare had demonstrated what death could look like, giving me a better appreciation of what life could really be. If that was true, I hoped I wouldn't waste the knowledge.

For today though there really wasn't much that could be said. Conversation seemed pointless. I didn't know the family well enough to reminisce about the man or his life and my connection with Andy only served to make me feel sad for the boy. I decided that it would be simpler to keep my thoughts to myself; at least for today.

A few days later, I heard a knock at the door. My life had resumed its normal routine, and our house was filled with a renewed happiness due to my successful fight with cancer. I still had things to do, and my newfound wisdom from the past few months, even the last few days, did not prevent me from falling back into familiar patterns. That was how it was meant to be; just part of living. I had spent some time speaking with Marie about Andy and his Dad dying but since she didn't know the boy it was more just story telling than a conversation. It was difficult to not feel sadness for him but what could I do? With those things in mind, I was surprised to see who was at my door.

"Mrs. Bell."

"Hello, Mr. Henry. I'm sorry to bother you."

"No bother at all. Would you like to come in?"

"No, thank you, but I wanted to ask for your help."

"Certainly; what can I do for you?"

"It's about Andy. He hasn't been the same since his father . . . well, you know." I nodded my understanding.

"I've kept him home from school thinking maybe he needed the time to absorb everything that has happened. My father and I have done the best to talk with him, but he's still a little boy. My boy . . ." she said with emotion. "He's been gone all day, and I'm worried."

I admired this young woman standing before me, and I could only imagine what struggles she was going through during this time. It was hard to lose a spouse no matter what kind of person they had been, and I was positive that it would be even harder when you have small children to care for. She didn't have much time to herself to mourn, because her daily responsibilities would give her no time to shed her own tears. I felt compassion for her.

"I'll do whatever you need, Mrs. Bell. What would you like me to do?"

A look of relief came over her face. "Well, I'm sure I know where he is. I just don't feel right going there."

I knew immediately what she was talking about.

"You think he's in his fortress."

"Yes. I just don't feel it is right for me to go on to Mr. Johnson's property, because even though Andy spoke about him, I have never met the man. I would feel awkward speaking to him. I know you are friends. Would you be able to go?"

"Absolutely, I'll go immediately. I'm sure everything is fine so go back home. And try not to worry." That was a dumb thing to say. What mother wouldn't continue to worry? It was the only thing that had come to my mind.

"Oh thank you, Mr. Henry. That means a lot to me."

"No problem." Grabbing a light coat from the closet, I walked out, locking the door behind me. Mrs. Bell walked with me to the street, where we both turned in opposite directions to continue our steps. "He'll be home for supper" I added with a sense of false bravado.

When I came on to Johnson's land, I decided to stop at his house to see if he was home. I thought it might make things better if both of us went to Andy's fortress and talked with him; assuming he was there. Something told me he was.

When Johnson answered the door, I briefly filled him in on the details of Mrs. Bell's visit. I told him everything I knew to that point, which of course wasn't much.

"She's sure he's there?" he asked. "I didn't see him or his friend walk by for days."

"I don't know why but she seemed almost certain about it. It's probably become his hiding place as well as where he plays. That would make sense for a small boy wouldn't it?"

"I guess so. Maybe he talked about the fortress with his Mom some time ago. Who knows and does it really matter?" he added as he took his own coat from the closet and stepped out the door.

"You're right of course. Now we just have to help find him. Hope he's there."

He nodded in agreement and we began the short walk to the tree where Andy's fortress sat high in the tree. It wouldn't take us long to get there because I could tell both of us were worried and had picked up the speed of our pace. No words were shared between us but this was one of those times when we understood each other just fine. Andy was the priority.

When we arrived at the spot, I called up to see if Andy was already there. Frankly, I didn't want to make the climb up the ladder if I didn't have to.

"Andy," I called. "It's Mr. Henry and Mr. Johnson. Are you up there?"

We heard no sound so Johnson spoke next "Andy, I know you're up there" he said with the confidence of an old man. "Just holler down so we know you're okay. Your mother is worried."

The last part of his statement must have struck a chord with the boy and even though it still took a moment longer than I expected Andy called back down to us, "Hi, Mr. Henry. George and I are both up here." I didn't want to express too much emotion but there was a small part of me that felt a wave of relief. I think the old man felt the same way because it sounded like he started to breathe again.

I looked up towards the fortress entrance where his voice had come from and saw Andy looking back down at us. There was no appearance of surprise in his voice, almost as though he had been expecting us.

"Can we come up?" I asked relieved to see our young friend safe.

"Sure," Andy said.

As both of us began to climb up the ladder, part of me was thinking about Andy, but part of me was also thinking that I would finally get to meet the mysterious George. I had not had a chance to meet him before and my curiosity was getting the better of me. For now though Andy was my first concern.

"Hello, boys," I gasped as I stepped onto the floor of the fortress. I was shocked at my physical response. Maybe I hadn't recovered from the cancer treatments as fully as I thought. I pushed any concerns about myself aside and turned my attention towards Andy.

"Your mom is worried about you, Andy" I repeated Johnson's statement in what I hoped was a compassionate tone. It was important to me that he didn't feel that I was admonishing him, just showing concern.

"I know, Mr. Henry. I'm sorry."

"How come you didn't tell her where you were going?"

"I just needed to come to our fortress and talk with George," Andy said.

I looked over at his friend standing in the corner. It was the same young man I had seen at the funeral. Turning back to Andy, I knelt down on the floor so I could be at eye level with the boy.

"I understand, Andy, but you need to let your mom know where you are. Things are hard for her now, and she needs to know you're safe. Mr. Johnson told me you never even let him know you were here, and you know that's wrong."

"I know you're right, Mr. Henry" he said in a sheepish voice. I avoided telling him he was the man of the house now; I always hated when people said things like that. It put a foolish burden on a young boy and was only said because people never knew what else to say.

"I'm okay, Mr. Henry," he spoke apologetically.

"I know you're okay, Andy. Just make sure you don't do this again, all right?"

"Yes sir."

I could have continued to lecture him on how important it was for him to behave and put less stress on his Mom or how he was just a little boy who can't be allowed to run wherever he wanted to without someone knowing where he was. I was good at lecturing so I was sure I would have thought of a good one. However something in the back of my mind told me this was not the time or was it necessary. I listened to the message and left things where they were.

As I stood up, it occurred to me that I had not been inside this structure since the last day of its construction. It hadn't changed much. A few pieces of furniture made from wooden crates. How the boys got them up here was a mystery.

There was something different, however. I wasn't able to put my finger on it, but something seemed out of place. I figured it would come to me later.

I didn't know what to say next, and Johnson wasn't giving me much help. Come to think of it he hadn't uttered a word since we had climbed the ladder into the structure. I made an attempt at changing the subject—somewhat.

"How's your mom being doing, Andy?"

"She's okay," he said. "Grandpa has been a big help, and I've spent a lot of time with my sister."

"And how are you?"

"I'm okay. Been busy with all the people around our house; Grandpa says that's normal."

"You think that's right?"

"Guess so. Grandpa always tells the truth so I believe him. He says I'm okay."

I was amused by the simplicity of a small boy's understanding of what okay could mean. I believed that children many times handled death better than adults. Maybe it was because in an ordinary chain of life the older you get the more death is on your mind.

Everyone denies it but if you looked deep enough into a person's soul I would challenge anyone to say the thought of death doesn't come to their mind from time to time. A child on the other hand only has the adults around them and their reaction to death to gauge their own reactions.

I didn't want to be a grown up in Andy's life that dwelled on the sadness of death. I wanted him to know that life went on and could be good. That's why I didn't voice my own thoughts to anyone in the fortress. Instead I carried forth with the conversation as though we were just making a visit.

So trying to change the subject I smiled at him and said "Nice place you have here."

"The best! George and I really like it" exclaimed Andy. It was so easy for this boy to change gears.

My statement and Andy's reaction broke some of the tension accomplishing what I was hoping for. I wanted to take Andy's mind off of his problems at home. It looked like it was working so I decided to continue with the same approach.

"Maybe you should bring your Grandpa here sometime, or even your Mom."

"No I can't bring Mom here" he spoke in a shocked tone.

"Why not?"

"She's a girl!" he exclaimed as though I should have already understood that.

"Oh I see" I looked up at old man Johnson as I spoke my words and I could see the beginnings of a huge smile coming to his face. I made sure I didn't laugh, even though I wanted to. "Well that makes sense" I nodded in agreement with Andy.

I was just about to say something else when Andy said "Besides George is a good friend. He's all I need right now."

When Andy mentioned George, It occurred to me that I had been so focused on Andy that I had neglected his friend. The old man hadn't said anything to him either since we had climbed into the fortress, which seemed strange to me. Johnson had at least met the boy; you would think he would acknowledge his presence.

I turned towards George, ready to introduce myself and ask him some questions, when I heard Johnson's voice speak my name before I could say anything.

"Robert," he said. He had never called me by my first name and never in such a quiet, gentle voice. It caught me off guard.

Turning towards him, he continued by saying "There's something I want to tell you. Remember how I told you that I had met George before?"

"Yes." I replied. "You met him at your house when Andy came by."

"Actually I met the boy long before that."

"Really?

"Yes and it wasn't here in the neighborhood. It was somewhere else."

Intrigued I asked "Where?"

"In the hospital, the night my wife died."

He had my attention. Staring at him with a look of disbelief, I asked him, "How can that be? You said she died years ago."

"That's right," Johnson nodded. The fortress seemed so quiet even with Johnson's words ringing in my ears. The birds had stopped singing; the sounds of the world no longer surrounded me. All I could hear was the silence of the room trying to understand what the old man was saying. He was making no sense; had he lost his mind? The mood had shifted from a simple visit to one of somber importance.

Confused, I turned from Johnson and looked over to the little boy. How could this young child be a part of his past? Hell he was barely old enough to be part of today. I thought once more had the old man gone crazy? Was I now supposed to deal with him as well as Andy? Was *I* the one going crazy? Had I even heard him correctly?

Before I could ask any of those questions the silence was broken as I heard my name once again. This time it was quieter and it was Andy's voice. I shifted my eyes from George back to Andy not knowing what I was about to hear.

"Mr. Henry. I have something I want to tell you too."

I crossed the room to Andy and kneeled in front of him once more. He gestured for me to move closer and then in almost a whisper, said, "He's a guardian angel."

I didn't know what to say. All I could think of was to ask him "What?"

"George is a guardian angel, Mr. Henry. He's our angel so you see everything will be okay. I will be okay."

"Our angel? What do you mean our angel?"

"I mean he is here for all of us—Mr. Johnson, you, and me." Andy spoke with such maturity and certainty that I almost believed him. But where was the proof of any of this?

I looked over towards Johnson, who looked back at me and nodded. I could tell that he believed the same thing Andy was telling me. Not knowing what to do next, I looked in the corner at the small boy known as George. He looked like any other boy his age. There was nothing special about him. Before I could open my mouth and dispute what I had been told, I heard Andy's voice once again.

"You see, Mr. Henry, we all needed him. I needed him because he knew I needed someone to help me with my fortress, so he gave me you. Mr. Johnson needed him because he needed to have more friends in his life like us and you Mr. Henry—"

Before he could finish what he was saying, I heard a third voice come from the corner of the fortress. It was a strange but somewhat comforting sound.

Stepping forward and speaking for the first time was George. He looked straight at me and finished Andy's thought, "And you, Robert, needed me so that you could remember the past," glancing at Andy; "see the future," turning his attention to the old man; "so that you could handle today. Miracles come in small ways; ways people often don't expect. They are the ones that matter the most and they are given to people when they need them."

I continued looking at this boy; this "angel" memorized by him and for the first time I saw something I hadn't seen before. It wasn't a halo of light or a levitation of his body or any other stereotypical event portrayed in movies. It was the look of wisdom in his eyes of an old man as though he knew what he was speaking of. It was as though I was looking into someone's soul; maybe *my* soul. He no longer looked like a young boy to me. It was as though nothing else in the room mattered in this moment. It felt like the truth stood before me.

His first words of wisdom had brought together all of my random thoughts and insights over the last few months. The things

I had spoken of and the things I had told no one. Everything that had happened to me began to make more sense. All the memories, the peeks at the future, and the things I had learned now came together as one message that awakened happiness in me I had never experienced before; awareness I had never expected and peace I had never felt before.

Still in disbelief, I continued to listen as he spoke again, "You see, Robert, everyone has their own fortress. They build walls to protect themselves and walls to keep people out. I help people come in. I opened the doors; you walked through. I've always been here and I always will be, if you let me."

No longer mystified by his message a wave of calmness fell over me and the room seemed alive. The silence was deafening but George's message was clear. For the first time I was hearing with my heart, not my head. I looked towards Andy, then over in Johnson's direction, and finally back to George. It all made sense to me now.

Everything seemed right—*my* world was right. Much like Andy I knew I would be okay. My world was safe and my future would be good. One final look around the fortress showed me all I needed to know; everything I would need was already there and the people I needed were always close by. It was then that I understood that my own fortress could be anything I wanted it to be;—and the walls came tumbling down.

ACKNOWLEDGMENTS

I have been fortunate enough to work with Trafford Publishing and all of their staff who deserve a warm thank you for aiding me in bringing this story from mind to paper. It is a story of fiction and is not meant to depict or represent any specific person or event but it is a story that has been influenced by people in my life whose actions often spoke as loud as their words. They have been a part of making me the person I am and I would like to acknowledge them for what they have meant to me.

It begins with my father who taught me all about accountability, responsibility and honesty. His humble guidance built a platform for my future actions. My mother who's sharp tongue came with a strong sense of humor that I enjoyed and inherited from her. The next to thank is my oldest brother Brian who lived his life in a way that set the bar high enough for me to see the possibilities and another of my brothers, Butch who learned the fragile importance of life and how to live it. My friend Howard was someone who served as my confidant and mentor. He listened to me when I needed him most and challenged me to find my own answers. My wife Lorna was always someone who demonstrated an inner strength that I could only admire. She shared my failures and cheered my successes. She often served as a light of hope even when she didn't know she was and has been the best partner I have ever had. Finally I thank God for blessing me with all of these people and so many others who have come—and gone—in my life sharing moments in time that helped shape the person I have become. I hope I make them all proud.

Ken Jackson

CPSIA information can be obtained at www.ICGtesting.com
Printed in the USA
LVOW130602121212

311187LV00002B/46/P